UNBRIDLED FEAR

"Runaway! Runaway!" someone on the sidewalk screamed.

Jason's gaze swept up the street and widened in alarm. As I turned in my seat, I gasped in fear, for an out-of-control wagon careened around the nearby corner and swung wide, putting its rear end on a collision course with our own vehicle.

Instinct told me to jump, but there wasn't time to return to Jason's side, and the street was certain death.

"Sit down!" Jason commanded. He leaped into the wagon and caught up the reins.

Instantly I dropped to my seat and clutched it for dear life. I remember feminine screaming coming from all directions and through the hazy blur of rising fright that dried my mouth. I remember seeing the runaway horses and how their eyes looked wild and their mouths strained in fright. But the last thing I remember is being thrown against the solid warmth of Jason Landry . . .

MORE SUSPENSEFUL GOTHICS

THE CURSED HEIRESS (973, $2.95)
by June Harris
When Melinda wears her priceless heirloom, the Montoya butterfly, she incurs the wrath of her relatives at Montoya Manor. Then someone tries to take her life—and she fears the culprit is the very man she loves!

THE CLAVERLEIGH CURSE (958, $2.50)
by Sandra DuBay
Alexandra never believed the rumor that every woman who married a Claverleigh carved her own gravestone—until she was certain that someone, maybe even her husband, wanted her dead!

THE SAVAGE SPIRITS OF
SEAHEDGE MANOR (940, $2.95)
By Dianne Price
The shrieks of the dead were Drew's nightly lullaby at Seahedge Manor. But as time passed, she wondered what she had to fear the most: the island's stormy nights, or her grim, unwelcoming relatives . . .

THE LOST HEIRESS OF
MERRIOTT MANOR (919, $2.25)
by Pamela Pacotti
When Delcia arrives at her isolated ancestral mansion, two men await her. And if she trusts the wrong one, she will seal the doom of her destiny and forever cloak the secrets of her past!

THE HAWKSMOOR HERITAGE (898, $2.50)
by Catherine Moreland
Innocent Katie never even thinks of the vast Hawksmoor fortune—but the greedy Hawks family thinks otherwise. They swear they'll drive her from Hawksmoor, even if it has to be in a hearse!

Available wherever paperbacks are sold, or order direct from the Publisher. Send cover price plus 50¢ per copy for mailing and handling to Zebra Books, 475 Park Avenue South, New York, N.Y. 10016. DO NOT SEND CASH.

THE VELVET SHADOWS OF JUSTIN WOOD

BY ANDREA HALEY

ZEBRA BOOKS
KENSINGTON PUBLISHING CORP.

To my husband, Del, who encouraged me to write. And to my children, John, Kim, and Lisa, for their patience.

ZEBRA BOOKS

are published by

KENSINGTON PUBLISHING CORP.
475 Park Avenue South
New York, N.Y. 10016

Copyright © 1982 by Irene Pascoe

All rights reserved. No part of this book may be reproduced in any form or by any means without the prior written consent of the Publisher, excepting brief quotes used in reviews.

Printed in the United States of America

CHAPTER ONE

In the twenty years of my life I never dreamed I would meet my grandfather, Martin Justin. But now in the spring of 1889, twenty-nine years after my father left Washington Territory, never to return, I stood on the wharf in Seattle, my two trunks at my side.

A cool blast of air whipped my skirt, and as I drew my mantle closer about me I noticed all the other passengers had departed. I was the only woman on the wharf now, and standing against the background of the square-riggers and steamships, I felt conspicuous. I could feel the eyes of dock workers rake over me as they clattered cargo on and off ships.

Until three months ago my father, William Justin, had never mentioned a visit to his family. In fact, he had rarely talked of them at all. Now there was only Grandfather, and it was because of him and the heart attack he had suffered that prompted Father to plan our journey.

When my father died suddenly of a seizure, I gave no further thought to his plans. After all, I knew little of my grandfather, and I had no reason to believe that he would even care to see me. As far as I knew, not once in all these years had he even inquired about me.

Nor did I expect a reply to my wire informing him of his son's death; but write my grandfather did, inviting me to make my home with him. Not only was I surprised but bewildered. He knew I wasn't alone.

I'd informed him that I would be living with my Aunt Helen and her family, so it seemed odd that after all this time he was concerned for me.

For the first time since I had boarded the steamship in San Francisco and set sail from the only home I had ever known, I felt uneasy.

Nervously my fingers wound around the drawstrings on my reticule, and I fought down the urge to pace in front of my trunks. Where was Mr. Landry? I looked about, studying the faces of the men who moved among the wooden crates and stacks of lumber. A silly gesture, of course, since I had no idea of what he looked like.

According to my grandfather's last telegram, Jason Landry was to meet my ship and escort me to the Justin home on Lake Washington.

The mere thought of that man's name shot a bolt of indignation through me. Several days prior to my departure I had received a letter from him, or perhaps a more apt description would be a hastily scribbled note. Without so much as an explanation he had requested that I postpone my trip. What the relationship between this man and my grandfather was and on what authority he based his request I did not know, but I felt certain Martin Justin knew nothing of that letter.

To my aunt, who was like a mother to me, my grandfather's invitation brought dismay. "He couldn't possibly care about you, Abby," she said when I showed her his letter. "He's selfish and arrogant and he'll try to dominate your life just as he tried to dominate your father's. You'll find no happiness in Seattle."

Her words were harsh and yet in part true. My grandfather had planned out his son's life and for two years they were in constant conflict. As far as Martin

Justin was concerned, his son's place was at his side at the Justin Mill Company, but to my father, his future was medicine. A bitter quarrel ensued and William Justin left his home for San Francisco and medical studies.

My father was a kind and sensitive man, and we had a special relationship. Perhaps this was because there were just the two of us, for my mother had died when I was only eight.

She was a beautiful woman and although people said I resembled her in almost every way I always felt she was far more attractive than I. Often I would sit and stare at the oval framed photograph Father had given me of her, noting the similarity of our thick black hair and deep-blue eyes. Mother's features, though, were softer and there was a sensitive look about her mouth which I did not possess. My lips were fuller and my jaw had a stubborn set to it. The Justin in me, I was told.

Startled by a clanking noise behind me, I swung around and saw a chain-entwined steel line being hauled aboard a square-rigger on the bay. The ship, loaded with freshly milled lumber, sat low in the water and for a moment I watched as seamen secured the line, then turned my attention to town.

In one respect this small community reminded me of San Francisco, for it, too, was built on steep hills. However, unlike San Francisco, it lacked beauty.

Seattle, to say the least, was a dismal place. The gray cloud-enshrouded sky hugged everything, obliterating all color from the buildings and the landscape. There was even a foul smell in the air, which spewed forth in the billows of smoke from the stacks of the sawmills crowded along the banks of Puget Sound.

Perhaps my aunt was right and I would find no

happiness here. I had considered her words carefully but as much as I loved her and respected her advice, I had no choice. I would fulfill my father's last wish—to care for ailing Martin Justin.

Raindrops spattered my cheeks and I stiffened, my anger rising. I had known it would irritate Mr. Landry to ignore his instructions as I had done, but to leave me standing in the rain and under the scrutiny of seamen and dock workers was spiteful.

As I darted a quick look around in search of shelter, I saw a short man wearing a dark suit step from the building at the base of the wharf and approach me.

At first I thought perhaps this man, whose age I guessed to be about fifty, was my escort to Lake Washington. However, the kindly smile he flashed dispelled that notion. No doubt the man who had scrawled that curt note was glowing and ill-natured.

"I seen you from my window, miss. Can I be of any help to you?"

I breathed a sigh of relief, then returned his smile. "Yes, thank you. Do you know a Mr. Landry? He was supposed to meet me here."

He nodded. "Why, I sure do; he runs the Justin Mill just up the road a piece, along the sound."

My lips parted in surprise, but before I could speak, he continued. "You'll catch your death standin' in the rain, miss. Why don't you come wait in my office?" He gestured toward the building he'd stepped from. "We can watch for Jason from the window."

Rain dashed against us as we ran across the rough-hewed planks into the small warm office, and stood before the potbellied stove in the front corner of the room. My shoulders went slack and my mouth clamped shut in the straight line as I looked down at my mantle and the skirt of my matching blue merino dress. I was drenched. I could feel the curls I had spent hours piling on top of my head drooping around the back of my neck. Painstakingly I had dressed this morning and now I looked a fright. Jason Landry, if he bothered to show up at all, would discover that I had inherited Martin Justin's quick temper.

"I'm Charlie Olson," the man beside me said. "If Jason isn't here soon I'll send someone up to the mill to see what's keepin' him."

"Thank you, sir. I appreciate your kindness. I'm Abigail Jusin. Martin Justin is my grandfather."

His faded blue eyes widened in surprise. "Why, I didn't know old Martin had any family left. He never spoke of 'em."

"Yes, well, my father moved away from here a long time ago. I don't wish to inconvenience you any further, Mr. Olson; would it be possible for me to hire a carriage to take me out to Lake Washington?"

"Why, yes, that's no problem. I'll be happy to help you in any way I can, but why not give Jason a few more minutes?"

Over my shoulder I looked up at the walnut octagon clock on the far wall; its black Roman numerals told me it was 2:50. My ship had docked at shortly after two o'clock. "Very well, sir. I'll give him a few more minutes, but then I really must leave. If I delay much longer my grandfather might worry about me."

"Yes, of course, I understand. Well, if you'll excuse me, I must get back to work. Please make yourself comfortable." He pointed to the oak chair beneath the window.

"Thank you, but I think I'll stand, perhaps my clothing will dry faster."

He nodded, then crossed to the vast oak desk heaped with ledgers and papers and, as he sat down, gave a sidelong look out the window. "I'll keep an eye open for Jason."

I gave him a faint smile of appreciation, then turned my attention to the wood-burning stove.

As I stood with my hands extended above it, listening to the crackle of the fire mingling with the sounds of rain striking the windowpane and the soft ticking of the clock as its pendulum swung back and forth, I felt uneasiness once again touch my nerves. Obviously Mr. Landry was going to make my stay here difficult. But why? Why should my coming to Seattle concern him? Unless, of course, he was up to something underhanded. Since he was, according to Mr. Olson, in charge of the mill, I could not overrule that possibility.

During one of my father's rare talkative moods, he had told me that the Justin Mill Company was one of the most successful in the Puget Sound area. If this was still the case, then Grandfather, seventy-one years old and ill, could well be easy prey for scheming fortune hunters.

So intent were my thoughts that I did not hear the office door open and close, or the sound of footsteps on the wide-board floor.

"Excuse me, are you Miss Justin?"

The cool voice from behind gave me a start. I whirled about to face a tall, slender man around thirty years old. His expression was aloof and his dark-brown eyes, heavily lashed, moved over me slowly. I felt self-conscious, remembering my limp curls beneath my velvet toque and my clothing spotted with moisture.

He arched a brow in amusement, plainly enjoying my discomfiture. "I'm Jason Landry. Are you Miss Justin?"

I stared at him in astonishment. He wasn't at all

what I had expected. From the moment I'd read his letter my mind had conjured up a picture of a much older man. He looked at me as though he were reading my thoughts and I felt the flush of embarrassment rise to my face. I straightened my shoulders proudly and looked him full in the eyes. "Yes, I am. I expected you some time ago. If it hadn't been for Mr. Olson,"—I waved a hand—"I'd have drowned in the rain."

He seemed startled by my sharp tone. His eyes narrowed and there was a grim set to his mouth. "I'm sorry, Miss Justin; problems at the mill detained me."

Mr. Olson broke in. "Did I hear you say trouble at the mill, Jason?"

"Yes, Charlie. It was nothing serious."

"Was anyone hurt this time?"

Jason Landry shot me a quick look. "One man, a minor injury." Although he replied in a casual tone I saw the angry glint in his eyes. He didn't want me to know about the trouble at the mill.

Mr. Olson leaned back in his chair and pursued the subject. "You know, Jason, if these accidents don't stop you'll lose the men. They're already thinkin' Justin Mill is jinxed."

Exasperation crossed Jason Landry's lean face, and he took a half-turn and looked out the window toward Puget Sound, his hands clasped tightly behind his back. His shoulders beneath his gray- and red-plaid mackinaw coat were broad, and he was dressed in brown trousers and brown leather boots. For a moment it appeared as though he did not intend to respond, but then he turned abruptly on his heel and threw the other man an icy look. "I'd appreciate it, Charlie, if you'd keep your opinions to yourself."

Color suffused the older man's cheeks. "Yes, of course, you're right, Jason."

Jason Landry turned his cool look upon me. "Now, Miss Justin, I presume those are your trunks across the way."

I was still seething with anger at his tardiness and rude manner. "Yes, Mr. Landry, they are."

He strode to the door and paused with his hand on the knob. "I'll be back for you as soon as I load them aboard the buggy, and please don't call me Mr. Landry. The name is Jason." With that he pulled open the door, stepped out, and let it bang shut behind him.

I stared after him for several seconds, thinking most women probably regarded him as ruggedly handsome. To me, however, he was simply an annoying person, and I hoped I would not have to see him often.

Already I felt protective toward my grandfather, a strange feeling indeed under the circumstances. Yet, at the same time I was flooded with doubt. Certainly I considered myself capable of caring for his physical needs, but what of his business interests? Was Jason Landry trying to take advantage of an aged and ill man? If he was, what then?

I pulled myself from my thoughts and went to Mr. Olson's desk. "Excuse me, sir, did you say that Mr. Landry ran the Justin Mill?"

He looked at me quizzically. "Yes, that's right; has ever since Martin took sick."

"Are the problems at the mill serious?"

"I can't say, Miss Justin; I only hear rumors." He glanced out the window and then in a nervous gesture pushed the books around his desk. "I'd best get back to work. I hope you enjoy your stay in Seattle."

"Thank you sir, and thank you for your kindness." He gave me a thin smile, then lowered his gaze to the ledger before him. I had the impression that he was afraid Jason would see us talking.

Just outside the window I saw the carriage come to a stop, and I left the office. Jason handed me in, then withdrew a lap robe from beneath the seat. "You'd better put this over you," he said, holding it out to me. Crisp air penetrated my still-damp clothing and I straightened the robe across my lap, grateful for its warmth.

Jason lifted himself onto the black leather seat beside me, then picked up the gray stocking cap from the dashboard. He pulled the cap down over his brown disorderly hair.

Rain fell lightly as we drove eastward on Yesler Avenue through what appeared to be the heart of town. The roads were muddy and the sidewalks filled with businessmen and late-afternoon shoppers.

"How far is it to Lake Washington?" I asked, breaking the awkward silence.

"Three miles."

"How is my grandfather?"

The carriage slowed as the dappled mare pulled a steep hill. "He feels pretty good most days. Fortunately, the two attacks he suffered—one shortly after the other—were minor, though they did take their toll on him. Mainly now, he's troubled with occasional swelling in the ankles and hands. And the rheumatism in his legs is a little more aggravating."

"I didn't know about the rheumatism."

"He's been plagued with that for years. At any rate, getting around on his own is out of the question and he's now confined to a wheelchair."

"How does he feel about that?"

"Angry at first, and frustrated. But he's come to accept it."

We were out of town now and it was quiet, the only noise that of our horse and buggy. The rain had stopped, but from the appearance of the sky not for long.

My mind ran backward briefly to Jason's note. I had to know why he had sent it. I summoned my courage and asked, "Why didn't you want me here?"

Jason gave me a sidelong look. "So you did receive my letter. I wondered about that. It would have been best if you had not come, at this time."

"But why? Your message was vague. I had no idea who you were, and I knew my grandfather wanted me."

"My error. I should have been more explicit. Your grandfather is still weak. Seeing you now, for the first time, might be too much excitement for him."

Anger flared in me. "Did you get a doctor's opinion?"

Jason regarded me from beneath his lashes. "No! I did not."

We lapsed into stony silence and did not address each other again until we came to a crossroad and Jason reined the horse to a stop. "This road circles the lake," he said. "Justin property begins here and extends a mile down to the water."

He urged the horse on and we moved slowly along the spongy drive. Douglas firs and hemlocks loomed over us, water rolling from their rain-drenched branches onto our buggy. A jungle of ferns and vines spread around their base. It was impossible to see more than a few feet, and it gave me an uncanny feeling. "Are the trees this dense around the house?" I questioned.

"No," he replied without looking at me.

It was getting late and I asked would he be returning to town this evening.

"No, Miss Justin." His tone was smug. "I live here and have from the time I was twelve years old."

I was shaken by his words and he knew it. He looked at me, his eyes bright with amusement. My face felt flushed and I quickly turned from his gaze.

"You needn't worry," he said. "You won't have to see me often. I'll be gone in the mornings before your pretty head is off the pillow and I won't be home until dinner."

I was silent, my hands clasped tightly in my lap, waiting for him to explain why he had lived here all these years, but Jason said nothing. I stole a look at him, noting the clean line of his profile and the set of his jaw. Clearly he intended to say no more.

I lifted my chin and looked straight ahead into the dark tunnel of trees, at the end of which was a faint radiance. Let him be silent, I thought. I'll find out about Jason Landry from my grandfather.

We came to a large clearing and I caught my breath at the beauty which lay before me. The white gabled house was immense and sat high up on a terrace overlooking the lake. The porch circled the house. To its right was a woodshed. Both were reached by a flight of stone steps. Outbuildings were scattered beyond the shed.

Jason pulled the horse to a stop in front of the house, alighted, and, after securing the reins to the hitching post, helped me down. I stood for a moment admiring the lake. It was huge, seeming to run in both directions for miles; its calm water as gray as the sky. A small boat was tied to a nearby dock.

As we climbed the steps to the house and entered, I was filled with nervous excitement. The thought uppermost in my mind was, would my grandfather like me? While I waited for Jason to close the door behind us I looked around. The hallway was large with many rooms opening from it. In the middle and to the right was the staircase. It curved gracefully upward. Beyond, I could see the dining room.

A round mahogany table stood in the center of the

hall. Upon it was a sculpture of a deer carved skillfully from wood.

At the sound of footsteps I looked up and saw an attractive woman, probably in her late twenties, descending the stairs. Her skin was fair and her plaited blond hair circled her head like a crown.

"Why, Mr. Jason," she said, and her blue eyes shone, "I didn't hear the buggy in the drive." As she crossed the hallway toward us her muslin skirt whispered over the highly polished hardwood floor. "I was just on my way to look in on Mr. Justin."

"How is he today, Leah?" He reached up and removed the stocking cap from his head.

"He's restless, didn't want to take his nap." She turned to me. "He's anxious to see you, miss."

Jason spoke up. "Miss Justin, this is Leah Hanson our housekeeper."

I smiled at her. "I'm happy to meet you, Leah. I hope my arrival won't be too upsetting to my grandfather."

"No, I don't believe so, miss." She regarded me with cool eyes, as if I were a threat to her. A threat to what? I wondered. To her and Jason?

"You go along, Leah," Jason said in a soft tone, "and check on Mr. Justin, and then would you please show Miss Justin to her room."

His courteous manner surprised me and my brow arched as I watched them. Obviously Leah brought out the best in Jason Landry.

"Yes, sir. I'll be right back." She hurried off toward the rear of the house.

Jason threw his cap on the table. "Now, if you'll excuse me, Miss Justin, I have some work to finish in the study. I'll have one of the boys from the stables bring in your trunks."

He was at the door and I called, "Jason." He

paused and looked at me. "Please don't call me Miss Justin. The name is Abby."

A grin lifted the corners of his mouth and I felt a strange warm feeling stealing over me. "See you at dinner, Abby."

I nodded with a faint smile, and watched him turn and leave the room.

It was so quiet standing alone in the high-ceilinged hallway. The door to my left was ajar so I crossed to it and gently pushed it open.

CHAPTER TWO

Immediately my eyes were drawn to the portrait over the marble mantel. A young woman stared down at me. Waves of long dark hair framed her delicate face and her eyes reflected the green from her dress.

I was so rapt in study that I did not hear Leah return. "She's beautiful, isn't she?" Her gentle voice lifted me from my trancelike state. I lowered my gaze and turned to face her.

"Is that my grandmother?" My voice was scarcely audible.

"Yes. She was twenty-eight when that was painted. It was just before the family left Missouri."

My eyes returned to the portrait, and upon closer scrutiny I noticed a resemblance between her and my father, which until now had eluded me. For in the photograph that he'd had of his parents they were older and Grandmother's features were not shown to advantage.

"If you're ready, miss, I'll show you to your room."

Leah's words roused me back to reality, and I became aware of the surroundings. We were in the parlor, and although it was huge, it maintained an air of warmth. Crimson velvet drapes hung from rods over the long windows, complementing the muted red arabesque design on the Brussels carpet. Two sofas, in rich damask, faced each other before the fireplace and here and there were mahogany tables and softly cushioned chairs. Upon the tables were hand-painted china oil lamps. I turned and followed Leah from the room.

As we climbed the stairs I asked about my grandfather. "He's asleep," she replied, "and I doubt he'll be awake before dinner." She led me to the end of the hall and stopped in front of the last door on the right. "Your grandfather used to have that room." She gestured across the hallway. "Now that he's in a wheelchair he has a room on the main floor."

She opened the door, and I followed her into the bright and cheery room. On my right, near the marble-topped washstand, was a dressing table with an oval gilded mirror. Between the two windows, adorned with pink satin tie-back draperies and organdy curtains, was a Queen Anne desk. The white papered walls sprinkled with delicate pink roses matched the organdy canopy above the mahogany fourposter bed.

"This was your father's room," Leah said. "Your grandfather had it redecorated for you."

"It's beautiful," I murmured, and looked about trying to visualize how it must have looked when my father had occupied it. Blinking back tears, I turned away from Leah and concentrated my attention on the two pink satin chairs before the crackling fire in the grate.

"I've instructed Dorothea to bring up tea," the

blonde woman told me. "If you'd like I can show you around the house before dinner and introduce you to the servants."

I cleared my throat. "Thank you, I'd like that. How many are there?"

"Two others besides me—Mrs. Brannon, the cook, and her daughter, Dorothea. Mr. Brannon is in charge of the stables and does most of the gardening."

I slipped from my mantle, and laid it across the crocheted bedspread. "Have you worked for Mr. Justin long, Leah?"

A touch of annoyance crept into her voice. "No, only since he took sick. Mrs. Gustafson had been with him for years, but she was too old to care for a sick man. So your grandfather pensioned her off." Leah stepped to the door. "If you'll excuse me, Miss Justin, I have to get back to work. Dinner is at seven. The gentlemen will be waiting for you in the parlor."

I gave her a warm smile, hoping to dissolve her reserved manner, but there wasn't a flicker of warmth in her eyes. She left just as two young boys were bringing in my trunks.

After they departed, I roamed the room admiring the furnishings. In a way this house reminded me of my Aunt Helen and Uncle Phillip's home. My room there had overlooked San Francisco Bay. My uncle owned a business in the heart of town and, as with my grandfather, his family lived in comfort. A life wholly different from my own.

My father's medical practice had been a large one. But like so many in his profession, a vast number of patients were impoverished. Tears pricked my eyes and I dabbed at them, sternly reminding myself that this was not the time to reminisce. Grandfather would be expecting me downstairs soon and I still had unpacking to do.

When Dorothea appeared at my door I was in the cedar-lined walk-in closet, hanging up dresses. Her knock was so light that I wondered if I had simply imagined the sound. But then she rapped again, and I hurried across the pearl carpet with its tangled clusters of pale pink roses, and opened the door. She looked at me, her blue-green eyes round and a timid smile on her lips. Grasped firmly in her slender hands was a silver tray; upon it sat a flowered tea service and a plate of cheese cakes. Her voice when she spoke was demure, little more than a whisper. "Good afternoon, miss. I'm Dorothea Brannon. Leah told me to bring you some refreshments."

It was a relief to be greeted by a friendly face, and I immediately returned her smile and stepped aside allowing her to enter.

Dorothea was thin and plain and she wore her dark-brown hair pulled into a knot at the nape of her neck. Both the hair style and her drab muslin dress were too severe, I thought, for a girl who did not appear to be more than sixteen. She came to a stop in the center of the room and darted a look around.

I hurried to the desk and moved aside the silver embossed ink well. "You can put that right here," I told her.

She set down the tray, then observed me from beneath her lashes. "Mama wondered if you needed any help unpacking."

"That was very thoughtful of her, Dorothea, but I think I can manage."

"Yes, miss."

After the young girl left I enjoyed the tea and cakes while I finished putting away my personal effects; then I freshened myself and made my way down the long hallway.

At the foot of the stairs I paused to stare at the

flight that went upward, wondering what was on the third floor. No doubt the servants quarters, I concluded, and continued to the parlor. The lamps were lit, but the room was empty.

A glimmer of light fell across the floor at the entrance to the dining room, and I moved toward it.

As I stepped through the wide doorway, I saw Leah placing china upon linen damask. She threw me a quick look, slantwise, then turned her eyes to the bronze clock on the mantel. "There's still time before dinner if you'd like to see the house," she said.

I nodded in acknowledgment, and while she finished setting the table, placing monogrammed silver alongside the china, I glanced about. Overhead a crystal chandelier with lighted white tapered candles spread a golden glow throughout the room, and the brilliance of the flames flickered over the walls. Dark wainscoting ran halfway up them, and above it was wallpaper in a country scene. French doors opened out onto the porch which overlooked the lake.

Leah moved to my side. "This way, Miss Justin. I'll introduce you to Mrs. Brannon." She led me through the swinging door to the left of the dining room, and I found myself in the spacious steam-filled kitchen. A short, heavyset woman, with rosy cheeks, busied herself stirring in a kettle on the stove. When she saw me a smile crossed her pleasant face, and she lowered the spoon to the counter.

"Why, you must be Miss Justin," she bubbled, and came forward. "We're so pleased to have you with us. I'm Elsie Brannon, been with Mr. Justin for over thirty years."

"I'm happy to meet you, Mrs. Brannon." I smiled. "You must have worked here before my father left for San Francisco."

"Oh, yes, miss, I did. He was such a fine young

man. Me and Mr. Brannon was sure sorry to hear of his death. You know," her voice took on a faraway sound, "your papa was so much like his mother, liked to read a lot and play the piano."

Leah shifted her weight from one foot to the other, clearly bored. Not wishing to irritate her further, I said to Mrs. Brannon, "Perhaps we could have a nice long talk some time soon. I'd very much like to hear more of my father's life here."

"Any time, miss." She smiled. "And if I can do anything for you, just let me know." I thanked her warmly, and as I turned to leave I saw Dorothea at a table in the corner, rolling out what appeared to be biscuit dough. We grinned at each other, and then I followed Leah back through the swinging door.

In the dining room she directed my attention to the carved wooden doors opposite the kitchen. "That's the ballroom. It's too dark to look at now, so I'll show it to you in the morning."

"Is it still used?" I asked, wondering if Jason gave parties.

"I don't know,"—she shrugged—"but I would doubt it. It seems to me only women would think of planning a ball. That's Mr. Justin's room. Mine is the one next to it." She flicked a hand at the doors to the right of the dining-room entrance. So her room wasn't on the third floor. But then I realized my grandfather would need someone nearby.

Farther down the hall and to the left she stopped and opened a door. "This is the library," she said, and stepped aside. A lamp near its entrance was lit, and I was able to see the book-lined walls.

As I moved back, pulling the door closed, the one next to me opened and Jason appeared. We looked up, both startled. Flustered, I said in a rush of words, "Leah is taking me on a tour of the house."

He looked from me to her, and I noted her disinterested expression had altered to a radiant smile. "I'll show Abby the study, Leah," he told her. "Would you please check to see if Mr. Justin is ready to join us in the parlor."

"Yes, sir." She squared her shoulders, straining the bodice of her plain dress; then reluctantly, it seemed, she moved away.

In comparison to the other rooms the study was small and dominated by an impressive mahogany desk. A painting of two young boys hung on the wall above it and glass doors opened out onto the porch. I returned my attention to the painting.

"That's your father and his brother, Jeremy," Jason remarked from behind me.

I had never before seen a picture of my Uncle Jeremy, and I was surprised to discover that he looked nothing at all like my father. Father's hair was dark and he was wiry, while Jeremy, on the other hand, was blond, broad-shouldered, and husky.

Jeremy, who had shared Martin Justin's interest in the mill, had died in a logging accident in his eighteenth year. It was then, my father told me, that my grandfather became insistent that his younger son, William, join him in the family enterprise.

I turned to face Jason. "Will my grandfather ever be able to return to work?" I questioned.

"No, I don't believe so. But you needn't be concerned, Abby. I'm sure Martin will insist I teach you the business. After all, you are his only living heir."

"Me?" I laughed. "Learn about the mill? Why I don't even know what the inside of one looks like."

"Well"—Jason grinned—"I'm sure your grandfather will see to it that I show you around Justin Mill in the very near future."

"But what about the accidents?"

The grin vanished from his face. "They're not serious, and I don't care to discuss them. Above all, I don't want you to mention them to your grandfather. I will not have him upset."

"I would never intentionally say anything that might upset him," I retorted.

"I certainly hope not, Abby. Now, come along." He took me by the arm. "Let's go wait for him in the parlor."

As we crossed the hallway in silence I pondered my ability to irritate Jason and yet why did he feel it necessary to be so evasive? Obviously he didn't particularly like me, and I wondered a bit apprehensively if my grandfather might share his judgment.

Cold and nervous, I sat down on the sofa near the fire and concentrated my attention on the four hand-blown decanters on the table before me. From his place on the opposite sofa, Jason lifted one of the decanters and offered me a glass of sherry. I declined with a murmured thank you, then turned my eyes to the shower of embers that fell in the grate. The ticking of the grandfather's clock adjacent to the entrance seemed to echo throughout the parlor, making me even more edgy.

I looked at Jason from the corner of my eye, only to discover him watching me; his expression softened.

A noise at the doorway caught my attention, and I jerked my head around to face Leah. She stood behind Martin Justin, who was seated in a wheelchair. Jason rose and went to his side. "How are you today, Martin?" he asked.

"Just fine. Just fine," he blustered, looking past the younger man to me. "Well,"—he waved an impatient hand at him—"don't just stand there. Push me closer to my granddaughter. I can't see her clearly from here."

Taken aback by the old man's brusqueness I flattened myself against the sofa, then remembered my manners and quickly leaped to my feet. His dark eyes, surprisingly bright, regarded me from under shaggy brows, and the royal blue of his dressing gown heightened the color in his face. He lifted his eyes to the portrait of his wife. "You don't look anything like her." He sounded disappointed. "I often wondered about that." He appraised me openly now, his stern face heavily etched with lines. Martin Justin reminded me of someone and then I realized who. Jeremy had been broad-shouldered and husky like his father.

Crestfallen, I eyed the two men with their ascetic faces. "No, I don't resemble her," I said quietly. "I take after my mother."

The old eyes returned to the portrait, and I noticed the muscles of his face tighten. My mouth went dry and my heart pounded furiously. I didn't dare look at Jason, for undoubtedly he was enjoying my misery.

However, it was he who alleviated my distress, and I viewed him with wonder. "Martin, don't you think Abby is almost as pretty as her grandmother?"

Grandfather looked from me to him, then back to me. A smile lifted the corners of his mouth, and I felt myself go limp with relief. "She is just as pretty as her grandmother," he declared with obvious pride. "And I am so grateful that she accepted my invitation. I've been a very foolish old man all these years, my dear, and I wouldn't have blamed you if you had ignored me. Please sit down and tell me—shall I call you Abigail or Abby?"

"Well," I grinned sheepishly, "the only time my father ever called me Abigail was when I got into trouble."

Jason couldn't resist saying, "With your curiosity and quick temper I suspect that was quite often."

I disregarded his caustic remark, certain I would never understand him.

Grandfather beamed. "Do you mean to tell me, Abby, that you've inherited the Justin temper?"

"Yes, sir. And, unfortunately, the Justin stubbornness."

He leaned forward. "What do you think of my foster son? Jason's been with me for eighteen years now and I don't know what I would have done without him."

Foster son? I looked at Jason in surprise.

He cleared his throat. "Now, Martin, I'm sure Abby isn't interested in discussing me."

"All right, Jason, all right." Grandfather grinned. "If it's going to embarrass you, we'll talk about something else."

Dinner was announced and we went to the dining room. The men were seated at the opposite ends of the table with me between them, facing the French doors. The draperies were still open and I noticed a strong wind had come up, sending ripples across the water. The evergreens bent and swayed as the breeze whipped through their branches and pushed dark clouds swiftly across the sky.

Even though it was overcast, I was amazed that it was still light. In San Francisco at this hour it would be totally dark. I mentioned this to my grandfather.

"That's because we're so far north," he explained. "During the summer months it remains light until ten o'clock and in the winter it's dark by four-thirty. You'll get used to it," he assured with a grin.

For a long while it seemed as though I did all the talking, for my grandfather asked so many questions about his son and our life in San Francisco. Jason remained aloof, making no effort at all to join in the conversation.

When we finished with the meal Jason rose and pulled the wheelchair back from the table. "All right, Martin," he teased, "it's your turn to push me."

On our way to the parlor I delighted in the playful banter between the two men. "Oh, by the way," Martin Justin said over his shoulder to Jason, "Nicholas will be out one day this week for a visit."

The mirth vanished from Jason's face and his eyebrows drew together in a straight line. "What does Wells want now?" he grumbled as he positioned the wheeled chair before the fire.

"He's just coming for a visit. He knew Abby was due to arrive this week and he expressed a desire to meet her. I don't know what it is you have against him, but I consider him to be my friend."

Jason turned sharply, and his eyes that searched mine were soft with concern, as though he felt a need to protect me. From what though? I wondered. Surely he didn't regard a friend of Martin Justin's as a threat to me. I shivered involuntarily, and lowered myself down onto the sofa beside my grandfather.

"I know he's your friend, Martin, but I don't happen to trust him. At any rate, let's not spoil the evening with talk of Wells. In fact, I'm sure you and Abby wouldn't mind some time alone and I could stand a bit of fresh air. So if you'll excuse me, I'll go out for a walk."

Before we had a chance to protest, Jason bade us good night and took leave of our company.

I was puzzled by his animosity toward my grandfather's friend and I asked, "Who is Nicholas Wells?"

Grandfather took my hand in his. "He's a young man around Jason's age. He moved here four or five years ago from Chicago. As I understand it, his father left him quite a substantial inheritance, which

27

Nicholas has used to purchase a mill. It appears he's making quite a success of it too, because he's certainly giving us plenty of competition. Tell me, Abby, what do you think of Jason?"

"Well . . . he's awfully serious and not very sociable either."

"Yes, I suppose you're right. He's always been serious, but lately even more so. I can't quite figure it out."

"Has this change taken place since he took charge of the mill?"

Grandfather ran a finger over his brow, considering. "Yes, I guess it has, but that's not the reason. Jason's pretty much had sole command of the mill for over a year now and he's doing an excellent job."

"May I ask why he's lived here all these years?"

"Why of course you may, Abby. Jason's father, you see, was foreman of the mill for many years and also my best friend. He and his wife and their two older sons drowned in a boating accident on the sound. Fortunately, Jason was here on that tragic day, finishing up some work for me in the stables. He had no other family, so your grandmother and I gave him a home. He's been like a son to me and a great comfort since your grandmother died. Didn't she ever mention him in her letters to your father?"

"Not that I can remember; but then she died when I was very young and I may have just forgotten."

"Bedtime, Mr. Justin," Leah said from the doorway.

Grandfather made a face. "Later, Leah, I'm not done talking with my granddaughter yet."

"Yes, sir, I understand, but you know what the doctor said about plenty of rest."

"I'm not tired."

"Please, Grandfather, go along with Leah," I

urged, "and get your rest. We can resume our visit first thing in the morning. Besides, I'm exhausted and could use some sleep myself."

"I'm sorry, my dear, I should have realized that. I'll see you in the morning then. Sleep well."

I kissed him good night and after Leah wheeled him from the parlor, I climbed the stairs to my room and slowly went through the motions of preparing for bed.

The wind moaned through the trees and flung rain against the windowpanes. It gave me an eerie feeling—a sensation I attributed to the immensity of my new home.

As I snuggled down under the covers my thoughts turned to Jason, and I reflected upon his comment on my being Martin Justin's only surviving heir. Did Jason believe I came here simply to inherit the mill? If so, then he must resent me. He has given years to it and should by all means be the one to inherit. I sank into sleep with that thought on my mind, only to be startled awake some time later by a harsh, grating noise from the room above. It sounded as though a heavy object was being dragged across the floor. Curious and a little apprehensive, I raised up on one elbow, then flew bolt upright when something smashed violently to the overhead boards.

CHAPTER THREE

Lightning zigzagged across the sky hurling its flash of brightness through the drapery-covered windows and as the electric arc retracted, the room was plunged back into darkness.

Gritting my teeth at the rumbles of thunder, I slipped from bed and ran my hands over the smooth surface of the bedside table, groping for the container of matches. With unsteady hands I lighted the lamp, then lifted it.

Slowly I moved my bare feet over the carpet, wondering even though the noise from the room above had ceased, if I should summon someone to investigate.

At the foot of the bed I was startled to a stop by the painful protest of a floorboard from beyond the door. I gripped the bedpost in an effort to still my quivering body and raised the light, illuminating the dark panel. Eyes widened and heart hammering a deafening staccato in my ears, I watched the china knob, waiting for it to be turned. Moments passed. Nothing happened.

A deep breath gave me a vestige of courage, and I went to the door and eased it open a fraction. There, at the entrance to a room near the far end of the dimly lit passageway stood a tall figure with his back toward me. From his size and clothing I could tell it was Jason. He opened the door, and, without a backward glance, disappeared from view.

I closed my door and leaned against it, contemplating whether I should lock it. But then common sense overrode fright and I dismissed the notion, certain I was safe in my grandfather's home.

When I replaced the lamp on the bedside table, I noticed it was shortly after midnight. What on earth was Jason doing up at this hour? And was he listening at my door? If so, then why?

A cold chill crawled through me, and I climbed back into bed and pulled up the covers. Tensed on one elbow I reached out to turn off the lamp, but decided instead to turn it low, at least until my nerves calmed.

No one had mentioned the third floor and I wondered if the Brannons lived up there. If not, then it must have been Jason prowling around. But why? Was he searching for something? Or was he simply trying to annoy me, to make my stay here as uncomfortable as possible? Just how much did the Justin wealth and power mean to him? I pondered before falling into a fitful sleep.

When I awoke in the morning a globe of light was spread across my pillow. The lamp on the bedside table still burned, its glow reminding me of the incident of the previous night.

I went to the window and drew aside its covering. The wind had subsided, but the rain came in torrents. I sighed and let the drapery fall over the window, closing out the gloom.

While I dressed in a striped shirtwaist and dark skirt, I repressed the thoughts that plagued me. I fastened my hair at the nape of the neck with a yellow ribbon, then went from the room.

At the end of the hallway I stopped short in front of the room I assumed was Jason's, and I found myself wondering what it looked like. A strange urge to open the door and peek in came over me. Good heavens, why should I want to do such a thing?

Bewildered, I gathered up my skirts and hurried down the stairs to the dining room. A hasty look around told me it was unoccupied, so I continued past the lively fire in the grate and pushed open the swinging door.

The kitchen was warm and friendly with its turkey-red tablecloth, glass cupboard doors, and polished black stove highlighted by gleaming chromium. Mrs.

Brannon was busy at the sink, washing dishes.

"Good morning," I greeted.

She flashed a cheerful smile. "Why, good morning, miss." She wiped her hands on her floral apron. "Did you sleep well?"

"Yes, once I got back to sleep."

Her brows knit together in puzzlement.

"Does your family occupy rooms on the third floor, Mrs. Brannon?"

"Why, no, Miss Justin. We have a cottage down by the lake, just over behind the stables. No one lives on the third floor. Why do you ask?"

"Someone was up there late last night and it sounded like things were being moved around."

"That's odd; there's nothing up there. Are you sure it wasn't just the rain and thunder?"

"Yes, I'm sure. Someone was definitely walking around and then something heavy crashed to the floor. Are those rooms used at all?"

"No, not since Mrs. Gustafson left. Besides, the attic is over your room. Why, I can't imagine anyone wanting to roam around in there in the dead of night. Come, sit down, miss." She withdrew a chair from beneath the round table. "I'll fix your breakfast and then go up and have a look around."

"Thank you; I'd appreciate it." I sat down at the table, then asked, "Is my grandfather awake?"

She responded as she took a box of oatmeal from the cupboard, "Yes, miss, he's an early riser."

While Mrs. Brannon prepared hot cereal, scrambled eggs, and a generous slice of toast laden with homemade jam, she talked of my father. I watched her in silence, wholly absorbed in her light rush of words.

Later, when I was nearly finished with breakfast and she and I chatted over coffee, Leah came into the kitchen. She surveyed the table, her nose wrinkled in disdain. "Meals are served in the dining room, Miss Justin."

"Oh, for heaven's sake, Leah." Mrs. Brannon scowled, and rose to her feet. "You know very well that we don't stand on formality here."

"Is my grandfather in his room?" I questioned the younger woman before she was able to hurl a retort.

She lifted her chin. "No, he's in the library." Leah swept past me on her way to the sink, her broadcloth skirt brushing my hand.

On my feet, I thanked Mrs. Brannon for the delicious breakfast and went to the library. Martin Justin sat before the window peering out at the rain. Even though the room was comfortably warm, he was bundled in a flannel dressing gown, with a bright wool afghan draped over his legs. He smiled broadly and motioned me to the chair beside him.

I was patient while we discussed many things, waiting for the appropriate moment to query him about Jason. I had to know if he had been the one in the attic last night. When at last Grandfather mentioned the mill I felt free to broach the subject without arousing suspicion. "There must be a lot of paperwork involved in operating the mill," I said in a casual tone; then asked if Jason ever found it necessary to work late into the night.

The sparkle in the old eyes told me we were now on Martin Justin's favorite subjects, Jason and the mill. "You're right about the paperwork, Abby, and I've always hated it. As for Jason working late, I don't really know about that, but I would imagine so."

Grandfather regarded me intently and I was afraid I might have piqued his curiosity, but then I breathed a sigh of relief when he continued, "It pleases me, my dear, that you're interested in the mill. One day soon

I'd like to talk with you about it." His voice faded, and he leaned back and closed his eyes.

I rested my chin on my fist and stared out the window at the mist, reflecting upon Jason's statement concerning the mill and Martin Justin. Would he be insistent that I learn its operation? I had the unpleasant feeling that now I would have to convince both him and Jason that I was not interested in the company. I hoped my grandfather would not be as stubborn with me as he had been with my father. And I wondered about Jason. Could the immense responsibilities entrusted to him account for his aloofness?

After lunch Leah wheeled Grandfather to his room for a nap, and I went to the kitchen to inquire if Mrs. Brannon had checked the attic. "Oh, yes, miss," she said. "I haven't been up there for a long time, mind you, but everything seems in order."

I thanked her, and as I moved along the hallway and mounted the stairs the events of the night raced through my mind, painting vivid pictures. Those noises had not been a product of my imagination; of that I was certain.

In my room I went straight to the desk, lighted the lamp, and began a letter to Aunt Helen. It would have to be cheerful, for if she knew of my doubts she would worry and as my guardian perhaps even insist I return to San Francisco. I suppose it was wrong of me, but I never told her of Jason's letter, for had she known, my journey undoubtedly would have been canceled.

Over the weekend sullen clouds produced an abundance of rain, and though I was disappointed that I was unable to venture out to explore the grounds, the inclement weather gave me the opportunity to come to know Jason better.

His complex nature was difficult to understand, but gradually I discovered that by avoiding the subject of the mill, he and I were able to converse in a more relaxed and friendly manner.

While I was pleased with this improvement in our relationship, I was, on the other hand, perplexed by the way our friendship was affecting Leah. She seemed to always be watching me, as if she suspected I had romantic designs on Jason. For the sake of harmony, I considered informing her that I was not so inclined, but it was such an awkward situation that I didn't quite know how to broach the matter.

On Monday morning I awakened to absolute silence, for the rain had finally stopped. But it wasn't until early afternoon that the sun peered over the edge of a gray cloud, transforming the raindrops on the windowpanes into glistening diamonds.

While Grandfather napped, I went out to investigate the grounds. The air was brisk and scented with the pungent aroma of damp evergreens and the flower beds were lined with crocus in full bloom. Red-breasted robins flitted about in the trees, then swooped to the ground in search of food.

At the back of the house a loud chorus of croaking drifted along the air from the lake. I wandered toward it, then strolled its bank. Every now and then a frog jumped from the grass and a ripple appeared on the calm water. Ahead of me was the Brannons' cottage. A canoe lay on the grassy slope nearby.

A section of land jutted into the water south of where I stood. From my position I wasn't able to discern if it was the end of the lake or an island.

The rustle of leaves from behind caught my attention and I turned with a start and stared into the shrubbery. The branches shook. I sucked in my breath and stepped back, half-expecting a bear or some other disagreeable animal to pounce on me. The leaves moved again, and I was about to make a hasty retreat to the house when a reddish-brown dog poked his head out from behind the huckleberry bush. "Oh, no." I laughed in relief and clapped a hand over my mouth. "Come here, fella." I leaned forward, my hand outstretched. He hesitated, then came toward me, his nose down and tail wagging. "My goodness, you're beautiful." I stroked his head. For several seconds he savored the attention; then he cocked his ear, listening and ran off toward the house.

As I straightened, following the dog with my eyes, I saw a lean man of medium height headed my way. He appeared to be in his early thirties. His hair was as black as my own and he was well-dressed in a dark-brown suit, white shirt, silk tie, and double-breasted vest.

He stopped a few feet away from me and said to the dog, "There you are, Old-Timer. Went wandering, didn't you?" At the sound of his master's firm, yet gentle voice the animal lowered his head and his tail drooped.

The man continued forward, regarding me with a warm and friendly smile. "I see you've met my dog," he said as he came to a stop before me.

"Yes." I grinned. "I wondered to whom he belonged. He's beautiful."

"No kind words, please." The man's smile broadened. "He doesn't deserve them. You see, he was supposed to stay in the buggy."

"Oh." I suppressed a chuckle.

"Allow me to introduce myself, Miss Justin. I'm Nicholas Wells. I believe your grandfather has mentioned me."

"Yes, he has, Mr. Wells. I'm pleased to meet you." I held out my hand.

He took it in his. "The pleasure is all mine. But please, I'd like it if you'd call me Nicholas."

"Very well." I withdrew my hand from his firm clasp. "And I'm Abby."

"Your grandfather wondered where you'd disappeared to, Abby. Leah couldn't find you in the house, so I said I'd look for you out here. What do you think of all this?" He gestured with his hand. "Quite a change from San Francisco, isn't it?"

"Yes. It's lovely." I took a half-turn and pointed across the water. "Perhaps you can tell me—is that the end of the lake or an island?"

"That's Mercer Island."

"Mercer Island," I repeated slowly. "That sounds familiar, but then maybe my father mentioned it at one time or another."

"The island was named after Asa Mercer and it might seem familiar because of the Mercer girls. Of course they were a little before your time, but then Asa and the girls did receive a lot of publicity in San Francisco."

"Oh, I remember now. My father told me that years ago there were very few women in this area and that Asa Mercer traveled east to recruit prospective brides for the men of Seattle."

"Precisely. He brought back about a hundred of them."

"Does anyone live on the island?"

"Yes, about half a dozen families, but they're mainly further south."

"Have you ever been there?"

"No, but I've given a trip over some serious thought. They'll be logging this end of it soon. Would you like to see it before the trees are eliminated? It might be fun to explore together."

Something in me responded eagerly and with rising

37

excitement. "Yes, I'd like that."

Nicholas smiled showing white and perfect teeth. "Then it's settled. Shall we go over on Sunday afternoon?"

"Sunday would be fine."

"Then I'll ask Martin for permission. Now, I'd better get you back inside before he sends someone out after us."

We wandered toward the house, the dog meandering ahead of us. "What's his name?" I asked.

Nicholas gave me a sideways look. "I just call him Old-Timer."

"What made you think of a name like that?" I laughed.

There was a glint of amusement in his eyes. "Well, he was given to me by an old-timer; at least that's what everyone calls him. So I just tacked the name on the dog."

I waited on the front porch while he tied Old-Timer to the buggy. And as I watched Nicholas I realized how differently he dressed from Jason; yet they were in the same business. Perhaps, though, Nicholas had donned a suit for his visit with my grandfather. I wondered if Jason ever dressed up for anyone. He certainly hadn't made any such effort for my arrival.

Nicholas climbed the stone steps. "All set, Abby." I turned to cross the porch, but he reached out and touched my arm, staying me. "How does Jason feel about your being here?"

"Not too pleased."

"I was afraid of that."

"Why?"

"Well, Jason's had the run of things around here for some time. Now with you here all that will change. I'm sure he felt one day he would inherit the mill."

Oh, not the mill again, I thought, and raised my eyes to the puff of white clouds against the background of bright blue sky. Now I could almost understand why Father left Seattle. I was silent for a moment, then said in a mild tone, "If you don't mind, Nicholas, I'd rather not talk about Jason and the mill right now."

"As you wish." He nodded, then slipped a hand beneath my elbow.

We entered the house. "Well, it's about time you showed up," Grandfather called from the parlor. "I thought maybe you forgot about me."

I went to his side and kissed him on the cheek. "I'm sorry we kept you waiting, Grandfather. But Nicholas was telling me about Asa Mercer and the island."

The old eyes sparkled. "Calling him Nicholas already, are you?"

"I make friends easily." I laughed as Nicholas and I seated ourselves on the sofa.

"And it's a known fact that I'm not shy." Nicholas chuckled. "Anyway, Martin, Abby was fascinated by the island and I wondered if I might have your permission to take her over for a while on Sunday."

Grandfather looked a trifle taken aback. "Well . . . I suppose it would be all right. But see to it that you take good care of my granddaughter."

"You needn't worry about that, sir."

The front door was closed with a thud as though shoved with annoyance, then Jason stepped into the room. I proffered him a smile, but he didn't seem to notice.

He surveyed us somewhat grimly. "Hello, Wells."

Nicholas rose and extended his hand. "Good to see you, Jason, it's been awhile."

After a brief handshake the two men sat down opposite each other.

Jason said, "You look well, Martin."

Grandfather pulled erect, a look of pride about his lined face. "Abby is taking excellent care of me. She'd perk up anyone's spirit."

"I'd have to agree with you there," Nicholas put in. "I can't tell you how much I'm looking forward to our outing on Sunday."

That brought Jason's head around to us. "What outing?"

"I'm taking Abby over to Mercer Island."

Grandfather spoke up. "How about having dinner with us, Nicholas?"

"Why, thank you, sir. I'd like that."

Jason stood up. "If you'll excuse me, I have some paperwork that requires my immediate attention. I'll see you at dinner." He left the room, passing Leah in the doorway. Her mouth drooped and I presumed she was nettled because he hadn't even tossed her a glance.

She managed to make her voice pleasant. "Dinner will be ready in about five minutes."

"Thank you, Leah," Martin Justin acknowledged, dismissing her.

On our way to the dining room a few minutes later, the door to the study opened and Jason stepped into its entrance. The doorway seemed dwarfed by his lean stature. "Abby," he called, "come in here for a moment, would you?"

I didn't appreciate his dictatorial tone and I opened my mouth to reply in the negative, but he didn't give me the opportunity. "I'll only keep her a minute, Martin."

"See that it's no longer," he returned, closing the matter.

I resented that. Why, neither one of them had given even one fractional consideration to my wishes.

I was tempted to assert myself—to inform the duo that I was capable of making my own decisions—but I restrained the urge, for I didn't want to involve Nicholas in a family dispute.

Wordlessly, I entered the study. Jason closed the door, then crossed to stand behind the desk. I could see that he was peeved about something. He stared at me in rigid silence, his eyes probing mine as though endeavoring to judge my character.

I was offended, but I would not allow him to detect that. "What is it you want?" I asked in calm dignity. "I don't want to keep the gentlemen waiting."

Jason's brows twitched. He came forward slowly, his intense gaze still on my face. "I don't want you going with Wells on Sunday."

"What?"

"You heard me."

"Now just a minute, Jason Landry, sole command of the mill does not automatically give you authority over me. I don't understand you at all. First you instruct me not to come here and now you won't let me out of the house."

"I didn't say I wouldn't let you out of the house! I said I didn't want you with Wells. There isn't anything on Mercer Island, but if you must see it, then I'll take you."

"No, thank you. I don't enjoy hostile company." I wheeled, flung open the door, and let it bang shut behind me.

CHAPTER FOUR

I sat in a chair on the front lawn, my eyes closed and face turned toward the sun. The book in my lap lay untouched. What was it, I wondered, about Nicholas that prompted Jason to regard him with a negative attitude?

Since our quarrel two days ago we'd both made it a point to avoid each other. So far we'd been able to conceal our antagonism, but logic told me that eventually the truth would become evident.

"May I join you, Abby?" Martin Justin penetrated my gloomy cogitation. I raised a hand to shield my eyes. He was on the porch, Leah behind him.

"Of course you may." I smiled and went to help Leah guide his chair down the ramp. "The sun's so warm, it's made me lazy," I confessed on our way to the rattan chair.

"After your trip, I'm glad to see you're relaxing. Besides,"—he grinned—"I've decided to put you to work."

I sat down and gave him a slow searching look. Grandfather was silent for a moment, his eyes watching Leah fidget with the brake on his chair. She seemed interested in what he was about to say. This didn't surprise me in the least bit, though it did add to my uneasiness. Between her and Jason I felt as if I were under constant surveillance.

Grandfather grew impatient. "Just leave it, Leah."

"Yes, sir." In one quick motion, as though her hand had been slapped, she pulled it from the brake.

Without looking at either of us, Leah took off across the sun-washed lawn to the house. A group of robins, alarmed by her rapid steps, chirped, fluttered their wings, and took to the air.

"Abby."

I blinked, throwing off the faraway feeling that had settled over me. "Yes, sir."

"Would you mind if I put you to work?"

"No, of course not. What can I do to help?"

"Well, I'd really appreciate it if you would take over the management of our household."

I gave his request careful consideration, then said, "I do want to be helpful, Grandfather, but I know nothing of overseeing a large home and servants."

"It isn't difficult, my dear, just time-consuming."

The sound of pounding hoofs disrupted our conversation and I slid around on the chair. It was only Jason, astride an Appaloosa. As he passed by on his way to the stables, Jason raised his hand in a friendly gesture. Grandfather waved back, then said to me, "Didn't you tell me the other day that you managed your father's home and his office accounts?"

"Yes."

"Then you'll have no problems here and it would be a big help. I'm afraid I haven't the patience to cope with it anymore, and Jason's so busy at the mill that I'm sure he'd be relieved to have you take over the responsibility."

"What responsibility?" Jason questioned as he approached and came to a stop in front of me.

Grandfather told him.

Jason regarded me carefully and to my astonishment I saw friendly lights in his eyes. Thrown off guard, I lowered my own. "I hope you accepted the job, Abby," he said.

At that moment it seemed important to prove to

him that I was capable and not merely an idle woman with idle thoughts. "I'll give it a try," I informed him.

"Good." Martin Justin slammed his fist down on the arm of his chair. "Jason can go over the books with you this evening after dinner and I'll let the servants know you're in charge."

"Abby,"—Jason chuckled—"do you have the feeling you've been rushed into this?"

"A little." I gave him a thin smile.

Grandfather grinned. "Well, I'll leave you two young folks alone."

"Oh, but that's not necessary," I said quickly. I had no desire to be alone with Jason. He seemed amicable, but I was wary.

"Actually, Martin, I would like to talk with Abby."

A devilish gleam came into Martin Justin's eyes. "I thought so. Just push me to the door, Jason, and I'll call for Leah. See you later, Abby." He winked at me as Jason turned his chair.

Absently, I picked up the book from my lap and held it tightly. This was ridiculous, I chided myself, I couldn't assume the worst every time Jason wanted to talk with me.

The front door closed, and he came toward me. "It's been awhile since I've been down to the lake," he said. "Would you walk with me?"

He noticed my hesitation, but his smile did not waver. A stroll along the lake would only prolong our conversation, and I didn't want that. On the other hand if he was trying to bridge the gap between us, then I could not turn my back on him. So once again I laid aside Emily Bronte's *Wuthering Heights*, and followed Jason across the lawn.

The air was still and the firs stood erect and tranquil, reaching toward the cloudless sky. We walked northeast, leaving the grass, and wended our way down a dark, narrow path. Trees loomed over us, and we were surrounded by a thick undergrowth. Puzzled, I asked, "Where are we going?"

"I didn't think you'd been this way," Jason said over his shoulder. "You can't see this path unless you're right on top of it. I thought you might like to see the apple orchard. It should be in bloom." He stopped without warning, and I bumped into him.

"What's the matter?" I blurted. He took hold of my arm and gestured for me to be quiet. I didn't know if I should be annoyed by his sudden, unexplained move or apprehensive.

Several seconds elapsed before he came around to face me, and then he regarded me in silence. There was a gentleness in Jason's eyes I had never before seen and as they held mine, I felt an unwanted stirring—a response I had no wish to feel. My heartbeat quickened as his hand slid down my arm and softly closed over my fingers. "Why did you stop?" I stammered.

"Hm?" He blinked. "Oh, I heard the rustle of bushes and I thought perhaps we might catch a glimpse of a deer."

"Oh." I swallowed hard, and pulled my hand from his. "Shall we continue to the orchard?"

He hesitated, then nodded and turned away.

At the edge of a clearing he stopped again and I came alongside him. The orchard was breathtaking. It was as if we had stepped into a painting. Apple blossoms sparkled in the sunlight and dark-green grass embraced the trees. At the end of the clearing rows of golden daffodils encircled a gazebo. As we leisurely moved toward it, I saw a fish jump nearby in the clear blue water, sending ripples across its surface. I entered the enclosure and crossed to the far side. "Abby," Jason said from the entrance, "I want to apologize for the other evening. I realize I was a bit harsh. It's just that since Martin isn't able to watch after you, I feel that it's my responsibility. And, to be perfectly honest, it would make it a lot easier on me if you didn't go gallivanting."

"Gallivanting?" I swung around. "You must have a very low opinion of me."

He came into the gazebo. "No, Abby, it's because I have a high opinion of you that I'm concerned."

"I appreciate that, Jason, but I really don't need anyone to watch over me. I'm a grown woman."

"Yes," he said, grinning, "I've noticed that."

I lifted my chin. "I can take care of myself."

"Ordinarily, I'm sure you can. But where Nicholas Wells is concerned, I have my doubts. He's shrewd and he's out to make a name for himself. Why, I honestly believe he'd do anything to get what he wants."

"How in the world can that possibly affect me?"

Jason moved to my side. "Look around you. Someday this will all be yours."

"Why do you presume that? You've given years to my grandfather and the mill. Everything should be yours."

"Your grandfather has already given me far more than I'll ever be able to return. He can't live in discord, Abby, so you and I are going to have to make every effort to get along."

"I realize that."

"Then we shouldn't have any further problems. And believe me, I won't say another word about Wells because I know by now you'll do exactly as you please. But I do hope you'll be cautious and view him objectively."

"Good heavens, Jason, I'm not stupid. And for my grandfather's sake I do want us to be friends."

He took a step closer. "Only for Martin's sake?"

This was too much. I had no wish to get involved with emotions I didn't understand. Most of all I was skeptical. What else could I feel when Jason had suddenly switched from open hostility to this?

I returned my attention to the lake and changed the subject to safer ground. "Where did you live before you came here?"

"In town,"—he sounded frustrated—"near the mill. My folks had a small home. In fact, I still own it. I lived in it my first year at the university."

I looked at him, impressed. "Did you graduate?"

"Yes," he said simply, then suggested we head back to the house. "If I'm to go over the accounts with you tonight, then I'll have to get them in order. What a relief it will be"—he grinned—"not having Leah shove those weekly menus under my nose."

We left the gazebo and wandered along the rim of the lake. "Do you think you'll like it here?" Jason inquired. "I mean, Seattle must seem backwoodsy in comparison to San Francisco."

"Well, it doesn't appear to be quite as exciting as San Francisco." I grinned. "But I do like it here. It's so beautiful and serene."

"You won't be bored?"

"No, I don't think so. Besides, I've always been able to keep myself busy and it means a lot to me to be with my grandfather."

Jason laughed. "Then I guess we're stuck with you whether we like it or not."

"That's an awful thing to say." I scowled at him.

He caught me by the arm and brought me about to meet his eyes. "I'm sorry; I was only teasing."

He looked sincere, but the fact that he hadn't wanted me here initially made me a little dubious.

"Come on, Abby," he soothed, "smile. Pretty

women shouldn't frown, you know."

Despite doubt, I succumbed to his gentle plea.

"Now, that's better." He grinned, and took my hand in his.

Back on the front lawn Jason retrieved my book from the rattan chair; then we climbed the stone steps to the house, cleaned the mud from our shoes on the scraper by the front door, and went inside. Jason excused himself and continued down the hallway to the study, while I crossed to the open parlor doors.

Grandfather sat alone before the fire. The sound of my footsteps on the polished floor drew his attention from the portrait of his wife. "Abby,"—his tone was thoughtful—"do you play the piano?"

"Yes, Grandfather. Would you like me to play for you?"

"If you would, please. There's some music in the cabinet next to the piano." I went straight to the rosewood cabinet, placed my book on top of its shiny surface, then pulled open the carved double doors. The sheets of music were yellowed and worn and my hands trembled as I removed a stack of them and stood up.

"Did my father play from these?" I asked.

"Both he and your grandmother played from them. Her favorite composer was Chopin. Can you play any of his pieces?"

"Yes, sir." I blinked back tears.

The music for "Polonaise" was particularly worn, so I presumed it must have been my grandmother's favorite. I played it first.

My last selection, the "Etude" in E major, proved to be an unwise choise, for it was a soulful song which brought back a rush of memories. When I left the piano and went to Grandfather's side, I noticed that his eyes were as filmed as my own.

He cleared his throat. "You play beautifully, Abby my dear. You must favor me with selections often. I've missed it. Jason took lessons for a while, but all he ever produced was an abundance of noise. Don't you dare tell him I told you, though." Grandfather grinned, and so did I.

At dinner Jason was more talkative and cheerful than usual. While Grandfather and I were favorably influenced by Jason's good mood, I could see that Leah was not. The relaxed atmosphere and occasional laughter seemed to annoy her. Her rigid expression made me uncomfortable, so I attempted to improve her disposition. I gave her a smile I hoped conveyed warmth and friendliness, than asked if she'd had a chance to enjoy today's sun.

She pressed her lips together, then responded as she rounded the table to pick up the fork which had slipped from my grandfather's hand. "No, Miss Justin,"—she managed to sound courteous—"I've been busy with housework all day." As she leaned forward to grasp the utensil, traces of mud on the hemline of her skirt caught my attention. Obviously Leah had not been entirely confined to the house.

Later in the evening, Jason and I went to the study where he attempted to acquaint me with the household accounts. Although they certainly were not difficult to understand, the spicy aroma of his cologne seemed to paralyze my mind and more than once he was forced to repeat himself. To my absolute chagrin, all my efforts to impress him with my competency crumbled before my very eyes.

After we finished, I thanked him and was about to take leave of his company when he suggested a walk along the lake. "Again?" I laughed, recalling our afternoon stroll.

"Why not?" He grinned. "It's the most peaceful place in all of Seattle."

I accepted his invitation, though I was a trifle hesitant. Was Jason romantically involved with Leah? If he was, then I certainly didn't want to cause her any more unnecessary distress. But surely if he cared for her, he wouldn't deliberately hurt her. Would he?

It was indeed peaceful by the lake, and from my seat on the lawn swing I dreamily stared at the silvery glow of the full moon on the placid water. Jason and I didn't talk much, and I imagined that like myself he was deriving a sense of contentment from the mild night air and the musical sounds of the frogs and crickets.

It was so pleasant there, that on the following evening I once again meandered over the moon-splashed lawn to the swing. As I neared it, I noticed Jason sitting on it, and I came to an abrupt halt. He must have heard the rustle of my petticoats, for he looked around. For one instant, before he flashed a smile, I saw annoyance cross his face. "I'm sorry," I said, "I didn't know you were here. I won't disturb you."

I started to turn away, but his voice stayed me. "You're not disturbing me, Abby. Come on over and keep me company."

I did sit with him for a while, but I have to admit I was ill-at-ease, for I kept wondering which of the emotions he first displayed was genuine—the annoyance or the smile.

CHAPTER FIVE

On Saturday morning I was pleasantly surprised by an unexpected visit from Nicholas. "I was on my way home from a business trip to Renton," he explained, "so I thought I'd stop in to see if you're still in favor of our outing tomorrow."

I sat down on the sofa and looked at him steadily. "Of course I am. Why? Have you changed your mind?"

He made himself comfortable beside me. "Definitely not! But I did notice that Jason disapproved and then after you spoke alone with him the other evening there seemed to be a strain between the two of you. I thought perhaps that during the week he might have talked you out of going with me."

"Well, he didn't. Besides, he's not my guardian. My grandfather's approval is all that is necessary."

Nicholas smiled. "Well, I'm glad to hear that. Since he and I are good friends I don't think he'll object if I come to see you—often." He held my eyes with his. "Would you mind if I did, Abby?"

I looked away, a little embarrassed by his boldness.

"I'm sorry; I shouldn't have been so forward. I have a habit of always saying exactly what I feel."

"I have the same habit." I grinned, and returned my attention to him.

"Really?" He laughed, and I nodded.

His expression grew serious. "Would you mind if I came to see you from time to time?"

"No," I murmured.

"Do you ride?"

"Yes, but not very well. I took lessons for a while, but I'm afraid I wasn't an apt pupil."

"Maybe you had a poor instructor."

"No." I laughed. "I think he had a poor student."

Nicholas eyed me with amusement. "In any case, would you consider riding with me sometime? The countryside is pretty at this time of the year, with the wild flowers in bloom."

"If you don't mind a slow rider."

"I'll not mind." His voice was light.

"I'll have to check with my grandfather, of course."

Nicholas nodded. "Where is he, anyway?"

"Down at the stables, chatting with Mr. Brannon. Would you like me to send Leah to fetch him?"

"Thank you, Abby, but I really can't stay. I have to get back to the mill and clean up some paperwork. I'll stop by the stables on my way out and pay my respects."

I accompanied Nicholas to the door. "Shall I have Mrs. Brannon pack us a picnic lunch for our outing?" I asked.

"Now why didn't I think of a picnic lunch?" He laughed. "It's a good thing one of us is farsighted. You know, I haven't been on a picnic since I was a boy."

"I haven't been on one for a long time either."

He regarded me from beneath thick, dark lashes. "I really am looking forward to tomorrow."

"So am I."

Nicholas studied my face for a long moment, then told me good-by and went from the house.

Dreamlike I returned to the parlor and picked up my book. But I could not concentrate on the author's words, for thoughts of Nicholas dominated my mind. He was so warm and friendly and above all, unlike

Jason, not complicated.

In the late afternoon we had another unexpected visitor. I was relaxing on the back porch with my needlepoint when Leah came out to inform me that a Mr. Taylor was waiting in the parlor. "Mr. Taylor?" I said.

"Yes, miss." Her face was impassive. "He's from the mill. I think he's the bookkeeper."

"Oh. Is he here on business?"

"No, I don't believe so. Anyway, when I told him Mr. Justin was still napping, Mr. Taylor asked if he might meet you. Shall I have him come out here?"

"No, thank you, Leah, that won't be necessary. I'll go on in."

"Yes, miss." She went back into the house.

I set aside the needlepoint, then left the porch. When I entered the parlor a meek-looking man, who appeared to be in his forties, rose to his feet. He adjusted his wire-framed spectacles, which I noticed blended with the sprinkling of gray at his temples, then came forward. "Good afternoon, Miss Justin." He smiled. "I'm Zachary Taylor, an employee of the mill."

I returned his smile and held out my hand. "I'm happy to meet you, Mr. Taylor."

He took my hand in his friendly clasp. "The pleasure is all mine."

"Please, won't you make yourself comfortable." I motioned to the sofa. "My grandfather should be awake shortly."

As we seated ourselves I asked Mr. Taylor if he would care for a cool drink. He graciously declined, then put a question to me. "Will you be coming out for a tour of the mill soon, Miss Justin?"

"I expect I will be, though no one has really said

much about it."

"Oh?" He arched a brow. "I guess your grandfather changed his mind then."

I narrowed my eyes. "I'm afraid I don't understand."

"Well, the last time I was here he was so excited about your seeing it. He told me he was going to have Jason show you around immediately." He leaned forward. "Is he all right—your grandfather, I mean?"

"Oh, yes, sir, he's just fine. I imagine he'll suggest I view the mill after he's certain that I'm all settled in."

Zachary Taylor sat back, a look of relief overspreading his sallow face. "Yes, I expect you're right."

"Have you worked at the mill for quite a while, Mr. Taylor?"

"It doesn't seem like it,"—he beamed—"but I've been an employee for twenty-seven years now."

"Taylor," Martin Justin called from the hallway, "what in the devil are you doing here at this hour? Are you neglecting your job?"

"Well, he *sounds* like himself,"—Zachary Taylor chuckled—"never letting anyone get away with anything."

Leah wheeled Grandfather into the room. "Well, Zach,"—he grinned—"are you?"

"Now, Mr. Justin, have you ever known me to neglect my duties?"

"Not in the past, but now that I'm not around to keep an eye on you, who knows?"

I came to my feet. "If you'll excuse me, I'll leave you gentlemen to your visit. I enjoyed chatting with you, Mr. Taylor, and I hope to see you again soon."

"Thank you, miss. I hope so, too."

Leah tucked the afghan around Grandfather's legs, then asked if he was comfortable.

He told her he was and as she and I made for the

door, Mr. Taylor said, "Your granddaughter is lovely, Martin. Now I know why Jason hasn't been working late the last few days."

If Leah was irritated by that remark I would not know, for I casually headed for the stairs and mounted without looking at her.

At dinner I only half-listened when Grandfather told Jason of our two visitors, for my curiosity over him and Leah kept me preoccupied. Each time she came into the room I watched Jason from beneath my lashes, looking for some indication of his feelings for her. He was polite and he smiled at her once or twice, but he didn't seem to particularly notice when she deliberately let her hand brush his.

"Zach was quite taken with Abby," Grandfather was saying. "He wanted to know when she would be coming out to the mill."

Jason looked at me quickly, catching me watching him. Flustered, I wanted to lower my gaze, but he held my eyes with his, his brow arched quizzically. "I hope Zach didn't bore you with shoptalk, Abby." His tone was casual.

"Our visit was brief," I told him in an even tone, and resumed eating. I did not regard Jason surreptitiously again, and at the conclusion of the meal he closeted himself in the study—to work, I presumed.

I didn't see him again until later in the evening when he came into the parlor to inquire if I would be going to church with him in the morning. I told him that I would like to, then went up to bed.

However, too many thoughts crowded my mind and I was unable to sleep. I tossed and turned for a long time and then I managed to relax a bit when I envisioned Nicholas' cheerful face. I snuggled down, pondering what it would be like to attend a formal affair with him—the theater or maybe a party. I had no doubt that he would look impressive in evening attire, and that he would be totally at ease in an elegant social environment.

I opened my eyes and frowned into the darkness, recalling Jason's look of displeasure when Grandfather had told him of our visitors. Would I be subjected to that disagreeable expression every time Nicholas came to call? Disturbed by that grim prospect I began to toss and turn again, until finally I decided to distract my thoughts by reading for a while.

I sat up and lighted the lamp. The absence of my book from the bedside table reminded me that I had left it in the parlor. Although I was in no mood to brave the cool night air to go after it, neither was I desirous of staring into the darkness for hours. So with one quick motion, I flipped back the quilt and caught up my wrapper from the foot of the bed. Pulling the silk garment about me, I thrust my feet into slippers, then made my way down the dimly lit passageway.

The staircase was shrouded in darkness, and I paused to grasp the rail firmly before I commenced my descent. When I was about a quarter of the way down, the heel of my right slipper came in contact with a hard object, turning my ankle and throwing me forward. A fierce bolt of pain surged through my arm as I fought to retain my grip on the slick banister. And as the lower portion of my body struck the carpeted stairs, a scream from deep within my throat punctuated the silence.

Shaking uncontrollably I lay on the steps, clutching the balustrade, my firm grip having prevented my tumbling to the floor below.

The sound of running feet from the hallway above impelled me to shout, "Watch out, there's something on the stairs."

There was a moment of stillness, then Jason called, "Are you hurt?"

Before I was able to respond he was at my side, hauling me to him. "Are you hurt, Abby?"

"No. . . . I don't think so."

"What happened?" Leah cried from somewhere below.

"It's Abby. She fell on the stairs. Light the lamps in the parlor," he ordered. "I'm bringing her down."

I kept my head against the warmth of his flannel dressing gown as he gently lifted me and carried me to the sofa.

Jason knelt at my side, his face soft with concern. "What happened? And what on earth are you doing up at this hour?"

My arm throbbed, my ankle was sore, and what was worse, I felt utterly foolish. "I couldn't sleep," I murmured. "And I was on my way to get the book I left on the table over there, when my slipper caught on something."

He frowned, then stood up. "Take a look at her ankle, Leah. I'm going to see what it was."

She nodded, and sat down on the edge of the sofa. Leah's golden hair hung down her back in one long plait, and her blue cambric wrapper was drawn tight, enhancing her full figure. "Which ankle was it, miss?" she asked, and our heads came up at the jangle of Martin Justin's bell.

"I'm all right," I assured her, and urged her to look in on my grandfather.

As she slowly rose to comply, I said, "Tell him I slipped. I wasn't injured, and that I'm returning to bed."

On her way past Jason in the doorway, he reached out and seized her by the arm. "Where are you going?" he demanded.

"To look in on Mr. Justin." Her voice shook.

He released her. "Go ahead then, but see to it that you come right back."

She nodded, her eyes fixed on the feather duster in his hand.

Jason returned to my side and stood over me, brandishing the hard-handled object. Even though I still trembled, the sight of a robust man waving a feather duster about struck me as funny, and I had to hold my breath to suppress laughter. "This is what you stumbled on, Abby. There's no excuse for such carelessness. You could have been severely injured — or worse."

Leah came back into the room, and he shook the duster at her furiously. "How do you explain this being on the stairway?"

"I don't know," she stammered. "I was in the pantry most of the day. I didn't ask anyone to dust. Maybe Mrs. Brannon knows. I'll ask her in the morning."

"You needn't bother! I'll talk with her myself. Now go on up and see that Miss Justin's room is ready."

She squared her shoulders, drawing attention to her heavy breasts. "Yes, sir."

"Is my grandfather all right?" I asked before she left; she assured me that he was.

"Can you walk, Abby?" Jason wanted to know.

"I think so." He took both of my hands in his and helped me to my feet. A sharp pain coursed through my ankle, bringing a moan to my lips.

Jason slipped an arm about my waist. "I'd better carry you up."

Even though I had likeed his holding me, I was, nevertheless, embarrassed and quickly declined the offer.

Strangely enough I slept well that night. Perhaps

that was because I drifted into sleep remembering the warmth of Jason's body when he had held me close.

In the morning I awoke with a dull ache in my arm, though I was relieved to discover that my ankle bore no traces of pain or tenderness.

When I went down to the dining room for breakfast Jason and Grandfather were already at the table. Jason rose at my entrance, and for a fractional moment my eyes lingered on him, admiring the fit of his well-tailored suit.

"How are you?" he asked simply.

"Fine, thank you," I told him with a smile.

Grandfather beckoned, and I moved to the table and sat down in the chair beside him. He took my hand in his dry clasp. "Jason told me what happened," he said softly. "I'm so sorry, Abby. I really don't understand it. Nothing like this has ever happened before. We've questioned Mrs. Brannon and Dorothea, but they were no help."

The unnerving events of my first night in the Justin home pressed forward in my mind. I sank back on my chair, drawing my hand from Martin Justin's. Had someone deliberately placed the duster on the stairs? That thought seemed incredible, and yet was it really? I glanced down the length of the table to Jason, hoping to see the gentle and concerned expression I had observed last night, but he sipped coffee, his face devoid of emotion. A thread of suspicion crept forward in my mind. Was it possible that my stumble on the stairs was linked in some way to his midnight appearance at my bedroom door? And had he been the one causing the disturbance in the attic prior to that? Twice since my arrival he had stressed my right of inheritance to the Justin wealth, giving the impression that in time he would relinquish his authority to me. But could a man who has experienced such power surrender it so easily?

Grandfather broke in on my ruminations. "Abby, you'd best help yourself to some breakfast or you'll be late for church."

Wordlessly, I came to my feet and went to the sideboard. As I helped myself to small portions of ham, scrambled eggs, and blueberry muffins, it suddenly occurred to me that no one could have known I would descend the stairs last night.

I returned to the table feeling guilty that I had suspected Jason of wrongdoing. However, my sense of guilt was of short duration, for another thought struck me. He could have placed the duster on the stairs believing perhaps that the object would go unnoticed beneath the hemline of my billowing skirts.

Had I fallen down the dark carpeted stairs in the light of day, Jason could have claimed innocence by merely stating he had not seen the obstruction. After all, his stride was long, and I'd noticed that he generally ascended and descended two or three steps at a time.

I didn't want to believe he wished me harm, but the salient fact remained: Jason and I were the only ones who used the staircase at night. My stomach churned as I forced myself to consume the food on my plate, and I felt overwhelmed by a desperate desire to flee from this house.

Jason rose and came to my side. "If you're finished, Abby, then we'd better be on our way."

I hesitated. I didn't want to be alone with Jason, and I wished that Grandfather were able to accompany us. If not him, then at least somebody.

With a heavy heart I kissed the aged man good-by, then followed Jason out the front door.

"The church is up the road about a mile and a half," he informed me as we left the drive and headed northward on the main road. "I'm sorry about last night, Abby. I don't know how to explain it. One of the servants must have been careless and is afraid to admit the truth."

"Perhaps," I said between stiff lips and focused my attention on the sun-brightened woods. Chipmunks chattered and scampered over fallen logs and occasionally a rabbit dashed across the rutted road.

As we approached a clearing, a young boy around eight years old, jumped out from behind a vine maple and ran alongside our buggy. "Hello, Mr. Jason, who's the pretty lady?"

Jason slowed the carriage. "Hello, Joey. This is Miss Justin."

I flashed a smile. "I'm pleased to meet you, Joey."

He returned the expression, then ran off when someone from behind called to him.

"That's Doc Sims's boy," Jason remarked. "Doc has seven more youngsters at home." We passed a general store, several houses, and what appeared to be a schoolhouse.

At the end of the clearing, sheltered between tall cedars, was the small whitewashed, steepled church. Jason reined in alongside the other carriages, alighted, then handed me down. We walked over the cedar rounds, which formed the pathway to the church, and up its wooden steps to the narrow entrance.

Later, after the service, Jason stood tall and erect at my side, introducing me to most of the congregation. My head reeled, attempting to remember all their names.

"This is Doc Sims, Abby," Jason said as a short man stepped forward, his dark hair flecked with gray and his face weathered. Two adorable young towheadead girls clung to him.

Dr. Sims smiled warmly. "I've been looking forward

to meeting you, Miss Justin."

I matched his expression and held out my hand. "Thank you, sir."

"I heard your father was also a doctor."

"Yes, he was." By now most of the congregation had departed, and Jason and I were able to talk with Dr. and Mrs. Sims for several enjoyable minutes. He seemed particularly interested in the fact that I had assisted my father in his office.

"I could really use some help straightening out my office." He laughed. "If you ever get bored, Miss Justin, please don't hesitate to come on over and see me."

"Perhaps I will." I smiled. "I loved the work and miss it very much."

On our way home Jason was distant, seemingly absorbed in thought. I made no attempt to engage him in conversation.

When the carriage rounded the drive and the house and a buggy came into view, he scoffed, "Hm, looks like Wells is here already. He sure isn't wasting any time."

Jason pulled the horse to a stop behind the other conveyance. When he came around to help me down, his hands lingered on my waist, and he looked at me grimly. "Remember, Abby, what I told you about Wells," he warned.

CHAPTER SIX

The front door opened and Nicholas came out on the porch. Jason's hands on my waist tightened and he stiffened with annoyance. I tried to step back, but he held me firm. I had the distinct impression he desired to draw me into his embrace, but for some unexplainable reason, he held himself in check.

Jason looked down at me with a protectiveness that frightened me a little and yet at the same time revealed tenderness—an emotion I suspected he seldom surrendered to.

In that brief space of time in which he stood so close that his breath touched my cheek, I felt my suspicion of him recede. I knew it was unwise to allow my pounding blood to influence my mind, but I was unable to help myself.

"Thought I heard you pull in," Nicholas called from the porch. "We've picked a beautiful day for our outing, Abby."

Jason seemed about to say something, but then he changed his mind and stepped back. "Have a nice afternoon," he said politely, then reboarded the carriage and drove off toward the stables.

I hurried up the steps, somewhat embarrassed that Nicholas had seen that moment of closeness between Jason and me.

Nicholas regarded me with raised eyebrows. "Looks like you and Jason are friendlier."

I could feel the color come to my cheeks. "We understand each other better. Besides, it's important to my grandfather's health that Jason and I get along."

Nicholas fell into step beside me. "Yes, I'm sure you're right."

We joined Grandfather in the parlor. He sat before the open window overlooking the drive. As I leaned forward to kiss his papery cheek, I wondered if he'd seen Jason and me, or if he'd overheard my words to Nicholas. Perhaps it would not upset Martin Justin to know that Jason and I had frequently been at odds, but I didn't want to take that chance.

I came erect and asked in a light tone, "Did you miss me?"

He took my hand and gave it a gentle squeeze. "Certainly, my dear. Nicholas came along, though, and we've had a nice visit."

To my relief he gave no indication that he'd overheard Nicholas and me. In fact, the grin Grandfather flashed reminded me of the expression on the face of a cat who had cornered a mouse and was toying with it.

Nicholas crossed to my side. "I'll keep Martin company while you go up and change, Abby."

I gave him a nod in acknowledgment and left the room. After donning a gingham dress and sturdy boots, I returned to the parlor and kissed Grandfather good-by.

It wasn't until Nicholas and I were settled in the boat that I became aware of how differently he was dressed. Even though he was casually attired in a buckskin coat and corduroy trousers there was still a dissimilarity between him and Jason.

Nicholas noticed my sharp appraisal, but he gave me a smile that told me he didn't mind. Nevertheless, I was still embarrassed and strangely tongue-tied.

"Did you meet your neighbors this morning?" he

asked, trying to put me at ease.

My head came up. "Yes, I did. Do you know Dr. Sims?"

"I've come across him a couple of times at logging camps."

"It seems he needs help in his office, and I thought perhaps one day this week I might go over and volunteer my assistance."

"I take it you've helped your father in his office?"

"Yes, I did, and I miss working with people. Although maybe it wouldn't be the same assisting another doctor." I paused as a recollection of my father's kind face came forward in my mind, and a twinge of loneliness touched my very being. "There were quite a few people at church," I managed, "but I didn't see many houses along the way."

Nicholas straightened, lifting the oars from the water. "There are more houses as you travel further north, and a logging camp beyond the church. But I suggest you not venture that way alone."

"Why not?"

"Because loggers are a rough breed, Abby." He plunked the oars back into the water. "They have no families and live in the poorest conditions. Most of them work just until they've earned enough money to spend in town, then quit. When the money's gone they move on to the next camp. But enough talk of loggers." He smiled. "Tell me, do you think Martin will allow you to work with Doc Sims?"

"I hope so. The serenity of the country is nice, but I'm used to the active life of the city. Besides, my father taught me to be useful and independent. He didn't admire frivolous or docile women."

A mischievous smile tugged at the corners of Nicholas' mouth and his eyes, sparkling in the sunlight, were as blue as the water. "I have the feeling you're going to give the two men in your home quite a time of it."

"I expect you're right." I grinned and turned my attention to the view. The sun glistened on the cedar-shingled roof of the house. It looked majestic nestled among the enormous firs. Dreamlike, I let my gaze move along the shoreline, past the gazebo and the trees abundant with apple blossoms. From the chimneys of the houses to the north, wisps of blue-gray smoke rose; and to the south, soft plumes of clouds overwhelmed the horizon.

"Abby," Nicholas said, sounding serious, "has Jason said anything to you about the accidents at the mill?"

I looked at him quickly. "No, not really. He prefers not to discuss them."

"I see. Well, doesn't it seem odd to you that they began immediately after Jason took command?"

"I wasn't aware they began then. In any case, what difference would that make? Jason wouldn't do anything detrimental to the mill; it's his life."

Nicholas held the oars steady. "Perhaps he isn't capable of managing it."

I responded in swift defense, which surprised me a little. "My grandfather told me Jason is doing an excellent job."

Nicholas was silent. His eyes watched me, considering. "Martin hasn't been to the mill for several months now," he said at last. "And doesn't it seem strange, too, Abby, that Jason is hiding this trouble from him?"

"He isn't hiding it. He's only trying to protect my grandfather's health."

"Are you sure?"

I sat back, stunned. And why in heaven's name was I defending Jason? Good grief, for all I knew he could be plotting to do away with me.

Often, throughout the afternoon, my thoughts wandered from Nicholas and our exploration of the island to Jason. Was I right in following his instructions not to inform Grandfather of the accidents? But then, since he was an invalid confined to a wheelchair, what purpose would it serve if I did tell him? As much as I dreaded it, the only way it appeared that I might be able to determine the cause of the trouble would be to spend time at the mill, observe and learn.

I tried not to let that dismal prospect influence my mood, but apparently I wasn't successful, for on our way back across the lake, Nicholas said, "You've been awfully quiet, Abby. Have I upset you with my remarks about Jason?"

His face, soft with concern, brought a lump of regret to my throat. "I'm sorry if I haven't been very good company."

He gave me a half-smile, his eyes holding mine. "I always enjoy being with you, and I hate to see the afternoon come to an end."

"So do I," I admitted boldly. "And you haven't upset me. It's just that I'm not sure what course I should follow. Grandfather says Jason is capable and yet you don't seem to think so."

"Look at it this way, Abby: if Jason has nothing to hide, then why is he purposely keeping you uninformed? He certainly doesn't have to worry about protecting *your* health."

We came alongside the dock. "Of course he doesn't. But maybe he feels it's pointless to involve me in something I probably wouldn't understand anyway. I mean, aren't the accidents due to mechanical malfunctions?"

"Yes, and that could be his reasoning. But then it seems to me that he would just say so."

As Nicholas helped me from the boat I considered

telling him of the incident with the feather duster, but I rejected the notion. After all, I had no proof that Jason was involved, and I simply could not bring myself to cast suspicion on Grandfather's foster son without positive evidence.

On the dock Nicholas looked down at me and said, "I understand your grandfather wants you to observe the operations of the mill, so why not use that as a reason to go there and speak with Zachary Taylor, the bookkeeper. He's been with the company for a long time and he knows what's going on."

"Yes, I know. I met him yesterday when he came to the house for a visit. But I can't bombard him with questions regarding Jason's competency."

"You don't have to bombard him, Abby. Your grandfather founded the company and as his heir it would be only natural for you to be interested and inquisitive."

He looked so serious, I couldn't resist a grin. "Undoubtedly I'll ask a lot of moronic questions because I know absolutely nothing about a sawmill."

Nicholas laughed and hugged me to him. "Moronic questions would be an excellent cover-up. Zach would never suspect a thing. Besides, he loves to talk about the company, so he'll be pleased by your interest."

"You sound as if you know him quite well."

On our way to the front of the house, he took my hand in his as he responded. "As a matter of fact, I do. You see, when I first opened my business I couldn't afford a full-time bookkeeper, so your grandfather suggested that I approach Zach about handling my books on a part-time basis. He was more than willing to give me a hand, and I think he was very flattered that your grandfather recommended him so highly."

At the base of the front-porch steps Nicholas

stopped and turned me about to meet his eyes. "Go to the mill," he urged, "and talk with Zach. And don't worry." He lifted my chin. "Jason won't be able to deceive you. You're too intelligent for that and he probably knows it."

I felt a chill, despite the warmth of the late-afternoon sun. If it was Jason's intent to deceive me and he realized he wasn't being successful, what then?

"Smile," Nicholas prodded, his hand still beneath my chin, "and say you'll go riding with me next Saturday."

The thought of another outing with him brightened my spirits. "I'd love to. And who knows, maybe then I'll finally sight a deer. They sure seem to be scarce around here."

"Scarce isn't the word." He laughed.

"What do you mean?"

"The early settlers killed off all the deer for meat."

"Oh." I gulped. Why then had Jason stopped so abruptly on our way to the gazebo last week? What had he heard? Obviously not a deer, as he had claimed.

The front door closed with a resounding thud and I turned from Nicholas' touch. Jason was on the porch, looking me up and down with disapproving eyes.

I inhaled a deep breath, then tried to hide my exasperation behind the brightest smile I could muster. "We had a lovely time on the island, Jason. You should take a young lady over for a picnic lunch someday."

"I already have," he tossed back, his gaze lingering on the ripped flounce across the bottom of my dress. Certain that he suspected Nicholas of ungentlemanly conduct I altered my expression to a frown. Jason glared at me, then addressed my companion. "Wells," he said, "Martin would like you to come in for a while, if you have the time."

Nicholas replied that he did, and as we climbed the steps Jason moved along the porch headed for the rear of the house.

About half an hour later Nicholas excused himself to tend to some errands in town. I accompanied him to his buggy and it was while I was on my way back to the house that I again encountered Jason. He was coming toward me from the lake, a picnic basket clutched in his hand. "You must have been awfully distracted to go off and leave this in the boat," he said bluntly, and held up the wicker basket.

"Oh." I laughed, trying to make light of the oversight. "I guess Nicholas and I were too immersed in our conversation."

"Obviously." Jason was not amused.

He came to a stop in front of me, and I thanked him for bringing up the basket.

He regarded the hemline of my dress, then asked in a civil tone, "How did that happen?"

"I caught the flounce on some vines," I told him truthfully, and took the basket. "I'll take this in to Mrs. Brannon. And, Jason,"—I looked him in the eyes—"I really would appreciate it if you would not question my every action." With that I turned away and made for the kitchen.

The remainder of the day passed uneventfully, though my sleep that night was spasmodic. I simply could not dismiss my conversation with Nicholas, and I was more confused than ever. Was Jason incapable of managing the mill? Was he trying to deceive me? Or merely endeavoring to spare me from the aggravating problems there? And what of his negative attitude toward Nicholas? Did Jason truly distrust him? Or was he afraid of the questions Nicholas could kindle?

In the morning those thoughts were still sharp in my mind. I didn't want to think about them any more, so I hurriedly dressed and went down to breakfast. Grandfather had already eaten, so I partook of the meal in the kitchen where I could enjoy the company of Dorothea and Mrs. Brannon. Both mother and daughter seemed to be excited about something. Dorothea's eyes were bright and Mrs. Brannon was in and out of the pantry, checking provisions and jotting down needed supplies. I watched them curiously, waiting for one of them to comment on the reason for their excitement. But neither one of them did, so I presumed it was a personal matter.

After breakfast I went to the library to spend some time with my grandfather. Leah responded to my tap on the door. Her eyes twinkled and she looked exceptionally happy. Immediately I wondered if Jason had been paying her some attention.

"Come on in, Abby," Grandfather called from his chair near the window.

"What in the world are you up to?" I teased, noting the pile of papers on the table beside him.

"Have a seat and I'll tell you. Leah, you can go now. Abby will take over."

When we were alone he shuffled through the papers, then lifted his gaze to me and said, "We're going to have a party."

"We are?" I grinned.

"Yes." He nodded. "I thought this would be the simplest way for you to meet our friends and also give you the opportunity to become acquainted with some nice young ladies. After all, you can't go gallivanting the countryside with Nicholas all the time. It wouldn't be proper."

Gallivanting? My shoulders went slack. Hadn't

Jason accused me of that last week? Was my meeting young ladies his idea? Was he going to see to it that I spent my time at sophisticated tea parties? "Did Jason suggest the party?" I wanted to know.

"Why, yes, he did. And I should have thought of it myself."

"You don't think it's too soon after my father's death?"

"No, I don't believe so. At any rate, Jason and I discussed it over breakfast this morning and we felt it wouldn't be out of line. It's important for you to meet people of our community and besides, I don't think your father would have wanted you to mope around the house."

"No, he wouldn't."

A smile brightened the lined face. "Then we'll have the party. Now these are the names of the people I intend to invite." He pushed the papers across the table. "Jason has a list of the younger people and he'll go over it with you when he gets back."

"Back? From where?"

"He didn't tell you?"

"No."

"Well, it seems there's been a delay in logs coming in from one of the camps and he's gone to check on it. We handle a lot of government contracts, you know, and we can't afford delays."

"Does Nicholas handle government contracts, too?" I was curious.

"Yes." The word came slowly. "Tell me, Abby,"—Grandfather narrowed his eyes—"is this interest in Nicholas Wells more than just friendship?"

"He's been very kind," I said quietly, "and I like him a lot."

"I see. And how do you feel about Jason?"

"Well,"—I sighed—"he's a little difficult to

understand. I mean, he's so intense and rather aloof. But, for the most part, he's also been kind."

"Then the two of you are getting along all right?"

"Yes, sir," I lied, not wishing to upset him. "It's important to you that Jason and I be friends, Grandfather, isn't it?"

He placed a hand over mine. "Yes, it is, my dear. I love you both. You must be aware of that."

"Yes," I murmured. "I am."

He smiled, then returned the conversation to the party. "Now, then, when Jason comes home at the end of the week I thought maybe you and Dorothea could go into town with him one morning and start the arrangements. And I insist you order yourself a new ball gown."

I beamed, and asked if he'd selected a date yet for the event.

"Well, I was thinking of about three weeks from Saturday. There will be so much to do. Several friends from town will stay overnight, so we'll have to prepare the guest rooms. Knowing Mrs. Brannon,"—he chuckled—"she'll insist the house be scrubbed from attic to basement."

"This won't be too much of a strain on you, will it?"

"Good heavens, no. I'm looking forward to it. Why, we haven't had a party here since Jason graduated from the university and he didn't even want that. So you should be pleased he was considerate enough to suggest having one for you."

My mouth drooped, for I was certain Jason Landry had not suggested the party out of consideration for me. It was undoubtedly a means by which he felt he could choose my friends and be assured he had me under his thumb. Well, he would never accomplish that. A knock sounded on the door, and I came to my feet and went to it.

"Why, Dr. Sims, I smiled. "It's nice to see you again. Please, come in."

"Checkup time, Doc?" Martin Justin questioned. "Or just a friendly visit?"

"Both," the doctor replied as he came into the room. "I've been at the Jensens' for the last few hours, delivering their sixth child. So I thought I'd stop by here on my way home and see how you are. Mind if I sit down? I'm exhausted."

As Dr. Sims crumpled into the wing chair, I noticed his eyes were dull and there were deep lines formed around his mouth.

"Can I get you anything?" I offered. "Coffee or maybe some tea?"

He raised a declining hand as if it took a good deal of effort. "No, thanks. I must have drunk at least three gallons of coffee at the Jensens'."

He watched me as I drew up a straight-back chair, then said, "You know, Martin, I'd surely like to steal this granddaughter of yours."

"Oh?" Grandfather arched an eyebrow.

"She and I discussed your son's medical practice when we met yesterday and I must say she could be a tremendous help in my office."

"I'm afraid I don't understand."

"Well, for one thing, I haven't the time or the energy to keep my office or the accounts in order. Oh, Molly used to help, but with eight young ones to tend, she can hardly keep up with her own work."

Excitement coursed through me. "I really would like to help, Grandfather. May I?"

He looked at me in surprise.

Dr. Sims slipped father down into the chair. "Would you mind, Martin?"

"Well . . . I don't know."

"It would only be for one or two afternoons a week."

Martin Justin drew a short breath. "I'd do almost anything for you, Doc. After all, if it weren't for you I might not be alive today."

"I don't want you to consent on that basis."

Grandfather gave me a long and thoughtful look. "I had hoped, Abby, that you'd spend time learning the operations of the mill. Wouldn't it be too much for you to do both?"

I stared beyond him to the book-lined walls, giving the matter careful consideration. "No, I don't think so," I said at last. "Perhaps I could spend one afternoon a week at Dr. Sims's office, with the remaining afternoons devoted to whatever it is you want me to learn."

"Well . . . I don't want to be as strict with you as I was with your father; yet it does seem that a young lady shouldn't be running around so much. Jason said—" His voice trailed off.

My spine stiffened. "What did Jason say?"

He flicked my question aside with a wave of a hand. "Oh, nothing, dear, nothing. You can give it a try for a couple of weeks and we'll see how it works out."

"Oh, thank you." I hugged him.

"I appreciate it, Martin," Dr. Sims put in, then said to me, "If your grandfather doesn't mind, Abby, would it be convenient for you to come back with me this afternoon? I have some free time, or at least I think I do." He laughed. "And I can show you around. John, my eldest, can see you home."

I looked at Grandfather. "Would you mind?"

"No, I guess not, if that's what you really want."

A few minutes later I left the library and went to the kitchen to inform Mrs. Brannon that the doctor would be staying for lunch.

When I entered, Dorothea was busy sifting flour into a large bowl. Her cheeks were rosy from the warmth of the room and her eyes were still alight with excitement. "You know about the party, "—I smiled at her—"don't you?"

"Yes, miss, your grandfather told me before you came down to breakfast. He said you and me could go shopping. Is that all right with you?" Her voice dwindled as if she feared I might rescind the invitation.

"Of course it is, Dorothea. It'll be such fun making all the arrangements." We chatted gaily while I helped her prepare corn bread for the noon meal.

It was about one o'clock when the doctor and I boarded his buggy, and as we made our way over the rough road toward his office, I asked about the results of my grandfather's checkup. "He's doing amazingly well, Abby. Part of that is due, I'm sure, to the excellent care all of you at the house lavish on him, and part from his following my explicit instructions."

"He's very good about that," I confirmed with pride.

"Well, it's made the difference. Oh, by the way, I noticed his medication is getting low."

"Yes, I was going to mention that."

"I'll send some along home with you."

I nodded, then sat back and let my gaze wander over the moisture-laden evergreens and the canopy of gray clouds that overshadowed the sky as the doctor spoke reverently of his practice. His dedication reminded me of my father's.

Within twenty minutes Dr. Sims reined the horse to a stop in front of a medium-sized log house. Smoke billowed from its rock chimney. Adjacent to the house was a smaller log building; the shingle on its door identified it as the doctor's office.

Without warning rollicking children bounded from

the house and gathered around us. Their father scooped up the youngest and swung her up onto his shoulders. "You all remember Miss Justin, don't you?" He smiled down on them with paternal pride.

"Oh, yes," they chorused, jumping up and down.

After a brief visit with Mrs. Sims I followed her husband to his office. It was clean, and he appeared to have all the latest medical equipment, but it was very disorganized.

The oak desk in the far corner of the room was cluttered with an abundance of papers, and the diploma, centered on the wall behind the desk, hung askew. In the middle of the wall was a doorway. Beyond, I was able to see one corner of the examining table and a cabinet bulging with supplies; its glass doors hung open.

Dr. Sims went to the desk and placed his Gladstone bag on it. "As you can see, Abby, I am in desperate need of help, and I certainly hope this mess isn't going to scare you off."

"This *is* a bit overwhelming." I laughed. "But not enough to scare me away."

I set to work immediately, and by the end of the afternoon the instruments were in their proper places and the supply cabinet no longer bulged to the extent that its doors were unable to be closed. Before leaving for home I gathered the account books. "My project for tomorrow," I told the doctor.

That evening I retired earlier than usual. Lack of adequate sleep on the previous night coupled with an active day had left their effects on me. I had no trouble falling into a deep sleep. However, my slumber was of short duration, for I was rudely awakened by thumping noises overhead—the same sounds I had heard on my first night in the Justin home. I threw back the quilt and swung myself off the bed. "This is ridiculous," I complained out loud, and thrust my feet into slippers. I pulled my wrapper about me and stormed across the semidark room to the desk.

The thumping noises continued as I lighted the candle, but this time I was too irritated to tremble. I was determined to discover who was disturbing me, and why.

Slowly I moved along the hall and up the flight of stairs to the third floor. Darkness enveloped me. I raised the light aloft and watched the long shadows which the flickering flame threw against the wall. The passageway floor, bare of carpeting, prompted me to tiptoe. And cold air penetrated my wrapper, urging me to retreat to the warmth and safety of my room, but anger prodded me on.

The last door on the right would be directly over my room, and I inched toward it. A floorboard squeaked beneath my right foot and I withdrew it instantly, as if a rodent had scampered over it. For what seemed like eons of time I stood absolutely still, my ears strained, listening. Dead silence persuaded me to continue forward.

At the attic door I gave a gentle twist to the cold brass knob and stepped across the threshold. A splash of moonlight beamed through a window, spreading a silvery glow on the floor below. Declining courage influenced my shortened stride and motivated my gaze to dart about the darkened interior. Near the window was a chest of drawers and a mahogany coat rack. Both were covered with a network of spider webs and what appeared to be an accumulation of years of dust.

Footsteps clattered on the boards behind me. Before I was able to react, hands struck the middle of my back, impelling me forward with a force that flung the silver candlestick from my grasp. It hit the floor, dropping the attic into blackness at the precise moment that the door banged shut. I stumbled several feet across the wooden floor before I was able to catch my balance and pull to a stop. For timeless seconds utter silence seemed to press in around me and then the sound of heavy breathing began to drum in my ears.

CHAPTER SEVEN

Waves of fear welled in me, and my head reeled, terrified by the thought that perhaps the intruder was still in here. Fright kept me rooted to the floor, even though logic contradicted that emotion. Obviously, unless the other person were to light a lamp, darkness would keep my whereabouts a secret.

For what seemed like a long time I remained motionless, my ears attuned to the sound of labored breathing.

As the time lengthened and no other noises rent the stillness, I began to suspect it was my own erratic respiration that throbbed my ears.

I drew myself erect and inhaled a deep gulp of stale air. If silence prevailed, then I would know that I was alone.

In my misery I experienced one measure of relief. Jason was not home, so I was able to eliminate him as the person who had hurled me into this frightening predicament.

It was quiet, and I felt like a dolt. I had allowed my

own breathing to wrap me in terror. My lungs felt as though they were about to burst, and I slowly exhaled, easing the pain in my chest.

The dim circle of moonbeams that spilled through the window offered some comfort, but that was all. The illumination was too faint to light my way to the door.

Arms extended, I moved forward, slowly placing one foot before the other. A halo of moonshine danced over the sleeves of my silk wrapper as I crossed in front of the window, and I hastened my steps to lose myself again in the darkness. Several more steps brought my stiff fingers in contact with the wall. Somewhere to the left should be the door. I moved toward it sideways, my fingers running over the rough surface of the wall until I reached the smooth panel. The doorknob was as cold as ice and my shaking hands fumbled in their urgency to yank open the door. I paused, forced myself to be calm, then gave a sharp twist to the knob.

At the far end of the passageway a disk of light gleamed through the organdy curtains, creating an eerie ghostly effect.

As I groped my way blindly down the passage I stopped briefly in front of each door, wondering if the intruder might be behind one of them.

Several times I experienced the strange sensation that someone was following me. Would he reach out for me? I glanced over my shoulder into the blackness. It was like peering into an inkwell.

At the foot of the stairs I came to an abrupt halt. The fingers of light that filtered through the window were dim and the stairway obscure, reminding me of my encounter with the feather duster. Was the person who had placed it on the step that night the same one who had just been in the attic? Could there be an object on one of these steps?

Not taking a chance, I went to the outer wall and put my hand on its cold surface. Carefully I lowered one foot after the other until I reached the second-floor landing; then I quickened my pace.

My body trembled uncontrollably, forcing me to pull to a halt in front of Jason's bedroom door. I leaned against it, fighting back the tears that stung at my eyelids.

Without warning the door flew open, and I screamed as I lost balance and fell into the room. Strong arms caught me about the waist, and then it was dark.

Way off in the distance I heard a voice calling my name, and my eyelashes fluttered in response, then closed again when a sharp pain shot across the back of my head. And why was my forehead wet? I raised an arm to examine it, but a rough hand pushed mine down. "Don't, Abby!"

The voice was familiar. It was Jason. "I'm so glad you're here," I said without thinking, and opened my eyes.

"Oh, Abby," he sighed with gentle concern, "what am I going to do with you?"

Jason was home. That thought streaked across my mind and came to rest. I looked up into the face that was close to mine and I felt more wretched than ever. "What are you doing here?" I asked in an uneven voice, and wondered if it was his hands that had struck my back. Had Jason closed the attic door, imprisoning me in its darkened interior?

His eyebrows came together in a straight line. "You just said you were glad I was here. Have you changed your mind already?"

"Did I say that?" I stammered, and closed my eyes, praying that when I reopened them I would be alone.

I wanted to believe him innocent, but how could I with him here?

"Open your eyes, Abby, and look at me."

I obeyed the first order, but I could not gaze into the eyes that were so near to mine. I turned my attention to the wall behind the bed.

"Abby, look at me and for God's sake tell me what you're up to." His warm hand went to my chin and brought my face around to his. His grave expression did nothing to allay my rising suspicion.

"Where am I?" I hedged.

"In my room."

"What? I shouldn't be in here." I attempted to sit up on the bed, but Jason would not move. I had no alternative but to lie back down.

"Don't try to move until your head has had a chance to clear. You're perfectly safe." Safe from what? Bodily harm? Or familiarities? My breath seemed to be suspended, for suddenly I realized that it was the latter from which I didn't want to be safe. I wanted him to put his lips on mine. His mouth was so close. I had the overwhelming desire to throw my arms around his neck and pull him down on me. I could feel heat in my face and my heart beat so wildly I was certain that he, too, could hear it.

"Are you going to tell me what happened?" he persisted. "You were terrified when I opened the door."

His sharp tone dissolved my desire. "Please, Jason, can't I sit up? I can't talk lying down."

He removed the cold compress from my forehead. "Very well, if you insist."

As I came erect, my eyes surveyed the room. It was furnished in heavy mahogany with a carpet in muted blues and grays. On the wall opposite me hung a glass-enclosed photograph of a man, a woman, and three young boys. Dimness made it impossible for me to view the picture clearly. "Is that a photograph of your family?" I asked.

"Yes. Now are you going to tell me what is going on?"

"Noises in the attic woke me."

"What kind of noises?"

"Someone was walking around and banging things."

His dark eyes narrowed in disbelief. "Are you sure you weren't just dreaming? I mean, what logical reason would anyone have for prowling the attic at this hour?"

"Well, how should I know?" I exploded. "And I wasn't dreaming. This is the second time this has happened." My voice dropped to a whisper. "Someone is trying to scare me."

"Why would anyone want to scare you?"

"I don't know, but I'm sure someone doesn't want me here."

He regarded me with suspicion. "You think it's me, don't you?"

"No. Oh, I don't know, Jason. You didn't want me to come to Seattle."

"Admittedly I didn't at first. But now—" He stopped abruptly, his eyes holding mine. For one electrifying moment I had the impression he was going to take me in his arms; but then he looked away, breaking the spell. "Anyway, do you honestly believe I'd go lurking around up there?"

"No, I suppose not."

"What do you mean, you suppose not? Oh, never mind, we'll discuss that another time. Right now I want you to tell me why you didn't inform me of the noises when they first occurred."

"Well, for one thing, we weren't getting along very well."

"Is that the only reason?"

I hesitated. "No."

"Well, go on," he prodded.

"On that first night when the commotion in the attic ceased I heard someone at my door. Then when he went away I opened it a crack and I—" I let my voice dwindle.

"And what?"

I swallowed hard. "I saw you going into your room."

"So you assumed then *I* was the cause of the disturbance?"

"I wasn't sure. You were up! Who else could it have been? Unless,"—I paused— "it was Leah."

He stared at me in astonishment. "Why in heaven's name would she be thumping around in the attic trying to scare you?"

I felt foolish. His words and expression made my remark seem far-fetched. "She's been very cool to me," I stammered, "and obviously doesn't want me here." Immediately I regretted that statement, for I sounded like a spoiled child, whining.

"She's only a servant, Abby. What difference would it make to her if you're here or not?"

Did Jason really regard Leah as "only a servant"? I considered telling him I suspected she was in love with him and perhaps felt that I posed a threat, but I dismissed the thought. I didn't want him to think I was prying. Worse yet, I didn't want to give the mistaken impression that I was conceited. "Other than you and I and Grandfather she's the only other one in the house at night," I said finally, "unless the doors are left unlocked."

"If you're wondering could anyone let themselves in, it's possible. We don't generally lock up the place at night. But from now on I'll see to it that the doors are locked. At any rate, Abby, it was me at your end of the hall the other evening. I was on my way to bed when I heard a sound and I went to investigate."

"Then you must believe me if you heard the noise too."

"Yes, I believe you, although at the time I attributed the cause to the scraping of a branch against the house. If you recall we did have high winds on that night."

"High winds and branches had nothing to do with it. I'm positive of that because I went up to the attic tonight."

"You what?"

I made a feeble attempt to defend my impulsive action. "Well, you weren't here and there wasn't anyone I could send to investigate. Besides, I was angry and wanted to get to the bottom of this."

"So you flounced off up the stairs, giving no consideration to what you'd do if you should confront someone. Well, what happened?"

"Somebody pushed me into the room."

Jason took me by the shoulders. "Were you harmed? Did you see who it was?"

I shook my head. "No. It was too dark for me to see anything or anyone. Do you suppose it could have been the same person who placed the feather duster on the stairs?"

"No, I don't," he answered quickly—too quickly, I thought. "I told you to forget about that, Abby. It was just a careless oversight by one of the servants." He narrowed his eyes at me. "Why were you standing in my doorway?"

"I was trembling and I leaned against it for support."

"Oh." He sounded disappointed.

A hint of suspicion still nagged at me. "When did

you arrive home? My grandfather told me you'd be away for several days."

"Those were my plans, but for some strange reason I felt the need to rush home." He frowned. "Maybe that's because you're such a handful. Lord, I wasn't home more than ten minutes when you fell into my arms. Abby," his voice grew grave, "I want you to promise that you'll inform me immediately if you should be disturbed again. And for God's sake stay away from the attic!"

"All right, Jason. But aren't you going to go up and investigate?"

"I will in the morning. By now whoever was up there is undoubtedly gone."

He rose and took my hands in his, pulling me to my feet. "Come on, I'd better get you out of my room before we create a scandal and your grandfather insists you marry me." Jason's proximity and his voice as soft as a caress sent a tremor through me. "Was that such a bad thought, Abby? You're trembling."

"No." The word was scarcely audible. He was teasing me, I was certain.

"I think it would be wise for you to stay within range of the house for a while," Jason said at my bedroom door.

"But why? *This* is the only place where anyone has bothered me."

"True. But at least here, if you should encounter trouble, help is just a call away. Don't look so alarmed." He touched my arm, grinning. "I doubt you'll have any more problems. Still, it doesn't hurt to be cautious. As soon as I determine what is going on, you can resume a normal routine."

"Are you going to inform the authorities?"

He glanced down at the floor, seemingly in deep thought. "I don't know; I'll have to think on that."

"But why? This is—"

"Do you always have to ask so many questions? Can't you trust in my judgment?"

I lowered my gaze, momentarily speechless. On impulse I wanted to respond in the affirmative, but I was still dubious. He could have been in the attic. After all, if he did manage to frighten me back to San Francisco there would be no one to upset his control of the mill. And why did Jason return home sooner than planned? And in the dead of night? It seemed to me that it would be dangerous to traverse the rutted and narrow roads of Seattle after dark. As much as I wanted to believe it, I was not convinced he would inconvenience himself for me. Especially when he didn't appear to be too concerned over my fall on the stairs or this incident tonight.

"Abby, I'm not trying to make light of what has occurred since your arrival." Was he reading my mind? I wondered, and raised my eyes to his. "I just don't want to upset your grandfather unnecessarily. Having the authorities roaming about the premises is bound to have some adverse affect on his health. Let me see what I can uncover on my own, all right?"

I scrutinized his face, but my mind seemed unable to function. Jason was too close, and I was too aware of his lean body and the brightness of his eyes. "Do whatever you think is best," I managed finally, and wasn't even sure if what I said made sense.

A slight smile upturned the corners of his mouth, and when he reached out and gently took me in his arms, I did not resist. For moments that passed too rapidly he held me in his tender embrace; his heart pounding as furiously as my own. Jason lifted my chin and put his mouth close to mine. "Will you stay near the house?" he breathed.

I nodded dumbly, too mesmerized to even respond verbally.

For one fractional moment I considered informing him of my volunteer work for Dr. Sims, but then Jason's lips touched mine, erasing all thoughts from my head. His kiss was light and brief—too brief, I thought as I entered my room a few seconds later. But how in heaven's name could I long for him to kiss me passionately when suspicion dominated my brain?

It wasn't until the following evening that I saw Jason again and then it was under unpleasant circumstances. I had just descended the stairs headed for the parlor to join him and Grandfather, when Jason's raised voice brought me to a sudden halt. "She did *what?*"

CHAPTER EIGHT

I was in trouble again; there was no doubt about it. And I suspected that my failure to inform Jason of my commitment to Dr. Sims was the reason.

The voices from the parlor were faint now and I forced myself forward. The heels of my shoes echoed on the polished floor, so I tiptoed. There was no need to attract attention to myself, for Jason Landry would pounce on me soon enough.

For several seconds neither man noticed me in the doorway. Jason stood before the window overlooking the porch, his back toward me, and Grandfather sat near the fire. "Why do you worry about her so?" Martin Justin wanted to know. "I believe she's perfectly capable of taking care of herself. Abby is like her father—independent. If I had realized thirty years ago just how independent my son was I'd never have lost him. I do not intend to lose my granddaughter."

"So you'll spoil her instead." Jason swung around and caught sight of me. He looked me up and down as if he suspected that I had been deliberately eavesdropping. "How long have you been standing there?" His accusing tone brought the color to my face, giving a false impression of guilt.

I swallowed the lump that had formed in my throat. "I'm sorry, I didn't mean to interrupt."

"Come over here, Abby," Grandfather called. I moved to his side without looking at Jason. "That young man over there seems to think I'm spoiling you. Jason's upset because you were assisting Dr. Sims yesterday."

"I'm not upset, Martin. I simply believe Abby will have enough to occupy her time and it hardly seems proper for a young woman to be traipsing around the countryside."

"I am not going to be traipsing about the countryside! Working with the doctor is gratifying. I can't live in society without contributing something to it."

Jason sat down on the sofa opposite me, a look of exasperation about his face. "Why didn't you tell me about this yourself?"

Grandfather broke in. "Well, how could she? As I told you, Abby went to Doc's place yesterday and you didn't get home until late."

Jason and I exchanged glances and I felt a little panic-stricken, wondering how he would respond to that. Surely he wouldn't mention that he and I were alone in his room last night, would he?

"You're right," he told my grandfather, "I'd forgotten, time goes so quickly. In any case, there's no need to discuss it now. Abby and I can talk about it when we go over the invitation list later."

"Now's your chance to thank Jason for suggesting the party," Martin Justin urged.

I regarded Jason from beneath my lashes. His smug expression infuriated me. Evidently he felt assured that I had not detected his clever scheme to select my friends. I wanted to grab up one of the stoppered decanters on the table in front of me and hurl it at his head, but I managed to retain a ladylike demeanor. For Grandfather's benefit I thanked the complacent man, though I did so between stiff lips.

His eyes met mine squarely. "The party will be a lot of work; think you can handle it?"

I shot him a frown. "Of course I can. When will it be convenient for Dorothea and me to go into town with you to begin the arrangements?"

Jason ran a finger over an eyebrow, considering. "Well, the next couple of mornings I plan to be at the mill early. We're working long hours to meet a deadline. How about Friday?"

"Friday will be fine."

Martin Justin leaned forward and addressed the other man. "Do you think you'd have time that afternoon to show my granddaughter around the mill?"

"Yes . . . I suppose so. Are you interested in seeing it, Abby?"

"Yes, I'd like to."

"Then plan on bringing an old pair of boots along. The yard is muddy and the sawdust, you'll discover, adheres to the boots like glue."

I nodded, then asked, "What about Dorothea? Do you think she'll want to tour the mill?"

Grandfather shook his head. "No, she's lived around them all of her life. It wouldn't interest her. I'm sure she'd much rather spend that time visiting with her sister and new niece. They live just a block from the mill." He looked at Jason. "I saw the pile of papers you brought home this evening. What's going on?"

"I'm working on a bid which concerns the Kimberley Diamond Mines in South Africa."

"Really?" Grandfather looked impressed.

"The corporation just went under new control. They're abandoning the practice of open-pit mining and are converting to shafts and underground pits. The conversion will require a great amount of lumber; plus, the corporation is also busy constructing a town for its employees. So the mill that is awarded the contract stands to gain a substantial profit." Jason turned his attention to me. "I'm sorry. I'm probably boring you with this shoptalk."

"No, you're not. It sounds interesting."

Grandfather suggested, "Abby, why don't you play for Jason and show him how a piano should sound?"

I smiled at the devilish gleam in the old eyes. "If you both would like?"

Jason nodded approval, and Grandfather, who was grinning at me wickedly, said, "You'd better play something other than Chopin or Mendelssohn. Jason's more the lumberjack ballad type. We wouldn't want to put him to sleep."

"I'm afraid I'm not familiar with any lumberjack ballads." I suppressed a giggle.

"Just as well." Martin Justin tilted his head back and laughed. "They're terrible and most of them aren't for the ears of young ladies. How about 'Hot Time in the Old Town', or 'Strawberry Blonde'?"

Jason was impatient. "That will be enough from you two. Play whatever you like, Abby. I guess if you can attempt to acquaint yourself with the operations of the mill, I can try to appreciate good music."

" 'Greensleeves' was my father's favorite," I told the

duo, and went to the piano. "I'll play it."

Later, after my grandfather retired for the evening, Jason and I went to the study to go over the party list. The door was locked, which was unusual, so I promptly asked why.

He held his answer until we were inside, with the door closed behind us. "Those concern the Kimberley bid." He pointed to the neat stack of papers centered on the desk. "I have some rough estimates and we must be careful they don't get into the wrong hands."

He drew a chair to the front of the desk and as I seated myself, I asked, "But who would bother them here?"

He pushed the coals around in the grate and threw on a log. "No one probably, but we have to take every precaution. I believe we'll be able to outbid our competitors. That is, unless someone gets hold of these figures." He sat down behind the desk and gave me a long look. "Don't tell anyone that I have these estimates here, Abby—especially Wells."

"Are you saying you think he'd break in for those papers?" I protested.

"No, he's hardly the type to skulk about, but I wouldn't put it past him to hire someone."

"That's a horrid thing to say about Nicholas. You can't be serious."

"Oh, but I am. Wells, you see, has been trying to win larger contracts for the last couple of years without much success. He can't afford to bid too low, but if he should discover the amount of our estimate he could underbid us by a few dollars and the contract would be his."

I sat up ramrod straight. "You make it sound as though someone has already stolen company information."

"They have," he said simply. "The office has been broken into twice in the last six weeks."

I stared at him. "And you presume Nicholas is the culprit. Why? There are so many other mills around—"

"I haven't singled him out; but he is the most aggressive, and he does head my list."

"Well, being aggressive doesn't automatically mean he'd stoop to stealing!"

"How readily you defend him, Abby, and yet you find it so difficult to trust in me. And another thing; why didn't you tell me last night about Dr. Sims? That was pretty clever of you to promise to stay close to home after you'd already made a commitment to him."

"Now you're implying I did something underhanded and I resent that! I see no need for me to remain near the house, and I don't understand why you're so insistent upon that. Especially when you adamantly tell me to forget about my fall on the stairs and don't appear to be too concerned about my encounter in the attic."

His jaw hardened and I was grateful the desk separated us, for he looked as though he wanted to shake me. Jason came to his feet and moved to my side. I didn't look up, but I could feel his angry eyes boring into the top of my head.

He sighed deeply. "I'm just about to give up on you, Abigail Justin. Your obstinate refusal to trust in me is making it difficult for me to protect you."

My head came up. "Protect me? From what?"

"From whoever wants these figures. Although if I'm right and it is Wells, then his romancing you toward the ultimate goal of marriage would provide him with far more than just the contract."

I sucked in my breath and was about to lash out at

him, but he cut me off. "Don't get riled! I didn't mean that as an insult. I'm only trying to remind you to view him objectively. After all, you've been here less than two weeks and he's already been out to see you three times. It seems to me that he's moving your friendship along rather rapidly."

"That is none of your affair!"

"Maybe not, but I would rest easier if you would go home until the bids for the Kimberley contract are in and the trouble at the mill is resolved."

I set my mouth in a straight line of determination. "I *am* home! And I want to know what is going on at the mill."

"All right, Abby, all right." He sat back down and gave me a long look. "I didn't want to burden you, but you give me no choice. The machinery breakdowns have not been accidental. I'm certain someone is out to discredit me and the reliability of the company."

"But why?"

"Because the breakdowns, besides being dangerous to the employees, hinder our production. No organization, government or private, is going to award contracts to a mill that not only can't keep commitments but is also having serious labor problems." He leaned forward, his eyes holding mine. "What do you suppose would happen to the mill if you and I were not here to oversee it?"

I ran my tongue around inside my dry mouth. "I would imagine it would have to be sold."

"Precisely. In the meantime Martin would probably put Zachary Taylor in charge. He knows a great deal about the operations of the company and he is an excellent bookkeeper. However, Zach doesn't know how to handle employees, and if the breakdowns should persist he'd no doubt lose the contracts by default. Some clever individual could then snatch them up."

"Nicholas, you mean, don't you?"

Jason nodded. "He and Zach, you see, are pretty close friends, and Zach does have a rather loose tongue. It wouldn't take much for Wells to draw pertinent information from him."

"Then why doesn't he simply cajole the Kimberley bid from Mr. Taylor?"

"He can't, because Zach doesn't know what it is. I never share the amount of our bids with anyone; it's too risky."

I lifted my chin. "Well, think whatever you'd like, but I'm positive Nicholas would never wish me ill."

"Physically I'm certain he would never harm you. But if he's not sincere he could make you terribly unhappy in time." He frowned. "In any case, I'm sure he wouldn't mind having me out of the picture, one way or the other."

"He wouldn't wish you ill either," I defended. "Nicholas is too kind and gentle to even consider such a thing."

"We're talking about a lot of money, Abby. People often do some very strange things to gain wealth and power."

"Yes, I know; but I can't believe that of him. And I know my grandfather wouldn't believe it either."

He sat down and regarded me through his veil of lashes. "Do I have to inform you of all the grizzly details before you'll be convinced of the gravity of this situation?"

I parted my lips to speak, but he raised a silencing hand. "Never mind; your answer is written all over your face. The other day," he paused, "someone took a pot shot at me."

"What? Were you hit? I mean, you look unharmed,

but then you're so reserved you'd probably hide an injury if you could."

He seemed pleased by my concern. "I wasn't harmed."

"When did it happen?"

"Last Monday on my way home home from the mill. Fortunately I ducked to avoid a low-slung branch at the same time that the shot rang out."

I remembered the incident on our way to the gazebo. "Is that why you stopped so suddenly on our way to the apple orchard last Wednesday? You said you thought you heard a deer, but Nicholas told me there are none in this area. Did you suspect someone might be lurking in the woods?"

"The thought crossed my mind. Really, Abby, I'd feel so much better if you'd stay near the house."

"But you said yourself that if Nicholas is behind all this, he wouldn't hurt me."

"True. But if by some chance I'm wrong about him, then who knows what a money-hungry person might do to get what he wants? Now, will you stay close to the house?"

"Yes, I guess so."

"What about Dr. Sims?"

I considered for a moment. "I really would like to continue working with him, Jason. Now, more than ever, I'll need to keep my mind and my hands busy. I won't be on the road alone, if that's what has you concerned. Mr. Brannon offered to drive me over, and Dr. Sims's son will see me home."

Jason deliberated for several seconds, then agreed. "Very well. But see to it that you never venture out on the roads alone."

I nodded.

"We'd better get to the party list," he said; "it's getting late." He withdrew a small leather-bound book from the center drawer of the desk. Jason ran his hand down each page, placing check marks beside various names, then gave the book to me. It felt smooth and warm in my hand. "You can copy down the names I've marked, at your leisure."

"Thank you, I'll do it tomorrow." He started to rise, but returned to his chair when I spoke again. "Jason, can I ask you one more thing?"

His eyes sparkled. "You certainly have a bagful of questions. I've never met anyone as inquistive as you. You must have been a very precocious child."

"I probably was." I grinned.

"Well, go ahead and ask your question."

"Did you inform the authorities of your being fired upon and are they investigating the accidents at the mill?"

The sparkle evaporated from his eyes. "They've been investigating the accidents, but with no success. At this point I believe they've abandoned their efforts. Even though they haven't said so, I have the distinct impression that they consider faulty equipment responsible for the mishaps."

"But wouldn't your being fired upon change their opinion?"

"Not necessarily. Besides, I didn't inform them of the gunfire."

"But why not?"

"What good would it do if I did? The authorities have been no help so far. Chances are they would attribute that to a careless hunter, which is possible. The countryside is loaded with idiots toting weapons. Oh, by the way, I went up to the attic this morning, but I didn't discover any evidence of anyone prowling around. The only thing unusual was your candle and its holder lying on the floor. I've returned them to the kitchen where I want them to stay. Perhaps lack of illumination will discourage you from roaming the house after dark."

With that, Jason stood up, gathered the papers on the desk, then withdrew two tarnished keys from his trouser pocket. He held up the pieces of metal. "The attic door is locked, and these will be put in the safe along with the estimates."

From my seat I watched him cross to the closet and open the safe which stood inside. "If nothing else," he said over his shoulder, "at least you shouldn't be disturbed again at night."

I derived no comfort from his statement, and when I climbed into bed a short time later sleep eluded me. What was I to believe? More to the point, whom was I to believe? Jason or Nicholas? The latter accused Jason of mismanagement and a desire to inherit the mill. Jason, on the other hand, charged Nicholas with thievery and even possible attempted murder. I was not convinced of that. I didn't know Nicholas well, but still for some unexplainable reason I was not able to picture this friendly and good-natured man in a shady light.

What of Jason though? I didn't want to believe him guilty of wrongdoing either. In spite of the threads of suspicion that looped through my mind, I liked him. In fact, I felt a growing attraction for him. In a way, trying to unravel Jason's complex nature was becoming a challenge. I admired his self-assurance and lately there had been times when even his dominance had aroused exciting and unfamiliar emotions. But how did he really feel about Leah? He was quick to come to her defense when I suggested she might have been the one in the attic. Still, that didn't necessarily signify that he was in love with her. Could Leah be jealous enough to go to childish lengths to harass me? To make me appear like a high-strung schoolgirl? Clearly Jason would abhor that immature quality.

I plucked at the covers, remembering the mud I'd seen on her dress on that day Jason claimed he'd heard a sound in the woods. Could Leah have been spying on us? If not, then why did she lie? Why did she tell me that she had been indoors all day?

CHAPTER NINE

Over the next few days, Grandfather and I saw little of Jason. He'd arrive home after we'd eaten our dinner, exchange a few inconsequential words with us, then retire to the study. There—while working, I assumed—he would partake of the evening meal which Leah brought in on a tray.

Last night it seemed as though she remained in the study for some time and I found myself pacing the floor. When she did depart Jason's company she caught me standing at the parlor door. Leah's eyes were bright, as if she were excited and I felt as though I would burst ridiculously into tears.

For a long time after that I continued my pacing, speculating upon the relationship between our attractive housekeeper and the man who sent my emotions into a turmoil. Was Jason in love with the buxom blonde? I pondered this question for the one-hundredth time, feeling absolutely miserable. And why the secret meetings? Was their relationship of a purely intimate nature, so that discretion was paramount?

The only way in which I was able to free myself

from my wretched contemplation was to keep my brain immensely occupied. The most pleasant means I found was to seek out Dorothea. She and I would talk at length over our outing to town and the impending party. Even now I find myself smiling in remembrance of the confession she had made two days previous. "You know, miss," she had said, "I hate housework and I don't want to get married for a long time, either. My sister got married when she was sixteen and now she's only eighteen. She's got a baby and she sits home all day like a little old lady. I'm in no hurry to wind up like that." Inwardly I had to admit it was a comfort to see someone less mature than myself, for Grandfather and Jason had a way of making me feel younger than my twenty years.

In between those times I spent with Dorothea and my grandfather I managed to work on Dr. Sim's accounts. As with my father, Dr. Sims had more patients who didn't pay than who did.

On Friday morning I hurried down the stairs to join Jason and Dorothea for our outing to town. When I entered the dining room, my boots in one hand and reticule in the other, my attention went from Jason, at the table, to Leah who was on her way to the kitchen. Was she serving him his breakfast? A glance at his plate told me that was unlikely, for he was nearly finished with the meal. He greeted me with a half-smile, then lowered his gaze to the paper that lay before him on the table. I had the distinct feeling he considered our plans for today a bore and my spirits declined.

Through breakfast, however, I managed to lift myself from the doldrums by simply ignoring the dark-haired man engrossed in his reading. Actually that wasn't too difficult, for Dorothea came into the room and kept me company. She was almost attractive this morning in a pale-green frock and white shawl. Her long dark hair was released from its usual knot at the nape of the neck and lay in soft waves about her slender shoulders. Perched atop her head was a straw bonnet with garlands of flowers across its front. The excitement that shone in her eyes helped to revive my enthusiasm.

In the carriage I sat between Dorothea and Jason. We were somewhat crowded and I wasn't pleased to be practically pinned against him. As long as there were doubts in my mind, I knew I had to view him objectively; but how could I do that when his nearness made my blood pound furiously in my veins.

Scarcely had we rounded the drive when Leah emerged from the house. "Jason," she called, and ran down the steps waving an envelope in an upheld hand. I was surprised that she had eliminated the title "Mister," though I shouldn't have been. Jason pulled the dappled mare to a halt under the shade of a hemlock.

Leah circled the back of the buggy and came to a stop beside him. She was breathless and her cheeks were flushed. "Could you please have someone at the mill give this to my brother? It's kind of important." She handed the letter up to Jason. Leah glanced past him and regarded me with warmth. Apparently she no longer considered me a threat, I thought, and turned away.

Jason slipped the envelope into his coat pocket. "I'd be glad to," he told her.

She thanked him; then started back to the house.

With a flick of the reins we continued on our way. The air was pleasantly warm and I felt cool and comfortable in my light camel's-hair dress. A slant of sunlight filtered through the trees and lay over the lawn like a golden halo. In its center birds fluttered, basking in its warmth; their singing blended with the sounds of the horse's hoofs and rolling carriage wheels. "Does Leah's brother work at the mill?" I asked.

Jason turned his attention from the road. "Yes, Carl's been one of our employees for several years. Oh, by the way, Abby, I'm not certain if I can meet you and Dorothea for lunch, as planned."

"Why not?" I tried to keep disappointment from my voice.

"The last of our shipment to Hawaii is being loaded aboard ship this morning and the captain is irate about something. He insists I meet with him or he won't set sail. I have no choice because we barely made this deadline and we can't have the vessel sitting in the harbor."

I spoke with my eyes focused on the golden blooms of the Scotch broom bushes that lined the dusty roadway. "Will your talk take that long?"

"It could. This particular captain isn't easy to talk to and he's pretty difficult to pacify. If I can get away for lunch, I'll meet you at Alden House at 12:30. If I'm not there by then, go ahead without me. I'll come by as soon as I can and take you out to the mill."

"Very well."

He leaned past me. "Dorothea, please see to it that Miss Justin doesn't get anywhere near Skid Road."

The young girl squirmed on the seat, seemingly embarrassed. "Yes, sir."

I was perplexed by the gentle order, but I made no attempt to query Jason. I didn't want him to tease me again about my bag of questions, especially in front of Dorothea.

We entered town. The streets and the waters of Puget Sound were splashed with sunshine. How splendid Seattle looked hugged by the golden brightness, I thought. Oh, it wasn't as grand a city as San Francisco, but it did have a special magic all its own.

As we passed the blacksmith's shop, the high-pitched ringing from the anvil flowed from the entrance and combined with the whistles from the steamboats and tugs in the harbor, and the laughter of children playing at a nearby watering trough.

Jason reined the horse to a stop in front of the printer's office, jumped down, and after tethering the animal, returned to help Dorothea and me. He escorted us to the office door, promised he would try to meet us for lunch, then reboarded the carriage and headed for the mill.

The business transaction with the printer took only a few minutes and after I was assured the invitations would be ready on the following Thursday, Dorothea and I left the establishment.

Back on the sidewalk, I let my gaze wander over the buildings across the street, searching unsuccessfully for a dressmaker's shop. "Dorothea," I said, "Grandfather suggested I ask you about a dressmaker. It seems"—I smiled at her—"He and Jason are at a loss in this area. Can you recommend anyone?"

"Why, yes, miss. Mrs. Soper's shop is just around the corner on Second Street. She's a good friend of Mamma's and the best seamstress in these parts."

A group of loggers passed by and Dorothea and I turned from their glittering eyes and waggish smiles. Their calked boots vibrated the planks beneath our feet. "Fine," I responded, "we'll go there next."

On our way to Second Street, I remembered Jason's order to Dorothea about 'Skid Road' and rising curiosity prompted me to ask her what he had meant. She pulled up short and regarded me with color suffusing her cheeks. "Well, miss," she hesitated, and looked around, apparently reassuring herself that no one was within earshot, "Skid Road is a terrible place. It's down along the waterfront. It's where the men go to drink and gamble; and all the bad ladies are there, too." She spoke so softly that I had to lean forward to catch her words.

"I see," I said, straightening up.

As we continued toward our destination, I wondered why Jason would even think for one moment that I might venture there. But then I recalled he considered me highly inquisitive.

The bell over the door of Mrs. Soper's shop jangled as Dorothea and I entered, and the steady hum of sewing machines sang out from the back room. Row upon row of wall shelves were filled with an assortment of fine fabrics in a variety of colors and in the center of the room were several racks of women's and children's garments.

The print curtain at the rear of the shop was pulled aside by a tall, heavyset woman of middle years. Her coarse gray hair was fashioned into a knot at the nape of the neck. "Why, Dorothea Brannon," she said, and her brown eyes glistened, "where have you been keeping yourself? I haven't seen you in ages."

"I don't get into town much anymore, Mrs. Soper. I came with Miss Justin. She needs a new ball gown."

"I heard you were here," Mrs. Soper said to me. "Seattle is getting big, but word still gets around."

We chatted for a few minutes, then moved about the shop giving careful consideration to the assortment of fabrics. "You don't want anything too heavy," Mrs. Soper advised. "Sometimes the month of May can be pretty warm." After a lengthy deliberation I selected pale-blue silk. Mrs. Soper suggested a princess-style dress with three-quarter-length sleeves and a square-cut neck filled in with white Spanish lace. My measurements were taken and a fitting arranged for the following Thursday, when I planned to pick up the invitations at the printer's.

My companion and I left the shop and, at leisure now, made our way down the block to Alden House. It was a huge hotel elegantly decorated in rich crimson velvet and colored crystal chandeliers.

For fifteen minutes we lounged in the softly cushioned chairs inside its entrance, waiting for Jason. "It's 12:35, miss," Dorothea pointed out. "It don't look like he's going to come."

The corners of my mouth drooped, despite my resolve to regard Jason impersonally. "No, it doesn't," I agreed. "We may as well go in for lunch."

We were just about to step into the dining room when a familiar masculine voice called, "Abby." I turned and saw Nicholas approaching. His warm smile dispelled my flagging spirits. "Hello, Dorothea," he greeted. "My, don't you look lovely today."

She blushed and looked at him from beneath her lashes. "Thank you, sir."

"And you, too, Miss Justin." His gaze went over me approvingly.

"Why, thank you, kind sir." I beamed at him.

"So, tell me, are you ladies in town on business or pleasure?" he wanted to know.

"Both," I told him, and explained our errands. "We were just going in for lunch."

His smile broadened. "Well, then, how fortunate for me. I was about to do the same. I'd be delighted if you would join me."

"I'd like that," I replied. "Is it all right with you, Dorothea?"

She nodded approval, her eyes wide with excitement as she glanced about the high-ceilinged, dimly lit dining room.

We were seated at a corner table graced with a

linen cloth and crystal vase filled with tulips in a multitude of colors. After Nicholas placed our order, he said to me, "I was going to come out to see you later this afternoon, Abby."

"Oh?"

"I received a note this morning from a friend in Portland. He's going to be in Seattle this weekend. Would you mind if we postponed our ride for a few days?"

I felt disappointment, but I didn't show it. "No, of course not."

"Would next Wednesday be convenient for you?"

"Oh, I'm sorry, I can't then. I'll be assisting Dr. Sims. And Thursday I'll be in town."

"Well . . . Monday is bad for me and I certainly don't want to postpone until next Friday. How about Tuesday, say later in the afternoon, around five?"

"Tuesday would be fine."

"Well,"—he grinned—"I'm glad we got that settled."

From then on Nicholas made it a point to include Dorothea in the conversation and her eyes beamed in admiration. Unlike Jason Landry, this man exuded compassion, and in the pleasant hour in which we conversed over luncheon my respect and friendship for Nicholas intensified.

When we emerged from Alden House he offered Dorothea a ride to her sister's home.

"Thank you, sir," she replied, "but she doesn't live very far from here and it's a nice day to walk." Dorothea expressed her appreciation for the lovely luncheon, then left our side.

Nicholas regarded me. "May I give you a lift to the mill, Abby?"

"Thank you, but I told Jason I would wait for him here."

"I hate to leave you standing alone. I'll wait with you."

I had no wish to observe Jason's usual look of displeasure at seeing Nicholas and me together, so I said politely, "You needn't wait; I'll be fine."

He hesitated. "Well, if you're sure."

I told him that I was, and while he accepted that, he did linger for a few minutes. And I became so immersed in our discussion of the party that I did not hear the approaching footfalls from behind. "Abby." Jason's disgruntled voice sent shivers down my spine.

Annoyed, and determined not to jump every time he opened his mouth, I told him over my shoulder, "I'll be with you in a minute, Jason."

Nicholas acknowledged the other man with a slow nod.

As with Dorothea, I also thanked Nicholas for the lovely luncheon; then I proffered my hand. "I'll look forward to seeing you next Tuesday afternoon, Nicholas."

He gave my hand a gentle squeeze, then turned away. I watched him go for several seconds, then drew a long breath and came around to face Jason.

CHAPTER TEN

He leaned against the building, his dark eyes assessing me with scornful amusement. "It didn't take you long to find someone else to take you out to lunch, did it? What did you do, get on the telephone and invite Wells to be your escort?"

My throat was choked with hurt and indignation.

"What an awful thing to say, Jason Landry." A woman brushed past me and stared with unabashed curiosity.

"Where is Dorothea?" he demanded, and I studied his rigid face. Did Jason presume that I had dined alone with Nicholas? Was this man jealous? I wondered, then quickly put the absurd notion from my mind. Jason Landry did not impress me as a man who possessed even one shred of sentiment or kindly feelings. For one fractional moment I was tempted to allow him to believe whatever he wanted, but it was against the training my father had instilled in me. Even a tiny white lie, he always said, tended to entangle one's life.

I let my eyes blaze up at Jason. "I did not call Nicholas! We happened to meet by chance and he was gracious enough to invite Dorothea and me to join him for lunch." As hard as I tried to subdue my voice I was not successful. People were staring at us. "Where is the carriage?" I demanded, and swept past him, hoping I was headed in the right direction.

His hand flashed out and caught my wrist. "I'm sorry; I've a damnable tongue."

"Well, at least we agree on something!"

His eyebrows twitched. "Come on, the carriage is up the street in front of the tannery." He urged me along the sidewalk. As usual, his stride was long and I practically had to run to keep up with him.

A tall, brawny man approached and his eyes twinkled as he shot us a sly look. "Say, what you got there, Jason?" The man chuckled. "Why, she's a mighty pretty one. Where you hurrying her off to?"

Jason ignored the crude man, while I, on the other hand, glared at him.

At the carriage, Jason handed me unceremoniously into it, jerked the reins loose from the hitching post, and climbed aboard. Several seconds of icy silence passed; then I spoke with my eyes focused on a ramshackle building off in the distance. "You know, Jason, we might as well face the fact that you and I will probably never get along."

"Well," he rasped, "I can't say that thought hasn't crossed my mind more than once. Still," his voice evened out, "we haven't known each other for very long, and the stress we're having to endure is hardly conducive to friendliness."

"Perhaps," I temporized. "At any rate, I haven't been fair with my grandfather."

"Just what do you mean by that?"

"Well, I get the impression it's important to him that you and I become good friends and I've led him to believe that in time we would be. To me that's deceitful, and the next time he asks how you and I are getting along, I'm going to tell him the truth."

Jason pulled the horse to a sudden stop at the side of the road and stared at me. "Don't do that, Abby. Martin has plans, don't shatter them. If you honestly believe you and I can't be friends, then let him discover that on his own."

I eyed him warily. "What kind of plans?"

"I can't tell you that. I'm sure your grandfather would want to be the one to explain. Personally, I think his idea is ridiculous and I told him so."

I lifted my chin. "Very well, Jason; if you won't tell me, then I'll ask him in the morning."

"For Martin's sake, Abby, don't get angry when he explains. He loves you and he means well." I was more puzzled than ever, but I did not pursue the matter. By now I knew Jason well enough to know when he closed the door on a subject it was a dead issue.

The deep blast of a whistle from a tugboat on the

bay brought my head up, and I noticed an enormous sign on the building to our left. It was the Wells Mill Company. I was impressed by its size and the hubbub of activity.

"Did Wells ask you anything about Justin Mill?" Jason questioned slowly.

I viewed him through narrowed eyes, wondering if he had been angry earlier because he feared I might have divulged the scant knowledge I possessed of the mill. Did Jason think I could be cajoled into betraying a confidence? "We never discussed business," I told him flatly. "Nicholas is intelligent and witty. He can think of other things to talk about besides mills and logging. When I said I would not discuss company business, Jason, I meant it."

"I never doubted that for one minute. I simply wondered if he pressed for information."

"Well, he didn't." We lapsed into silence.

A short time later we approached a cluster of white clapboard buildings spread in a semicircle along the waters of Puget Sound. Clouds of white smoke rose from the three stacks projected above the structures. Beyond, masts of ships were visible, and the sweet fragrance of freshly cut wood mingled with the pungent sea air. The whirring of saws set my teeth on edge.

Jason reined the horse to a stop before a large cedar-shingled building. While he tethered the animal, I saw a man step to the window, then move back out of sight. After helping me down, Jason reached under the seat for my boots. "You can put these on inside," he said as we stepped onto the porch.

The office was huge, with several desks and tables scattered around. Across the back of the room were two doors. My attention lingered on the one bearing Jason's name in broad gold letters.

Three men, who had been busy working when we entered, now stood and waited for Jason to introduce us. Their greetings were kindly, and to my surprise I found myself drawn to their work.

The door adjacent to Jason's office opened and Mr. Taylor emerged. He grinned broadly when he saw me, then came forward.

I matched his expression and held out my hand. He took it in his. "It's good to see you again, Miss Justin. Jason tells me you'll be spending some time here learning the operations of the company." Chairs scraped on the floor as the three men returned to their seats and resumed work.

"Yes, and I hope I won't get underfoot."

"Oh, don't let that worry you." He smiled. "It will be a pleasure having a pretty young lady in the office. We get tired of looking at these critters, don't we, Jason?"

He responded with a nod, then said, "I'll put Abby in your charge first, Zach. She can learn more about the company from the accounts than she can in any other department."

"Fine, I'll be happy to work with her."

"Thank you, Mr. Taylor," I said. "I'll try not to consume too much of your time."

Jason took a half-turn. "If you'll excuse me, I just remembered something I forgot to take care of this morning. Zach, would you show Miss Justin around the office? I'll be back in a few minutes."

"I'd be glad to."

When Jason was gone the older man and I moved about the room. I was particularly fascinated by the bulletin board on the west wall. On it was a list of ships, their estimated times of arrival at distant ports and their due dates back in Seattle. "Are these ships owned by the mill?" I asked Mr. Taylor.

"Yes, miss. The company owns six barkentines and two tugs. Quite a difference from when I first began work here."

"Were you a bookkeeper then, too?"

"Oh, my, no." He grinned. "I was only a mere lad of fifteen then. My apprenticeship began with a broom, though I must say we won't start yours off that way. Did you know that I helped train Jason also?"

"Jason an apprentice?" I repressed a giggle. "Somehow I had the feeling that all this just came naturally to him."

Crinkles formed at the corners of Mr. Taylor's eyes. "No, not quite. We worked together for a long time."

"He's so intelligent that I expect he learned very rapidly."

"Faster than most, I guess you could say. But sometimes,"—he laughed—"Jason thoroughly tried my patience."

"Why is that?" I asked, and wondered about the false ring in his laughter. Was there friction between this man and his superior?

Mr. Taylor cleared his throat. "Well, I suppose I just couldn't keep up with him. Jason, you see, has to know about everything. Why, he'll even leave the office to go out and help the men repair equipment."

"Shouldn't he? I mean, do the men think he's interfering?"

"Heavens, no. Most of them are delighted to be relieved of such trying and dirty jobs. But, you know,"—he regarded me with amusement—"I'm getting too old now to go chasing about the mill for Jason. It seems like he's always roaming around out there when I need his signature on an important paper."

"I don't imagine you had that problem with my grandfather."

"Fortunately, no. He was always right there in his office,"—he pointed to the door that bore Jason's name—"seated behind his desk."

I returned my attention to the bulletin board and inquired nonchalantly, "Is Jason as good a manager as my grandfather was?"

There was a long silence. "I think it's too soon to tell," he said finally. "Jason hasn't been in command for very long."

Wasn't one year ample time to make a reasonable determination? Was Mr. Taylor being evasive? Was he trying to protect Jason's position, and in so doing protect his own? "No doubt you're right," I told him, and began to move around again.

At the conclusion of the tour Mr. Taylor showed me into Jason's office. It was small, though perhaps the massive oak desk tended to dwarf its surroundings. Atop the desk were neat stacks of papers and what appeared to be an account book. Two rigid chairs stood beside a wooden cabinet on the east wall and along the opposite wall were a well-stocked bookcase and a safe. Above it was a map of Washington Territory.

Since I preferred not to keep Mr. Taylor from his work any longer, I thanked him for his courtesy and assured him I didn't mind waiting alone for Jason.

The soft-spoken man left the room, closing the door quietly behind him. For a minute I stared at the impressive desk, picturing Jason seated behind it absorbed in the mountain of papers upon its smooth surface. I took a long breath, disappointed that I had gained no significant information about Jason and his managerial ability. Apparently I would have to spend quite a bit of time here so that I could make my own determination. But would I be able to? There was so much to learn. I was beginning to wish that I had not agreed to my grandfather's recent request for me to become acquainted with the company.

Noises from beyond the window drew me across the room and I gave my attention to the waters of Puget Sound. It was crowded with logs sectioned off by tall, upright poles placed at intervals, reminding me of a corral for horses or cattle. In the distance the snowcapped Olympic Mountains rose majestically and puffs of smoke from the mills marred the otherwise clear blue sky.

To my left, along the edge of the water, was a long building. A portion of its front was open and a conveyor belt extended from it into the water. Opposite the conveyor was a dock with two ships moored to it. On the dock men moved about stacking lumber.

My thoughts returned to Jason, and I came around and placed my hands on top of his chair, my fingers caressing the hard wood. Overwhelmed with a sudden desire to seat myself in it, I swiveled the chair about and sat down facing the window.

The door swung open, giving me a start. I swiveled back to the desk as Jason plunked my boots down on the corner of it. "I'm sorry I kept you waiting so long," he apologized. "I have a couple of notes to jot down before we leave. In the meantime you can put on your boots." He opened the top left-hand drawer of his desk just as I leaned forward for my boots. Jason's face was within inches of mine and I wondered, with a warm rush of emotion that made me tremble a little, what it would be like to kiss him—to really kiss him, not just a brush of the lips like before.

I snatched up the leather footwear and sat down quickly. While I fumbled with the shoelaces I stole a look at him from beneath my lashes. Jason was preoccupied with the words he was committing to paper. He wasn't even aware of me. "Do you want to sit down here?" I offered. "I can sit in one of the other chairs."

"No, that's not necessary, I'm almost finished." After a few seconds he flipped his notebook closed, dropped it back into the drawer, then regarded me fidgeting with my shoelaces. "Can I help you?"

"No, thank you; I'll be ready in a minute." My fingers felt stiff and clumsy. Fervently I prayed he'd move away, but instead, he sat down on the corner of the desk. I could feel his eyes watching me and I had the distinct impression that they were alight with amusement.

Finally, my boots on, we left the office and crossed the muddy, sawdust-encrusted yard to the building that contained the blacksmithing equipment. A giant of a man, with huge shoulders and clothing soaked with perspiration, worked with expert skill at hammering a strip of metal on an anvil.

The opposite end of the building housed the machine shop, and I tried to remember the names of the various pieces of equipment as Jason briefly described their uses. Unfortunately, by the time we left the building all the names—lathe, planer, bolt cutter, and crucible—blended together and I knew it would be useless to attempt to straighten them out.

In the sawmill we were greeted by the squeal of circular saws, the booming thunder of rolling logs, and the low groan of moving carrier chains. Several seconds elapsed before I became accustomed to the almost-suffocating, sweet aroma of freshly cut wood.

Amazingly, there was little sawdust scattered around the plant. When I mentioned this to Jason he pointed out the chain conveyor that carried the sawdust and shavings directly from the machines to the fires beneath the boilers. "We're a city built on sawdust," he said laughing, "but we don't have to bury ourselves in it."

From the sawmill we moved out onto the wharf, where the thud of workmen's boots intermingled with the slapping sounds of lumber being stacked. "This shipment," Jason explained, "is destined for Australia."

"You know," I said, "I wasn't aware until today that the company owns ships."

"All the larger mills own their ships, or at least have part interest in them. Presently we're using barkentines,"—he swept his hand toward the vessels moored to the wharf—"but we have an order in with a shipbuilder on the East Coast for a schooner. Eventually we'll replace the barks with schooners; they require less men to operate."

There was a long silent moment as we watched a tugboat pull a three-masted square-rigger into the harbor; then Jason said, "Come along, I'll show you the main power plant." He led me back through the sawmill, to the far end. "This is the boiler room," he informed me over his shoulder. "The steam from these four boilers provides us with enough power to operate our equipment."

I opened my mouth to utter a question, but was interrupted by a shrill grating noise. Somewhere a man shouted at the top of his lungs, "Get down! The belt's going." Before I could react Jason wheeled and lunged forward, shoving me to the floor. A thunderbolt of pain surged through my head when it came in contact with the rough-hewed planks. In that brief gap of time before darkness claimed me I heard the whizz of of something overhead.

CHAPTER ELEVEN

A faint low moan echoed in my ears and I lay motionless, listening. As the sound grew louder I was startled to discover it was my own voice. It was as if it were attempting to draw me from the depths of blackness.

An unfamiliar sharp aroma touched my nostrils. As I jerked my head from side to side, a dull ache coursed through it. Clenching my teeth, I slowly opened my eyes.

Sunlight beamed through the window above me, causing my eyelids to flutter. From beneath them I glimpsed a green bottle and I raised my hand to push it away. The acrid aroma disappeared.

Even though I was aware someone sat nearby, I lay for a moment with my eyes closed, endeavoring to bring my thoughts into focus. The scream of saws rekindled the memory of Jason hurling me to the floor. Terrified, I opened my eyes at once and sat bolt upright.

My head reeled and patches of darkness veiled my vision. Through the blur I could see Jason sitting beside me, his expression grave. With a gentleness that seemed unlike him, he gathered me in his arms. "Don't pass out on me again," he whispered in my hair. "Are you all right, Abby?"

"Yes," I murmured without raising my head from the warmth of his flannel shirt. I lay still listening to the beat of his heart and hoping he would keep me within the circle of his embrace.

As much as I desired to know what had happened, I remained silent. For a while, at least, I wanted nothing to break this spell.

"The doctor will be here soon," Jason said, retaining his hold on me.

All my senses were aware of his strong body. "I don't need a doctor." My words were barely audible.

"In case you hadn't noticed, Abby, you have a lump on your forehead and it should be examined. I shouldn't have been so rough, shoving you to the floor the way I did, but there wasn't time to think."

Instinctively I wanted to reach up and touch the spot that ached on my temple, but I resisted the impulse. I was afraid my stirring might cause Jason to surrender his hold on me.

At this moment I didn't care about what had transpired in the boiler room. My soaring passion for this virile man overcame reason. Never before had I wanted a man the way I wanted Jason. His mouth was close and I moved my head slightly. His lips found mine. At first his kiss was light; but then as I snuggled closer and moved my arms up to encircle his neck, his embrace tightened and his lips became demanding. I sensed a feeling of surprise in him, which was replaced almost instantly by a tremor that went through his body. I reveled in the pain produced by his lips hard on mine.

Without warning Jason pushed me from him, and I saw the glint of anger in his eyes. "Get away from here, Abby! Go back to San Francisco."

I was trembling visibly, but I didn't know if it was from rising passion or my inability to fathom his words. Was Jason angry with me? Or himself?

"I don't understand," I managed, staring into his heavily lashed brown eyes.

He moved from my side as if he disliked all contact

with me. Bewildered, I watched the back of his head as he placed the bottle of smelling salts inside the white medical cabinet. A quick look around the small room crowded with three beds and a leather chair told me we were in the company infirmary.

Jason came about and regarded me from under his eyelids. A twist of excitement leaped in me. I lowered my eyes, embarrassed by my lack of emotional control. Women of high moral caliber did not throw themselves at men. What on earth must Jason think of me?

"Abby, do you have any idea of what happened in the power plant?" His voice was stripped of emotion.

I cleared my throat. "No, it all happened so fast."

"One of the belts operating the machinery snapped and whipped through the air narrowly missing us."

Chills prickled my scalp. "Does that sort of thing happen often?"

He leaned against the cabinet, his expression grave. "Occasionally, but I don't believe this was an accident. The belts were all inspected recently."

"Then you think someone deliberately tampered with it?"

"Yes, but I won't know for certain until I've had a chance to investigate."

"Is this similar to the accidents that have occurred previously?"

"Compared to the others, this is by far the worst. Someone could have been killed." He seated himself in the nearby chair, and I had the painful impression that he didn't want to be close to me. "Don't you see, Abby, you can't stay here? It's too dangerous."

I looked at him, startled. "Are you telling me that this accident was meant for me?"

He placed a calming hand on mine. "No, of course not. No one could have known precisely when we'd be in the power plant. That belt could have snapped off at any time."

"Then I don't see why you're trying to send me away."

He drew a long breath, clearly out of patience with me. "I am only trying to protect you. As long as these accidents persist you run the risk of being injured. Things could become much worse before the instigators of this sabotage are apprehended. I don't want to take a chance on anything happening to you. Go back to San Francisco. I'll send for you as soon as this situation has been resolved."

"I can't, Jason; my grandfather needs me. Besides, how would we explain my hasty departure without informing him of the trouble here? And what about the employees? I recall Mr. Olson mentioning that the men are beginning to believe the Justin Mill jinxed." I ignored Jason's look of annoyance and continued to press my point. "If I leave here now, so soon after being confronted by one of these numerous accidents, what do you suppose they'll think?"

"They'll think nothing! It's only natural for a woman to be frightened by an encounter such as yours. As for your grandfather, we can come up with a logical explanation for your departure. Illness in the family would—"

"No, Jason, I'm not leaving!" To my relief a knock on the door terminated our conversation, for I could see that my refusal to obey his instructions had escalated his anger. Jason rose abruptly and responded to the second knock.

A stocky bespectacled man carrying a medical bag came into the room. "Forgive my tardiness," he said. "We're having a dreadful day at the hospital." He turned his professional eyes on me. "I take it you're the patient, young lady?"

I nodded. "Yes, sir."

Jason introduced me to Dr. Caldwell; then he excused himself when the medical man began to probe the tender area above my right eye.

When Jason returned to the infirmary I knew by his grim expression that his suspicion concerning the accidents had been confirmed. Someone, he told me, had partially severed the belt that had nearly struck us.

Several hours later, his words still sent a chill down my spine. Who would do such a thing? I wondered, and turned in my bed. Although Jason had not speculated upon who the guilty party might be I knew he suspected Nicholas. I would never believe that myself.

My thoughts wandered back to that interval when Jason had left me in Mr. Taylor's care. Where had Jason gone? Could he have tampered with the machinery? Had he planned our entrance into the power plant at a time when he calculated the belt might snap? But then, would Jason have pushed me to safety? If his only intent was to frighten me back to San Francisco, then he might have.

I left the bed, ending my dismal cogitation, and went to the window. Overhead the stars glittered like sequins against a background of rich black velvet, reminding me of the twinkle I had observed in Dorothea's eyes this afternoon. In retrospect, it had seemed so easy to cast off the gloom induced by the accident and converse gaily with her.

When Jason and I had called for her at her sister's home, Dorothea had bounded down the flagstone walk. Excitement had been clearly evident on her face and in her hand she clutched a bouquet of spring flowers. "These are for you, miss," she had bubbled; then suddenly she regarded me with concern, noting the raised spot on my temple. "What happened to you, Miss Abby?"

When I told her of the incident at the mill the gaiety that had abounded in her eyes ebbed. Nothing, as far as I was concerned, was going to mar her day. I drew her attention from my injury by questioning her about the white silky flowers streaked with violet. A devilish gleam replaced the solicitude that had come into her eyes. "Those are trilliums," she informed. "I really shouldn't have picked them because they don't keep in water."

From that moment on, Dorothea literally bounced around on the front seat of the carriage, pointing out the lush green Cascade Mountains and the stately snow-encrusted Mt. Ranier.

When we arrived at home Jason and I were relieved to see Grandfather relaxing alongside the lake, enjoying the late-afternoon sun. Jason went down to visit with him, while Dorothea and I stole upstairs like two thieves in the night. There wasn't time to wash the sawdust from my hair, so Dorothea brushed it until it shone and fell into deep waves, covering the bump on my forehead.

The camouflage worked, and I knew Jason was pleased that we were able to keep the evidence of the accident at the mill from Martin Justin.

Back in bed I snuggled under the quilt and reflected upon the happiness I had observed in Dorothea today. I pondered, too, her remark about hating housework and wondered if in some way I could help her find employment she might enjoy.

Dorothea lacked a refined education. Nevertheless, her mind was sharp and I felt confident she would learn rapidly. Could Dr. Sims use her help? He needed more assistance than I would be able to give, and with Dorothea's patience and understanding she could be a valuable asset in his office. I drifted off to sleep, determined to broach the subject to her in the morning.

When I went downstairs for breakfast on the following day, I encountered Mrs. Brannon leaving Grandfather's room. "Is he awake?" I inquired.

She stepped away from his door, and responded in a soft, concerned voice. "Yes, he's awake and I'm afraid feeling a bit poorly. He gets these spells every now and then."

"What kind of spells?"

"Well, his legs are troubling him a little—the swelling and rheumatism, you know. But most of all he's feeling blue."

"Blue about what, Mrs. Brannon?"

"The mill. He misses his work there. He knows he can never return to it and just the thought of that sometimes drags down his spirit."

"Is there anything I can do to make him feel better?"

She gave me a gentle smile. "Your just being with him might perk him up, miss. He loves you so. Why don't you go on in?"

I nodded, and as Mrs. Brannon moved away, I tapped on Grandfather's door. Footsteps sounded beyond it; then Leah opened the dark panel. This morning her golden hair hung loosely, like a curtain down her back. She slanted me a quick look, then came out into the hallway and pulled the door closed behind her.

"Mrs. Brannon told me about Grandfather," I said. "Is he still awake?"

"Awake and staring into the drapery-darkened room, brooding. He won't talk and he won't eat his breakfast."

"May I see if I can change that?"

"Please do. I'll be in the kitchen if you should need me." She stepped away from the door, then paused and regarded me with a softened expression. "Tomorrow is my day off, miss, and my brother and I have plans to leave early in the morning for a visit with our parents. My mother's birthday is on Monday. If Mr. Justin isn't better in the morning would you want me to stay and watch after him?"

"No, that's not necessary, Leah. You needn't cancel your plans. We'll manage."

She proffered a smile as warm as the one she had cast my way on the previous day and again I wondered if she no longer considered me a threat to her and Jason. Leah left my side and for a long moment I watched after her, thinking how inordinately lovely she was with her hair loose about her shoulders. Had Jason ever seen her like this?

With that dismal thought in mind, I heaved a small sigh, then entered Grandfather's room. It was cloaked in darkness and the air was stale. Ahead of me, he lay motionless in the big fourposter bed. Dimness made it impossible for me to see his expression or if he even noticed my presence. "Grandfather," I said quietly.

He did not respond.

"Grandfather," I ventured again.

"Yes," he muttered, "what is it?"

"May I come in and sit with you for a while?"

He was silent for a long moment, then said, "If you want, but I'm not good company today."

"Let me be the judge of that," I insisted in a casual voice, and went to his side. "Is there anything I can do to make you more comfortable?" I kissed him on the cheek. "Or anything I can get you?"

"No."

"Have you had your medication?"

He nodded.

"Well, then, would you rather I just sit quietly while you try to get more sleep?"

"I'm not sleepy."

"Then may I open the draperies? It's a beautiful day and we should be enjoying it."

"Just leave them. I like it this way."

"It's gloomy and depressing," I pointed out, and before he could utter another objection, I went to the windows and gently eased open the blue damask draperies. Sunlight spilled into the room and cast golden patterns over the walls. "There now,"—I smiled at him—"isn't that nicer?"

"The light's blinding."

"Your eyes will adjust."

"Humpf," he grumbled in an undertone, "darn, bossy women."

With an inner grin, I shrugged aside the mutterings and glanced out the window, across the porch, to the rolling lawn and the lake. Mr. Brannon and Dorothea were on their way up from it. "Well, it appears as though we'll be having fish for dinner," I remarked, turning back to the aged man. "Dorothea and her father are on the way in with a string of trout."

Martin Justin stared up at the ceiling. Beside him on the night table was his breakfast tray. Sun shafts gleamed on the silver covers. Determined to rouse him from the doldrums, I asked on my way to the blue satin chair next to the bed, "Did my father often fish in the lake?"

Grandfather drew a short breath, then regarded me with dull eyes. "No," he replied as I sat down, "William wasn't an outdoorsman. I suppose that's why we were never close."

"I can't imagine anyone living in this beautiful country and not enjoying the outdoors."

"Oh, he enjoyed it, but in a different way."

"How's that?" I pressed.

"Well . . . William used to help Gus Brannon in the flower gardens."

"Really?"

He nodded. "That son of mine was forever digging up sickly looking plants and trees, then replanting them in sheltered locations and nursing them back to health."

"You know, Father never mentioned that, though his love for plants was always obvious."

"He was sensitive and gentle and I only wish I had realized then that he wasn't lumberman material."

"He was a fine doctor," I said softly, and a lump of emotion rose in my throat. "You would have been proud of him."

The old eyes brightened. "He gave me a warm and beautiful granddaughter and I'm grateful for that."

"And I'm grateful for you, Grandfather. But you must let me take proper care of you."

"Proper care? Why, you spoil me, my dear."

"Oh, I hope so," I told him truthfully, "because spoiling you makes me happy, though I'd be a lot happier now if you'd eat your breakfast."

He turned his attention from me to the tray, then back to me. "Well, I might be able to manage a little of it."

Delighted, I made Grandfather comfortable in the bed and sat with him while he partook of the light meal. When he finished, I asked, "Would you like me to help you to your chair?"

"Thank you, no," he declined. "My legs still ache a bit and I'd rather keep them outstretched. You might hand me my book, though." He gestured to the night table.

I gave him the book, then lifted the breakfast tray and, after reassuring him that I would be back again later, I left the room.

On my way to the kitchen I remembered Grandfather's plan—the one Jason had mentioned on our way to the mill—and I decided to withhold questioning the older man until he felt better.

The odor of fish dominated the kitchen when I entered. "Our dinner tonight?" I asked Mrs. Brannon, who was tackling the unpleasant task of cleaning the trout.

She turned with a start. "Oh, no, miss,"—she smiled—"lunch. And I must say Mr. Brannon is a mite put out because Dorothea caught most of these. Men don't take kindly to women outshining them, you know." She wiped her hands on her gingham apron and as she crossed to the stove, eyed the tray I carried. "You got him to eat." Her smile broadened. "I knew you could. Come, sit down, and I'll fix you some pancakes."

Over breakfast I decided it would be wise to approach Mrs. Brannon first in regard to my idea for her daughter and Dr. Sims.

Surprised by my interest in Dorothea's betterment, the older woman dropped into the chair opposite me. She smiled in a mist of tears. "Oh, Miss Abby, that would make my daughter so happy. She's such a good girl and deserves a chance to better her lot."

"I agree, Mrs. Brannon, but please don't raise your hopes too high. After all, I haven't discussed this with the doctor yet and he might shrug the idea aside."

She wiped her eyes with her fingertips. "I won't, miss."

"Would you prefer to discuss this with your husband before I talk with Dorothea?"

"No, that won't be necessary. He'll be as pleased as me." She reached out and touched my hand. "Thank you so much, Miss Abby."

"Oh, don't thank me yet." I grinned, then finished the last of the pancakes on my plate.

"Mr. Jason told me about the accident at the mill yesterday. Does your head hurt you?"

"No, Mrs. Brannon, but the lump I received certainly is a depressing shade of blue."

"You must have been scared half to death."

"No, not really. I was knocked out and by the time I regained consciousness everything had settled down."

"Just the same, Mr. Jason was furious when he told me about it. He left me strict instructions not to let you out of my sight."

I felt my spine stiffen a little and then relax. I didn't know if I should be pleased or perturbed.

"I've known Mr. Jason since he was a baby," Mrs. Brannon was saying, "and in all these years I've never seen him so angry."

Jason's face with its all too frequent scowl flashed across my mind. "He always seems to be angry with me," I confessed. "Sometimes I wonder if he even likes me."

She leaned forward. "I probably shouldn't say this, miss, but I think he's afraid of you."

"Afraid of me?" I almost laughed at that incongruous thought.

"What I mean is, he's afraid to care about you."

"But why?"

She hesitated. "It's wrong of me talk about Mr. Jason, but I love him and I've come to love you. I only want to help him. I believe he's in love with you, Miss Abby."

"Oh, but you're wrong." I stared at her in disbelief. "He doesn't even like to be near me."

Sadness came into her eyes. "Maybe if I explain what happened to Mr. Jason when his family died you'd understand him better."

"Please do, Mrs. Brannon, because I'm totally confused."

"Would you mind if I finish cleaning the fish while we talk?"

"Go right ahead. I'll clear the table for you." I rose and picked up the silver syrup pitcher.

"You don't have to do that, miss."

"But I want to. Please, tell me about Jason." She gave me a smile that reflected affection, then went to the sink.

"I'll never forget the day his family died," she began. "It was a miracle he wasn't with them. The Landrys, you see, were a close family. Ordinarily they went everywhere together, but on that particular day Mr. Jason was here working in the stables." She paused and stared out the window, a dreamy look in her eyes.

Quietly, I placed the dirty dishes on the counter. I wanted nothing to disturb her sequence of thought.

Mrs. Brannon lowered her gaze to the sinkful of water, resuming her explanation while she worked. "I remember so well that evening Mr. Justin brought young Jason home. He came running in here excited. For months he'd been saving for a new fishing pole and he told me that when he finished his work here he would have enough money. Even then he was like a member of the family. Jason liked it here in the woods and came often. He was a blessing to your grandparents. He seemed to fill the emptiness in their lives."

She sighed. "Anyway, when Mr. Justin told him of the accident, Jason ran away into the woods. He was twelve years old then and we all figured he would bear up under the tragedy. But it was too much for him. Men combed the woods, but they didn't find him. He returned on his own nearly two days later. The laughter was gone from his eyes."

Mrs. Brannon withdrew her hands from the water and reached for a towel to blot the fish. I leaned against the counter, wholly absorbed in her words.

When she spoke again I could hear the sadness come back into her voice. "Months went by before he took an interest in anything, but by then he was no longer a devilish young boy. He threw himself into his schoolwork and then later the mill. Other than your grandparents, he's never let himself become attached to anyone. Oh, he courted some nice young ladies,"—she smiled—"and a couple of times we thought he might marry, but then without a word of explanation he stopped seeing the girls."

She looked at me through moisture-laden eyes. "Can you understand him now, miss?"

I nodded, suddenly aware that tears also clouded my vision. Mrs. Brannon pulled me to her. "Oh, my dear," she said softly, "I believe you like him more than you're willing to admit." She led me to the table and then sat down across from me.

My cheeks felt hot. "I don't know how I feel about him." I sighed in dismay. "I can understand his aloofness, Mrs. Brannon, but why is he always angry with me?"

She burst out laughing. "You have a great deal to learn about men, my dear, but that's as it should be at your age. I'm sure Mr. Jason figures if he can stay angry at you he can keep his distance. I suspect he feels it's better not to love, than chance being hurt."

"But that's ridiculous."

"Of course it is. Perhaps, Miss Abby, you're the one who can make him see that. He's a good man; you'll find none better." She rose. "Well, now, if you'll excuse me I'd best get those fish into the refrigerator."

I stood up too. "And I'd better get my hair washed."

In the solitude of my room I flung myself full length across the bed and carefully considered her words. I couldn't believe Jason was in love with me. On that point, I felt certain, Mrs. Brannon was wrong. Did he push me away from him yesterday because he feared being hurt? I couldn't believe that either. To me it seemed inconceivable that anything could wound the feelings of rugged and strong-willed Jason Landry.

CHAPTER TWELVE

It was nearly dinnertime before I was able to consult with Dorothea over my desire to upgrade her employment. "Oh, miss, Abby,"—she giggled—"I can't believe it. Do you really think you can work it out with Dr. Sims?"

"Well, I'm certainly going to try. You must understand, though, that the entire plan hinges on whether or not he can afford to hire you. If he can't, or if he's not receptive to the idea, then maybe he'll allow me to train you in his office. I doubt he would mind that since he would be gaining free office help. If Dr. Sims doesn't employ you,"—the words came slowly—"perhaps Jason could help us find you a job."

Dorothea gave me a quick look. "Oh, I wouldn't want you to ask Mr. Jason."

"Why not?"

"Because he's already done so much for my sister. It wouldn't be right to ask him to help me, too."

"What has he done for your sister?"

"The house her family lives in is his."

"The house is his?" I said in surprise, and pictured the small white dwelling, with its trim picket fence, thick carpet of grass, and riot of color in the flower beds.

"Yes, it's his," she returned, and I wondered why Jason hadn't mentioned that when we stopped there for Dorothea yesterday. "Anyway," she continued, "Mr. Jason doesn't charge my sister and her family hardly any rent. He's a very kind man, miss. When he heard they were having hard times he told them to move into his house and not to worry about the rent. That was about a year ago. Things are better for them now, but he still won't take much rent. He told them to put their money in the bank so maybe someday they could buy a place of their own."

So there was a generous and compassionate side to Jason Landry's nature. "I can understand how you feel," I managed, a note of wonder in my voice. "And I won't ask him to help us."

Before the young girl left my room I requested that she not mention my proposal to anyone, other than her parents, until I'd had the opportunity to discuss it with the doctor. Dorothea agreed and left my side in a flurry of excitement.

Jason was not home in time for the evening meal, so Grandfather and I dined alone in his room. In spite of the continued dull ache in his legs, he'd managed to maintain a cheerful attitude, though his appetite had slipped a little. "Don't worry about it, Abby," he insisted. "My appetite will be back to normal in a day or two. You'll see. Now," —he grinned— "just because I'm not eating like I should, doesn't mean that I'm not up to a game of chess."

"Oh, but you always win." I feigned a pout.

He laughed. "Well, at least I'm still good at

something. Now bring on over the chess set, dear."

I gladly obeyed the gentle order and when Grandfather once again beat me at the game, I pretended another pout. "You're just going to have to get in some practice games," he teased.

"More than some," I admitted, smiling. "Now, off to sleep with you, it's getting late."

It was shortly after eight o'clock when Grandfather retired and I wandered down to the lake. Seated on the lawn swing, I fastened my mind on Dorothea. I could not disappoint her, but now I wondered if perhaps I had made a mistake in speaking with her before consulting the doctor. Often my impulsiveness had led me astray, and I wished now that I had sought out the advice of Grandfather or even Jason before declaring my plan.

The lush mat of lawn must have muffled the footsteps behind me, for I did not know anyone was near until Jason spoke my name. "Abby, I have a letter for you. I picked it up at the post office on my way home."

I slid around on the swing and at once my eyes went to the white envelope he held out to me. "Thank you," I said as I accepted it. "Oh,"—I grinned—"it's from my aunt in San Francisco."

"Judging from your expression, I can see you miss her a lot." He sounded tired and I looked up at him with concern. Jason's eyes were dull and there were deep lines of fatigue etched around his mouth. I wanted to reach out and touch him with a comforting hand. Instead, I held myself in constraint, afraid he would reject my sympathy.

A lump formed in my throat and before I could find my voice, Jason said, "I'll leave you to your letter."

I swallowed hard. "Please, won't you sit with me for

a while? I can read this later."

He tried to smile, but he wasn't successful.

"Have you had dinner?" I asked, after he joined me on the swing.

"Yes. I ate at the mill."

"You're later than usual. Is everything all right?"

"Everything is as normal as it can be under the circumstances. I hate to admit it, Abby, but you were right about your remaining in town."

I felt a tinge of smugness. Well, for once I was right about something where this man was concerned. "What prompted you to that conclusion?"

He took a deep breath. "The men were riled this morning over yesterday's accident, but they quieted down when I told them that you had taken it in your stride and would return next week for a day's work. No lumberman would ever admit a woman is braver than he." Jason managed a faint smile.

"I'm glad I was able to help,"—I smiled back at him—"even though I wasn't there."

A fish leaped in a glistening silver arc, drawing Jason's attention to the lake. I glanced past him to the grove of evergreens along the bank. Twilight was upon us now. "Jason, if you're not too tired," I ventured, "I'd like to talk with you about Dorothea."

"Hm?" He pulled himself from his thoughts and looked at me.

"May I talk with you for a few minutes about Dorothea? I need some advice."

He seemed pleased by my wish to consult with him. "What about her?"

There was a brief silence while I marshaled my thoughts. "I've become very fond of her," I began. "Dorothea is warm and considerate and she has a sharp mind. But most of all, she hates housework."

Jason appeared confused. "You mean she isn't happy here?"

"No, it isn't that. It's just that she would rather earn a living at a task other than housework."

"Like what?"

"I'd like to train her to work in a doctor's office." I held my breath, praying he would not laugh at my idea.

To my immense relief he did not, though he did regard me with surprise. "I would imagine you have Dr. Sims's office in mind."

I nodded. "Yes. Do you think he'll be agreeable?"

"I'm sure he'd like to have the help," Jason replied after several seconds of consideration. "However, I doubt he can afford to hire anyone. What of Dorothea? Is this what she wants?"

I told him of her excitement. "I realize Dr. Sims probably won't be able to employ her, but I'm hoping he will permit me to train her in his office. Once she's qualified, I can help her find a job."

"Maybe I can help too," he offered. "I know all the doctors around."

I smiled through a film of tears. "Oh, thank you, Jason." Overcome with a rush of warm emotion, I threw my arms around his neck, and kissed him on the cheek.

Momentarily he was taken aback, but then he pulled me hard against him, and kissed me as I had never before been kissed. This time I knew for certain he would not push me away; and I tightened my arms about his neck and clung to him with my body in the curve of his. His passion mounted faster than I was able to comprehend, and then I didn't think at all anymore. There was no suspicion in my mind, only desire that made me tremble with excitement I was unable to control. His hand moved from my back to the hollow beneath my breasts, and I shuddered with anticipation, wanting him in a way I knew was wicked for an unmarried woman.

Jason's hand trembled, and then he released me abruptly as if he sensed I was a little frightened. He kissed my cheeks, then held me at arm's length. Embarrassed by my conduct, I was unable to meet his eyes. I wanted to believe that I would have resisted any further advances, but my tingling body told me that was unlikely.

Jason's hand went under my chin, forcing me to look into his shining eyes. "Would you go fishing with me tomorrow?" he asked, and I knew he was trying to put me at ease.

I gave him a thin smile. "I don't know anything about fishing."

"There's nothing to it. Besides, it's almost a disgrace to live alongside a lake and not fish."

I hesitated. "Well, I don't know. Somehow I can't envision myself sitting in a boat on the lake for hours with a worm bobbing on the end of a line." I shuddered. "I don't think I'd be able to bring myself to stick a squirming worm onto a fishhook."

Jason frowned at me. "Your grandfather will be very disappointed to hear that. Your grandmother was an expert with a fishing line."

I turned from his touch, considering. "Well,"—I hesitated—"I guess if my grandmother could do it, then I suppose I can, too."

Jason hugged me to him and kissed my hair. "Come on, we'd better go in, it's getting late." He drew me to my feet and tucked my hand in the crook of his arm. "You'll need plenty of rest if you're going to battle those fish tomorrow. Besides, I'm exhausted. It's been a long day."

About a half-hour later, while I was preparing for bed, I heard the door at the far end of the hallway open and then close.

Quickly I stepped to my door and opened it a fraction. In the faint light I saw Jason descending the stairs, and I noticed, too, that he was still dressed in his work clothes. I watched him, eyes narrowed in bewilderment, until he disappeared from view. If he was as tired as he claimed—and looked, for that matter—then why wasn't he in bed? And where was he going?

CHAPTER THIRTEEN

In the morning I awakened earlier than usual and since there was ample time before Jason and I would leave for church I lounged around my room.

For timeless seconds I resumed my speculation on where he had been headed last night; but then I quickly terminated those thoughts when Leah came into my mind. He couldn't have gone to her, I told myself, not after the way he kissed me. Somehow I wasn't convinced and I was glad that I would not have to see our housekeeper today.

She was gone from the house already, for I had seen her and a tall, broad-shouldered man crossing the lawn to the dock a short time ago.

From my window I watched them until they disappeared into a cluster of trees. The man, whom I assumed to be Leah's brother, Carl, had hair as golden as her own.

When I finally emerged from my room and made my way down the stairs I was delighted to find Grandfather at the dining-room table. I smiled at him, then dropped a glance to his breakfast plate.

137

"Now, see." He beamed at me, and gestured to his breakfast of sausages, eggs, and hot buttered biscuits. "My appetite has returned. Just like I said it would."

I gave him a hug. "That's so good to see, Grandfather, and you look so well."

He gazed up into my face. "You look exceptionally well yourself, kind of a radiance about you. Any special reason for that?"

I thought of Jason's kiss and, despite my doubts of him and Leah, I knew that if there was a radiance it was linked to him. Nevertheless, I wasn't ready yet to openly admit that to anyone. "It's a beautiful spring day," I replied lightly, "and you're feeling better. That's reason enough. Oh, yes, and I received a letter from my aunt in San Francisco."

"A letter? When did that come?"

I helped myself to coffee from the sideboard. "Yesterday. Jason brought it home with him last night."

"Didn't he get home rather late?"

"Later than usual. It was just after you retired for the night. He saw me sitting on the swing down by the lake and he came down and chatted with me for a while."

"Really?" The old eyes sparkled.

Dorothea came in to check on Grandfather. When she saw me, a smile brightened her face. "Good morning, Miss Abby."

I returned the greeting.

"May I get you some breakfast now?"

"Please," I acknowledged.

When the young girl turned away, Grandfather asked, "So, tell me, Abby, how are your aunt and her family?"

"Very well," I told him, and was inwardly elated over my success at concealing my troubled thoughts from him.

"You must invite them up for a visit."

"Why, thank you." I beamed. "That would be nice, in time."

He swallowed a morsel of sausage, then said, "You know, dear, as frequently as we've talked about your life in San Francisco, you've never once mentioned suitors. Surely you had your share of them."

"Well, there were a few."

"No one special?"

"No, not really. Although my aunt thought a couple of the fellows who were extra attentive to me were, as she put it, 'excellent catches,' and she more or less suggested I give them some consideration."

"But you didn't?"

I shook my head. "They were nice and probably would have made good husbands, but I didn't love them, so there was nothing to consider. I just couldn't marry someone I didn't love."

"You made the right decision in that regard," he agreed. "And selfishly, I have to admit I'm glad you didn't find anyone, because then you probably wouldn't be here now."

"For that reason," I returned, as I also thought of Jason, "I, too, am glad there wasn't anyone." We exchanged contented smiles, then both looked up when Jason entered for breakfast.

"Well," Grandfather exclaimed, scrutinizing the younger man, "here's another exceptionally happy-looking face. Is your broad smile also related to the beautiful spring day?"

Jason's gaze swept to me and for an instant our eyes met and held. Was he happy because of our kiss? I wondered. Or maybe becaue of Leah?

He cleared his throat and returned his attention to Martin Justin. "Partly that," Jason responded.

"And partly what else?" Grandfather pressed.

139

"Well, this is a day off from work."

"Don't tell me you're becoming tired of running the mill already."

Jason grinned. "I'll never tire of that. It's just that a bit of relaxation is nice, too."

The conversation remained light throughout the meal, and I regarded the late-afternoon fishing excursion with Jason with mixed emotions. I wanted to be with him more than anything. Nevertheless, I was dubious of my ability as a fisherman. So when the time came to prepare for the excursion, it was with a bit of reluctance that I donned an old dress suitable for the occasion and joined him at the dock.

He gave me an appraising look and then a broad smile. "Congratulations," he said, "You've passed the first step."

I was bewildered. "I have?"

He nodded. "Yes, you're dressed appropriately. I was afraid you'd come down here in that ruffled thing you were wearing this morning."

"And get worms all over it?"

In a lightning motion he caught up the can of worms from the dock and waved them under my nose. They were long and slimy. My nose wrinkled. "These really bother you, don't they?" he teased.

I raised a hand and pushed the container away. "If you don't mind I'd rather not see them until absolutely necessary."

He smiled and I did too.

When Jason clasped my hand to help me into the boat I experienced a resurgence of the excitement his touch had kindled last night.

Some distance from shore he pulled the oars aboard and laid them on the bottom of the boat. "Was Martin still asleep when you left the house?" he wanted to know.

"Yes, but he told me earlier that he'd be down to

watch us as soon as he awoke." I glanced at the bank. It was still empty.

After Jason showed me how to use the fishing pole he placed the can of worms between us on the bottom of the boat. I had hoped he would offer to bait my fishhook, but that notion was soon dashed asunder.

He lifted a wriggling worm from the container. "This is the way to bait a hook," he said, pushing it through the middle of the worm. A shiver of distaste went down my back. He held one out to me. "You try it now." The corners of his mouth twitched with amusement.

Reluctantly, I reached out and then, with a shudder that shook my shoulders, withdrew my hand. "I don't suppose you'd do it for me?"

He could no longer suppress laughter. "No, I won't. Your grandmother baited her own hooks and there is no reason why you can't do the same." He thrust the dangling worm at me. "Now quit being so squeamish and take it!"

"Oh, very well," I grumbled, and snatched it from his hand. The worm felt like a piece of cold, cooked spaghetti. I squeezed my eyes shut and tried to ignore the hint of nausea in my stomach.

"Abby, you can't bait a hook with your eyes closed, you'll run it through your finger."

About ninety minutes later, I had, much to my delight, caught two trout to Jason's none. Laughter bubbled from me. "Would you like me to instruct you in the art of fishing?"

He smiled sheepishly. "Just beginner's luck."

"I prefer to call it skill." I turned my eyes to shore. "I wonder where my grandfather is? He should be awake by now."

"I'm sure there's no need to worry. He probably decided to remain indoors." Jason reached past me for the oars; his head so close that his breath touched my cheek. I did not move. "We'll row out a little further," he told me, and looked toward the house. His lips compressed and he came erect abruptly. "Looks like you have a visitor."

My gaze swept across the water, dazzled by sunlight, and I raised a hand to protect my eyes from the glare. Nicholas and Grandfather and even Old-Timer were leaving the back porch, headed for the dock.

Jason plunked the oars into the water and I stared at the ripples that rayed out. "I suppose you'll want to go ashore now?" he muttered.

"Heavenly days, no." I grinned. "We can't return until you catch at least one fish. Mrs. Brannon told me a woman should never outdo a man. Besides, why do you presume that Nicholas is here to see me?"

Jason threw me a sharp look. "You certainly are naïve, Abby. I can assure you he did not ride all the way out here to visit with your grandfather."

I didn't agree, but I kept the opinion to myself. So far this afternoon had been perfect and I wanted no friction to mar it. "I'm in no hurry to return," I confessed. "I'm enjoying myself and the company. Anyway, I'm sure my grandfather won't mind having Nicholas to himself for a while." I paused, then added hastily, "Would you rather I weren't so naïve?"

Jason gave me a slow searching look, then smiled into my eyes. "No, I guess not." Without further elaboration, he switched the subject. "Shall we try our luck farther out, then?"

"Yes, let's do."

In the hour that followed Jason caught one trout—but then, so did I. "Now I suppose you won't take me fishing anymore," I teased.

"I'm pleased you had a good time, Abby, but I

think I'd better get you ashore. You're getting a sunburned nose." He grinned.

Instinctively I put my hand to the area assaulted by the sun's rays. "Oh, what a sight I must be." I groaned. "A lump on my forehead and now a sunburned nose."

He laid his pole aside and reached out a slender hand to examine the bruise above my eye. "It doesn't look any better. Does it hurt?"

"No. The doctor assured me it would be gone in a few days." Jason's hand dropped to my shoulder and my heartbeat accelerated.

"Before we head back, Abby, I'd like to talk to you."

"About what?" My voice wavered.

"Have you told Wells that I suspect him of the trouble at the mill?"

"No."

"Good." He flicked a glance at the shore and I followed his line of vision. The two men were still on the bank.

Jason leaned closer. "I want you to promise me you won't discuss this recent accident with him."

"But why not? He must be aware of it, so what difference could our discussing it possibly make?"

"If Wells suspects either one of us is suspicious of him, he might panic and—"

"Are you implying he might harm us?"

"There's always that possibility. After all, if he is involved in the sabotage and is caught he'll go to prison."

"Aren't you exaggerating a little, Jason? Nicholas wouldn't hurt anyone and I'm sure he's not involved."

The dark eyes near to mine were brilliant with anger. "For God's sake, Abby, don't argue. Can't you just this once trust me?"

His words shook me to silence. "I'm sorry," I managed after a long moment. "I'll do as you ask."

"I'm only trying to protect you," he reassured softly.

"I know."

He took both of my hands in his. "For your sake, Abby, I hope I'm wrong about Wells. In any case, if he should question you about the accident, just shrug it off. It won't be easy, I know; but you can do it."

"Very well, Jason." I sighed. "I just hope this will all be over soon because I'm tired of evasive tactics."

"So am I. Oh, one more thing before we start back."

"Yes?"

"Wells may talk against me. I've seen the way he looks at you and I'm positive it irritates him that you and I live under the same roof. He wants you for himself."

I parted my lips to deny that, but Jason put a silencing finger on my mouth. "I'm sure he'll attempt to discredit me," he continued, "if he hasn't already. I hope you won't take his words seriously."

My throat constricted, making speech impossible.

When I didn't respond, Jason resumed, "If you're wondering why you should believe me instead of him, then I don't know what to say." He held my eyes with his and I could hardly bear his proximity. "I would never harm you or your grandfather."

My hammering heart influenced my brain. "I know you wouldn't, Jason."

He flashed a smile that sent the blood surging in my ears. Jason shot a quick look over the water and then not altogether gently drew me to him and put his mouth on mine. It was a sudden, quick kiss and yet fierce and tender.

For what seemed like too brief a moment he held me close, and then, as if he'd read my mind, he murmured near my ear, "Don't be embarrassed, Abby. We're merely vague figures to anyone viewing us from shore." I sighed with ecstasy and snuggled my head against his shoulder.

When we came alongside the dock Nicholas helped me from the boat. As always, he was dressed impeccably. Today he was clothed in a charcoal-gray suit and his blue eyes beneath dark brows regarded me soberly. I felt a stab of guilt and could feel my heart thumping in my throat, wondering if he had observed the kiss between Jason and me. "I must look a fright," I said, feeling the blood drain from my face.

"Never that," he reassured me with a smile.

The clatter of fishing equipment being transferred to the dock brought my head around and I could see that Jason was amused by the verbal exchange between the well-dressed man and me. I threw Jason a haughty look, even though the situation struck me as humorous, too.

"Can I help you with the gear?" Nicholas offered.

Jason stepped onto the dock. "Thanks, but I can manage."

"I didn't expect to see you until Tuesday," I said to Nicholas. "Has your friend from Portland left?"

"Yes, early this afternoon. I hope you don't mind my stopping by."

"You're always welcome," I told him sincerely. I raised a hand of greeting to Grandfather, who sat beneath the shade of a nearby fir, then stooped to brush the soft brown coat of Old-Timer.

Nicholas joined us for dinner and as he seated me at the dining-room table I felt my nerves tighten and my appetite diminish. For I was certain Jason would be remote and cool toward him, throwing a strain on the entire meal. But, to my astonishment, Jason's mood was not only light but he gave the impression of a man who didn't have a care in the world.

Apparently Nicholas was bewildered by the light mood because once or twice I saw him lift a quizzical eyebrow.

All through the meal I clung to the hope that I would not be left alone with him, for out of concern for me I was sure he would mention the accident at the mill. I did not want to be evasive with Nicholas and I feared that if he should detect a lack of straightforwardness our friendship would be weakened.

We had scarcely left the dinner table, however, when Jason neutralized that hope. In a casual tone he suggested to Grandfather that they venture down to the stables. "Jericho and Ginger are getting pretty old," he told him, "and I think we should replace them."

"Do we have to go down there right now?" Martin Justin grumbled. "We do have a guest, you know?"

Nicholas responded with eagerness. "No, please, go right ahead." He looked at me. "If Abby feels up to it, we'll take a walk down to the gazebo."

I didn't want to hurt this kindly man's feelings, so what else could I do but nod and give him a smile I didn't really feel.

Nicholas in turn gave Jason a look of gratitude for allowing him the opportunity to be alone with me. I was furious with Jason for hurling me headlong into a situation out of which he knew I would have to wheedle my way. Obviously he didn't care about me at all.

This evening my pensive mood dimmed the enchantment I felt for the gazebo. I entered and sat down on the whitewashed bench hardly aware of my surroundings.

"You've been awfully quiet, Abby," Nicholas said.

"Is anything wrong?"

"No, not really. I'm just a trifle homesick," I lied.

"I can understand that. I get a longing to see the family and friends in Chicago every now and then."

I sat dumbly, not knowing what to say.

Nicholas broke the awkward moment of silence. "Jason was certainly different tonight—friendly for a change. Are you the reason?"

I wanted to make a face at that remark, but I managed to constrain the impulse. "I doubt it." I sounded petulant. "I fully expected him to scowl through the entire meal."

"You don't want to talk about it, do you?"

"Talk about what?" I gulped.

"Don't be evasive; it's not your nature. You know very well I'm referring to the accident at the mill."

He put a hand beneath my chin and gently turned my face to his. Our blue eyes met squarely. "I'm worried about you, Abby."

"I appreciate your concern, Nicholas, but as you can see I'm all right."

"I want to hear your version of what happened yesterday."

I turned from his gaze. "There is nothing to tell. The accident was just that—an accident, one of those freakish mishaps."

"A freakish mishap? Is that what Jason called it?"

I shivered in dread. Obviously I was an ineffective prevaricator, and Nicholas would probably extract even the minutest details of the accident from me. "Don't be so serious," I told him. "I wasn't hurt."

"From what I understand, you could have been killed. And quit avoiding my questions!"

I looked him full in the eyes. "I'm not avoiding them. I can't explain what happened. I'm not familiar with the mechanics of the equipment. At any rate, from what I've heard, accidents aren't uncommon at sawmills."

"Yes, that's true, but Justin Mill has had more than its share lately. It's only a matter of time before someone is killed. In case you aren't aware of it, there were seldom accidents when your grandfather was in command. Watch out for Jason, Abby. He wants what he believes is rightfully his."

I didn't want to hear any more. I stumbled to my feet and made for the entrance, tears burning behind my eyes.

Nicholas intercepted me, blocking the archway with his lean body. "Did Jason brush aside the accident as if it were a common everyday occurrence?"

"If you're insinuating he had anything to do with it, you're wrong. Jason was the one who pushed me to safety. Both of us were threatened by the mishap."

"He's really charmed you over to his side, hasn't he?"

"Stop it!" I swung around.

Nicholas caught my arm. "I can see I'm right." He propelled me back to the wooden bench and gently thrust me onto the seat. He sat down beside me, retaining his hold on my arm. "I'm not going to let you make a fool of yourself over him, Abby. You may as well know that from all I've heard, Jason Landry does very well with the ladies."

I tried to get away from him, but his hand on my arm made that impossible. "Listen to me carefully," he ordered, "and above all, don't be angry with me. I care about you deeply and I cannot stand idly by and watch you get hurt. It isn't beyond Jason to make love to you to get what he wants."

I let my eyes blaze up at him. "Are you implying the only reason a man would be attracted to me is because of my grandfather's wealth?"

"Don't be ridiculous! You know what I mean. Your charm and beauty would captivate the heart of any man. But in Jason's case the mill is an added inducement. He's not going to simply walk away from something he's given half of his life to."

I lifted my chin. "If he's as cunning as you'd like me to believe, then why hasn't my grandfather noticed it? More to the point, why haven't *you* brought it to his attention?"

Nicholas sighed deeply. "To begin with I have no evidence to substantiate my accusations and what Jason does with the Justin Mill isn't really any of my business, except where you're concerned. Besides, in the absence of evidence to back up my claim, I'm positive your grandfather wouldn't believe me. He loves Jason like a son and where he's concerned Martin Justin is blind."

Clouds of confusion swam in my mind. I felt like a pawn bandied between two men. Which one of them was I to believe?

Nicholas slipped an affectionate arm about my shoulders and drew me against him. "Maybe you should return to San Francisco for a while."

I was so tired of hearing that. "I can't leave my grandfather," I told him in a tremulous voice.

"If you ever need me for anything, Abby, send word. I'll get to you no matter where you are, and as fast as I can." He tilted up my chin, and as he gently put his lips on mine, I felt a warm liquid sensation flow through my veins.

Later in my room I lay on the bed staring up at the canopy, my troubled thoughts jumbled in a sea of mist. Both men presented logical arguments and seemed sincere, and I was beginning to wonder if perhaps their intense antagonism toward each other had induced them to unwarranted suspicions.

A stab of pain pulsed over my right eye, and I raised a hand to the swelling, then sat up. On my feet, I shoved the cluttered confusion from my mind, and tried to make it a blank. Absently, I unbuttoned my dress and allowed it to slip to the floor.

A sharp knock on the door jerked me from my dreamlike state. "Who is it?" I called.

"Jason. May I talk to you for a minute?"

"Can't it wait until morning?"

"No, it can't."

"Oh, very well." I sounded irritable. "Just a minute." I slipped a wrapper over my camisole and petticoat, then opened the door. Jason stood in the flickering light, a stormy look in his eyes. I flinched. "If you're looking for an argument, I'm not interested."

He ignored my remark. "Were you in the study at any time today?"

"No, why do you ask?"

"Someone was rummaging around in there."

"Are you sure?"

"Do you think I have nothing better to do with my time than make up stories? I want to talk to you."

To my consternation, he strode into the room. "But you shouldn't be in here," I reminded, aware my mouth gaped.

"Don't be such a prude, Abby. Close your mouth and come over here."

CHAPTER FOURTEEN

I closed my mouth, but I did not close the door. The electricity between Jason and me clearly indicated that I couldn't trust either one of us.

He watched me cross and come to a stop in front of him, then looked over my head to the door. Amusement played at the corners of his mouth. "I can assure you, Miss Justin, if it were my intention to make improper advances, an open door would not discourage me. Especially when we're alone on this floor and it's unlikely anyone would come up here at this hour. Let's just see how much you really trust in me." In three strides he was across the room. The door clicked shut at the same time that my legs began to feel rubbery and my mouth felt as though it had been invaded by a handful of cotton.

Jason leaned against the dark panel and his eyes moved slowly over my nighttime-clad body. I felt so self-conscious I didn't know what to do with myself, except wring my hands. "Damn it, Abby,"—he started forward—"you look as though you suspect I'll lunge at you and—" His voice dwindled, then returned to normal "—seduce you."

I took a step back, keenly aware that if he put his hands on me I would be powerless. And here in the privacy of this room—in my bed—I would discover what transpired between male and female in the heat of passion. I wanted that because I now knew, regardless of the doubts I had harbored against this man, that I loved him. Still, I could not think only of myself and Jason; there was my family to consider. I could not bring possible shame to them. I had to do something quickly, before his outstretched hand was on me.

"Don't touch me!" He withdrew his hand as if it had come into contact with something hot. "How could you have been so insensitive? You deliberately threw me into an ordeal with Nicholas, one you knew I'd have to worm my way out of."

The color washed from Jason's face. "I'm sorry. If I had known it was going to upset you this much I would not have made it convenient for him to be alone with you."

"Then why did you?"

"I did it because I knew that eventually he would seek you out and question you. I preferred he do it here, with me close by." He gave me a crooked smile that set my pulses quickstepping. "I was on the porch, pacing most of the time you were with him."

"You were?"

He nodded. "What did you tell Wells about the accident?"

"Nothing, really. He did most of the talking."

"Good girl." Jason put his hand on the nape of my neck, then pulled me to him and kissed me. It was a light kiss that left me breathless and wanting more. I didn't dare dwell on that. "What prompted you to come to my room?" I asked.

He laughed, embarrassed. "I almost forgot about that."

"Hm, and you said it was important." I feigned a frown.

Jason sobered. "It was and it still is. Someone's rifled through my papers in the study and I wondered if you had seen anyone near there today."

"No, I didn't. Was anything stolen?"

"Not that I could tell. The Kimberley bids are in the safe and it's a tough one to crack. If Martin was still asleep when Wells arrived," he said slowly, "he could have sneaked into the study."

I took a step back. "Don't you dare accuse him."

"Still quick to jump to his defense, aren't you? Just what did he say to you? Or was it too personal to relate?"

"Yes, it was, to an extent." I purposely did not elaborate for Aunt Helen had said a woman should never let a man be too sure of her. It dulled a romance.

Jason seemed perturbed, but he did not press the issue. "Doesn't it seem strange to you, Abby, that the study was searched on the same day he was here?"

"It could be a coincidence. Besides, even if it was Nicholas, he wouldn't hang around leaving himself open to suspicion. He's too intelligent for that."

"Ah, but don't you see, perhaps he figured that would be our reasoning."

Now I was perturbed. "Think whatever you like, but I don't believe it. At any rate, couldn't the room have been searched last night?"

"Yes, I suppose so." Jason regarded me from under his thick lashes, and then I saw his eyes turn briefly to the bed. "I think I'd better get out of here, but first—" His voice trailed off as his eager lips came down on mine. It was evident from the way he held me hard against him that he wanted to direct our mutual passion to that mysterious end of which I had had no experience. But thank God he didn't allow his lips to linger on mine. We were both trembling when he released me and it was with mixed emotions that I watched him leave the room. One part of me desired him to remain, while the other part of me sighed with relief.

For the next two days I moved about almost oblivious to the noise of the house being readied for the party. Rugs were hauled out to the yard, thrown over a hemp line, and beaten. Crystal chandeliers were cleaned and everywhere was the aroma of beeswax and turpentine.

A dreaminess veiled my vision. I was hardly aware the skies had turned slate-gray and a thin mist sprinkled moisture about.

As much as I tried to keep my happiness to myself I could see Grandfather watching me covertly, his mouth turned upward into a sloppy grin. Once or twice I was tempted to approach him in regard to his plan—the one Jason had mentioned—but because of the endless activities that consumed my hours, time alone with the older man was limited. Whatever he had in mind, though, Jason had practically scoffed at it and I was steeled for the worst. I had the uncanny feeling that whatever Grandfather was considering could not be satisfactorily discussed in a short period of time.

As planned, Nicholas came by on Tuesday afternoon for our ride and I felt a little guilty about being with him. Since I was in love with Jason it didn't seem fair to either man that I was enjoying Nicholas' company. Yet there was nothing definite between Jason and me and I really wasn't ready to relinquish my friendship with Nicholas. I would miss him terribly and that troubled me.

"Well." He beamed when I met him at the front door. "You certainly do a riding costume justice."

"Why, thank you." I smiled in return and my eyes took in his fine-fitting casual clothes, most especially the buckskin coat I liked so much. "Please, won't you come in for a few minutes, before we leave, and say hello to my grandfather?"

"By all means." He entered.

The two men chatted for several minutes; then Nicholas and I left the house and set out on our horses. "You know," I said as we rode along the main road, "I'm beginning to feel like a native of Washington Territory."

"Oh?" He raised a quizzical brow.

"Well,"—I laughed—"I've noticed that after a few days of sunshine the main topic of conversation is: how much longer will the nice weather last? And like the natives I find myself searching the sky for ominous rain clouds."

Nicholas gave me a crooked smile. "Well, I'd say that just about qualifies you as a native. So, I take it then, Abby, you don't mind all the rain."

"San Francisco gets a fair amount of it, so I'm really used to it. Besides, we have the rain to thank for this beautiful greenery."

"The greenery and the abundance of trees."

"Hm," I teased, "always thinking of business."

"Oh, not always." He regarded me with sparkling eyes.

I felt a flush and glanced off to the wild flowers alongside the road. "You know,"—my voice became thoughtful—"I've been meaning to ask about the trees. Well, actually, the stumps."

"What about them?"

"I've been wondering why they're cut so high off the ground. At least those I've seen between here and town are about fifteen feet."

"They're all cut around that height."

"Isn't that a waste?"

"Essentially it is. On the other hand, the loggers don't have a choice. The butts of the trees, you see, are shaky and full of pitch."

We turned our horses onto an evergreen-lined

roadway that led to the lake. "How on earth, then," I questioned, "do the loggers get up high enough to saw them down?"

"They stand on springboards."

"Springboards? What are they?"

"Oh, they're boards about five feet long and eight inches wide. Notches are cut into each side of a tree and the boards inserted. And, as you might imagine, it takes a tremendous amount of balance to keep from tumbling off."

"No doubt." I laughed, then asked, "Did you ever try to balance on one?"

"No,"—he grinned—"and I'm not about to try. I'll just stick with operating a sawmill."

We reined in at the lake, dismounted, and let the horses drink of the cold water. "Well," I said, "I've managed to learn a little about sawmills since my arrival in town, but I still know nothing of logging, except that it's dangerous work."

"Extremely so," Nicholas emphasized. "But then loggers take the danger in their stride and they are quick on their feet."

Jason was quick on his feet, too, I thought, remembering that afternoon when he'd pushed me to safety in the boiler room.

"Shall we sit and enjoy the scenery for a while?" Nicholas gestured to a fallen tree at the water's edge.

I nodded, and as he tethered the horses, I moved to the tree and sat down. "I like it out here, around the lake," he remarked, taking up the spot beside me. "It's so peaceful and quiet. A real pleasure after the noise of the city."

"I think I like being among the trees the most."

"I'm afraid a lot of people west of the Cascades don't share your enthusiasm for them."

"Well, I would imagine they can be a nuisance,

what with trying to build roads and houses."

"A plagued nuisance, especially to the early pioneers and Indians. Why, the latter used to purposely set forest fires that would burn for miles until smothered by heavy rains. But then that was the only way the Indians knew to open up the country for better hunting."

"So, then, it was food over trees. No one can fault them for that."

"True," Nicholas agreed.

"Are the Indians here all from the same tribe?"

"No, there are many different groups."

"My father once mentioned the Duwamish tribe."

"Yes, there are the Duwamish, the Snohomish, Puyalluys, and many more."

"Wasn't Chief Sealth, whom this city was named after, from the Duwamish tribe?"

"I believe so."

"He and my father met once. They had to speak through an interpreter because Father didn't know the Duwamish language and Chief Sealth, I understand, refused to learn English."

"Well, actually, all I really know about the chief is that he was a big man. He wore a breechcloth and faded blue blanket and was the most important chief in the Oregon-Washington Territory."

"Yes, I'd heard that, too."

"Did your father talk much about this area?"

I shook my head. "No, he didn't like to look back. The only reason he even mentioned anything about the Indians here was because, at that time, I was studying Indian culture in school, and I persuaded him to help me with my lessons."

We lapsed into momentary silence as our gazes scanned the sun-dappled water and Mercer Island on the other side. Then Nicholas said in a voice that had grown soft, "Abby, I truly am sorry for having upset you the other day over Jason and the accident at the mill."

"Oh, Nicholas," I met his eyes, "you needn't apologize. I understand your concern and I do appreciate it."

"Still, for your own safety," he urged, "I wish you'd return to San Francisco for a while."

"I'm staying here," I told him firmly, "and I don't intend to change my mind about that."

"I worry about you."

"Please don't."

"That's not possible." He placed a hand tenderly over mine, and I wondered what in heaven's name I would do if he tried to kiss me again. I couldn't let that happen — not under the circumstances. Nor could I hurt him by pulling away from an outward show of emotion. To spare us both, I said the first thought that leaped to mind, "This place is nice, Nicholas, but I expect we'd best be heading back; it's getting late."

"Yes." The word came slowly, and his brows formed a frown. "I suppose you're right, though I wish you weren't. Our time together generally seems so short."

It seemed that way to me, too, and as we made for the horses, I reflected again on my reluctance to relinquish my friendship with Nicholas Wells. Was it normal to be in love with one man while experiencing a strong attachment for another? I needed time to consider this mystifying predicament. And, fortunately, it appeared I would have it, for the party preparations, as well as working at the mill and with Dr. Sims, would keep me too busy to spend any time socializing with either of the men.

On the following afternoon I went to Dr. Sims's

office where, to my dismay, I was confronted once again by utter confusion and disorder. Momentarily my spirits declined, then soared when it struck me that here indeed was positive proof that he did require full-time help. So rapt was I in thought that I was scarcely aware of the three patients who sat uncomfortably in the ladder-back chairs against the wall.

It was the cry of a child from behind the closed examining-room door that returned me to reality and plunged me headlong into an afternoon of daubing wounds and applying bandages. In between patients, I moved with haste, endeavoring to reestablish a vestige of order to the cramped office.

After the last patient left, I placed a kettle of water on the potbellied stove and set about preparing tea. When it was nearly ready, Dr. Sims emerged from the examining room and crumpled into the swivel chair behind his desk. Neither one of us uttered a word until after we had sipped the steaming hot liquid; then the doctor spoke first. "Thank you, Abby, for your help. It was a pretty hectic afternoon, wasn't it?" He tried to smile, but weariness pulled down the corners of his mouth.

"It was all of that," I agreed.

"You're as good as any doctor when it comes to bandaging. Your father trained you well."

"Why, thank you, sir. He was an excellent teacher and a patient one. You see, I was terribly awkward at first."

We sat in silence for several seconds, enjoying the respite and the soothing effects of the hot tea; then Dr. Sims reached into a desk drawer and removed a covered tin. He lifted the lid and held out the container to me. "My only vice," he confessed, "—my wife's cookies."

As I accepted an oatmeal-molasses cookie, I saw him lift his eyes and in one quick sweep, survey the room. "Well," he sighed, "I can see you've accomplished another miracle. The place is tidy again. Is there any chance I could badger you into working a couple afternoons a week? Ah, forgive me." He raised an apologetic hand. "I have no right to even ask such a thing of you."

"Oh, but I'm flattered you want my help. And if I had the time I would gladly give it." I paused; then, with excitement coming into my voice, I resumed, "I do have something in mind, though, that might interest you."

"Oh?" Curiosity narrowed the faded blue eyes.

I told him of my idea for Dorothea and the office, then said a small inner prayer as he leaned back in his chair and briefly considered. "Well,"—he cleared his throat—"I do like your idea, Abby, and nothing would make me happier than to help out Dorothea, but there is one obstacle."

"And that is?"

He lifted the account books. "These. My financial standing makes hiring anyone impossible. However, I do have a proposal, though I'm not sure you'll like it. It will mean a lot of work for you."

"I don't mind that, sir. Please, what is your proposal?"

He gave me a half-smile. "Are you a good bill collector?"

"Well." I frowned. "I did handle the billing for my father, but I can't brag about the response. Are you suggesting I take charge of your billing?"

"Precisely. If we can make this a paying practice and if Dorothea is able to carry out her duties here to my satisfaction, then I'll employ her." He inhaled a deep breath. "I'm afraid you'll have all of the work, while Dorothea and I reap the benefits. It hardly seems fair."

"I don't mind, really. And Dorothea can help with the billing. Do you think we'll be able to collect most of the outstanding sums?"

"Probably. This community has prospered well over the past year. I'd say the biggest problem with the accounts is me. I've let them fall into a deplorable state. Obviously I do need full-time help, and I'll assist you in any way I can, Abby. In the interim, you're welcome to begin training Dorothea."

When I reached home I jumped down from the carriage in an unladylike fashion, gathered up my skirts, and bounded up the stone steps and into the house.

Leah was setting the dinner table when I sailed into the dining room. Her unfriendly eyes raked over me. "Is Dorothea in the kitchen?" I asked in a breathless voice.

The blonde woman pulled erect, squaring her shoulders. "Yes, miss."

I tossed her a sweet smile which I hoped would ruffle the edges of her hostility and went to the kitchen.

Dorothea was at the stove, stirring a thick bubbly liquid contained in a heavy kettle. "What on earth is that?" I questioned, trying to keep my excitement under control. "It smells awful."

She wrinkled her nose in distaste. "I'm rendering lard."

With an air of nonchalance, I crossed to her side and peered into the kettle. I spoke with my attention fixed on the greasy bubbles. "It's all set, Dorothea, you can come with me to Dr. Sims's office next week."

Overcome with joy, her hand shot up off the wooden spoon and in a gesture that seemed unlike

Dorothea, she flung her arms about me. I watched helplessly as the spoon slipped slowly into the foul-smelling liquid.

We were both laughing with delight when Leah came into the steamy room. She viewed us with narrowed eyes that gave the impression she considered Dorothea and me on the verge of dementia.

CHAPTER FIFTEEN

Early on the following morning Jason and I left for town. I had the invitations to secure at the printer's office and a fitting at Mrs. Soper's shop for my new ball gown. But first I would spend some time at the mill.

Shortly after Jason and I arrived there, he placed me in Zachary Taylor's charge. "I have a desk all ready for you to work at," the older man said, and led me to the one near Jason's office. "You should be comfortable here, Miss Justin."

I thanked Mr. Taylor kindly, and as I took up the chair behind the huge oak desk, he moved away to secure the account books. They turned out to be more involved than I had anticipated. Fortunately, Mr. Taylor was a patient man. He slowly and methodically went over the books and filing system with me. At first I felt guilty about taking so much of his time; but then I could see that the responsibility of initiating me into the company procedures appeared to increase his feeling of importance.

All in all I was astounded by the immensity of the business and the constant flow of traffic in and out of

Jason's office. There were well-dressed businessmen, sea captains in dashing blue serge, and loggers wearing rumpled clothing and calked boots. Occasionally Jason stepped out from behind the closed door bearing his name in bold letters, and introduced me to an associate. Those men, I assumed were the most important of the lot.

When I was reasonably familiar with the accounts and filing system, Zachary Taylor hauled out a stack of correspondence for me to browse through. All the letters, of course, were addressed to Jason, and though they pertained to business, each one I noted bore a personal touch. It gave me a warm sense of pride to discover he was regarded with high esteem by his associates.

Shorty after noon Jason stopped at my desk. "So," he grinned down on me—"how is it going?"

"Oh." I groaned, and pretended a frown. "My brain is whirling."

His grin broadened. "I know what you mean. In the beginning I thought mine would never assimilate all that had to be learned. But you'll find it gets easier as you go along."

"I certainly hope so."

"Listen, Abby, may I take you to lunch?"

My heartbeat quickened. "Why, yes, I'd like that. Here, at the cookhouse?"

"No, I thought maybe someplace quieter."

Quiet and romantic? I hoped.

"Is there anyplace special you might have in mind?"

I pictured the dimly lit Alden House, but since Nicholas and I had dined there—and much to Jason's annoyance—I did not suggest it. "Actually," I said, "I'm not familiar enough with the eating establishments in town to make a choice."

"Then I'll pick out a place. Are you ready to leave?"

"I will be as soon as I straighten the mess on this desk and freshen myself."

"That's fine, no hurry. In the meantime I'll fetch the buggy, then meet you out front."

I nodded and set to work gathering the correspondence. I placed the stack safely away in a desk drawer and before leaving the office I expressed my appreciation to Mr. Taylor for his time and patience, then told him, "I'll be back before closing and refile the correspondence."

"If you'd like, Miss Justin, one of us can do it for you."

I gave him a warm smile. "Thank you, sir, but I'd just as soon do it myself and save inconveniencing the rest of you any more than is necessary."

"As you wish," he responded, a look of appreciation overspreading his sallow face.

I slipped on my cape, and as I left the office I was surprised to find Jason hadn't come around yet with the carriage. What could be keeping him? I wondered. Not that it really mattered, for as he'd said, there was no hurry.

I moved to the edge of the porch and watched the lumber wagons rumbling in and out of the yard. One of the drivers called a greeting, and I raised my hand in a friendly gesture. The air had grown warmer and drier, for the early-morning fog had been dissipated by the sun, though the ground was still spongy from the previous day's rain. As always there was the sweet aroma of freshly milled wood, and the incessant sounds of saws and bells and strident whistles that occasionally set my teeth on edge.

With a faraway sensation settling over me, I turned my attention to the stables across the way and to the right, and after eying the open entrance for several seconds, I saw Jason emerge in a company wagon.

Where was the carriage? I inwardly questioned. Before I could ask, Jason explained as he pulled to a stop and set the brake, "I hope you don't mind,"—he gestured to the wagon—"but a tire problem developed with the buggy."

He jumped down, and as he handed me up, continued. "It's being repaired now and will be ready for the ride home." I moved to the far side of the vehicle, and he boarded and took up the reins. "I'm afraid these wagons lack comfort," he told me in an apologetic voice, then released the brake. "And you'll notice every bump in the road."

"This is fine," I reassured him, for what did a few bumps matter as long as I was with Jason? I glanced at him from the corner of my eye, admiring the clean line of his profile and his broad shoulders beneath the lightweight coat. He was dressed in brown today, the color I felt most enhanced his dark hair and eyes. Jason looked at me and flashed a smile that warmed me clear through; then he gave his attention to maneuvering the wagon onto the main road and into the heavy flow of traffic.

The clatter of traffic, combined with the other loud and familiar sounds, made talking in normal tones impossible, so we rode in silence. Inwardly I smiled with contentment and satisfaction, for today I had dissolved Nicholas' theory about Jason's capabilities in managing the mill. The ledgers clearly indicated that production and profits had risen sharply under Jason's command. Why, though, hadn't Mr. Taylor mentioned the improvement when I questioned him about Jason's managerial ability? Was the older man thinking of machinery malfunctions? Had the equipment been allowed to fall into a state of disrepair? Jason was so efficient and meticulous that this did not seem likely.

He reined to a stop in front of Ericson's Harbor Inn and Restaurant. It was a red brick, two-story structure, elaborately trimmed with white gingerbread and black wrought iron. The restaurant was flanked by a hotel and a bank. Across the street were several department stores, and shoppers and businessmen moved along the sidewalks.

"I think you'll like this place," Jason remarked as he helped me down. "They offer a good selection of dishes, especially sea food."

"That's my favorite," I told him.

"Then you might want to try the salmon, it's prepared over a wood fire, Indian style."

We entered and I was delighted to find that Harbor Inn, with its rich velvets, crystal, and linen cloths, was as romantically lighted and elegantly decorated as Alden House. On our way to a secluded table, I saw several women cast admiring glances Jason's way. The most attractive and fashionably dressed female of the lot lifted a slim, bejeweled hand in greeting, which he acknowledged with a nod.

Both Jason and I ordered the salmon, served with potatoes, Indian bread, and green beans with almonds and mushrooms. "So," he said over the meal, "were you able to gain much insight into the business after one morning of poring over paperwork?"

I nodded. "Yes, I think so and I'm impressed. The company has really flourished under your command."

The compliment brightened his eyes, though his reply was modest. "Economically, these are good times for the lumbering industry."

"Especially the Justin Mill." I smiled at him.

"We're faring better than most."

"Yes, I can see," I agreed, then commented on the meal. "The salmon is delicious. The best I've ever eaten."

"I'm glad you like it, Abby."

We ate in silence for a long moment, then I said. "By the way, did I mention that my grandfather insisted I invite my family up from San Francisco for a visit?"

Jason's eyebrows drew together in the all too familiar frown. "I don't think that would be wise—not right now."

"I hadn't planned on right now, Jason. Not with the party and the strain that's bound to produce in Grandfather. And not until this Kimberley diamond business is settled."

A smile superseded his frown. "I'm glad we agree on this."

I was glad, too, I thought, recalling all the unpleasant encounters.

When we were nearly done with the meal, Jason asked, "Where are you headed for next, Abby?"

I consulted my pendant watch. "Mrs. Soper's for the fitting. After that, I'll pick up the invitations and probably do a little shopping. Then it's back to the mill to finish up some odds and ends."

"Shall I send someone around to fetch you back there?"

"No, that's not necessary, I'll hire a carriage."

On our way from the dining room, a few minutes later, I noticed that the attractive woman who had waved at Jason had already left and I offhandedly wondered if he had also taken note of that.

Out on the sidewalk my eyes blinked, adjusting to the bright sunlight that now bathed the city. Traffic was as brisk as before and there was the faint aroma of salt from the bay. A male passerby, dressed in casual attire like Jason's paused to exchange a few words with him. Introductions were made; then the man excused himself and made for the bank next door. Ahead of us a shaggy black dog, darting across the street, was nearly struck by a conveyance hauling beer. The driver slowed the vehicle and, with a raised fist, cursed the animal.

"I'll drop you at Mrs. Soper's," Jason offered as he helped me into our wagon. As I stepped to the far side and he prepared to board, the thunderous sounds of rolling wheels and pounding hoofs came to us from behind. Then a man, from somewhere on the sidewalk, hollered, "Runaway! Runaway!" Jason's gaze swept up the street, and when his eyes widened in alarm, I quickly looked about. My own eyes also widened, for an out-of-control wagon careened around the nearby corner and swung wide, putting its rear end on a collision course with our own vehicle. Instinct told me to jump, but there wasn't time to return to Jason's side, and the street was certain death.

"Sit down!" Jason commanded. He leaped into the wagon and caught up the reins.

Instantly I dropped to the seat and grabbed the back of it—for heaven only knew, with no dashboard on the conveyance, there was nothing else but the seat to clutch. Feminine screaming came from all directions and through the hazy blur of rising fright that dried my mouth, I glimpsed people scampering to the safety of the sidewalks. The runaway horses were abreast of us now, their panting like drum rolls in my ears. There was a driver in the box, but he was vague, for my attention was riveted on the horses. Then I involuntarily closed my eyes and gritted my teeth.

"Hang on," Jason shouted, and I heard him release the brake. There was the snap of reins. We lurched forward, then jarringly stopped abruptly. The runaway vehicle sped on by without even grazing us.

Startled, our horses whinnied and pawed at the ground.

"Whoa," Jason ordered in a voice in which I could sense his struggle to keep calm.

I inhaled a long tremulous breath, and shaking from head to toe, slowly looked around. Directly in front of our excited team was a parked carriage. I had forgotten it had been there when we had exited the restaurant. Dear heaven, if that carriage had initially been parked any closer, we probably wouldn't have escaped unscathed. I felt my lips compress and my gaze automatically darted up the street, searching for the vehicle. It was nowhere in sight. In its wake, however, the traffic it had brought to a sudden halt had begun to move.

"Whoa," Jason ordered the horses again, and as he brought them under control, several concerned citizens came forward to see if we were unharmed. A woman on the sidewalk exclaimed in a shocked tone, "I thought for sure something terrible was going to happen."

I shivered, though the sun was warm.

Beside me Jason drew a deep breath, then expelled it, and looked at me with anxious eyes. "Are you all right?"

I nodded, too shaken to speak.

Jason placed a comforting hand over mine. "Did you notice the driver?" he queried gently. "Or any identifying markings on the wagon?"

"No." I gulped.

He put the same question to those gathered near, and again the response was negative, for everyone agreed the driver's wide brimmed hat was pulled too low to discern his face. "And there weren't no markings on the wagon," a man offered. "That was a damned good driver in the box, though, the way he weaved in and out of traffic without causing an accident."

"There would have been one," insisted an elderly woman, "if this young man here hadn't jumped into his wagon and done what he done."

Jason thanked the group for their concern, then turned to me. "Would you like to go back into the restaurant for a sip of brandy to settle the nerves?"

I shook my head. "I'll be fine in a minute."

He gave my hand a gentle squeeze, then urged our horses into the stream of traffic.

"Jason," I managed, "thank you for what you did, for coming to my rescue."

"I'd go to any lengths to protect you, Abby."

The tender declaration brought tears to my eyes and a lump to my throat.

"You know,"—his brow furrowed—"at a quick glance, and that's all I saw of that wagon when it rounded the corner, it looked to be in a deadly line with ours. Yet it missed us by a foot."

I swallowed, and then moistened my dry lips. "Wasn't that because you pulled our wagon forward?"

"I didn't pull forward that much. I couldn't because of the parked carriage. Believe me, I honestly thought the rear of our wagon, if nothing else, would be clipped."

"Well, then, obviously that runaway wasn't as close to us as it appeared. Except,"—I moistened my lips again—"most of the witnesses you questioned, and I include myself, had expected the worst."

"Initially it could have been closer and the driver somehow managed to straighten it up. Still, that doesn't dim the fact that the worst could have happened whether we'd been struck or not. You see, the horses could have bolted—and very nearly did—causing untold damage to life and property."

"They would have bolted if you hadn't jumped in and taken command of the reins. Oh, Jason, I shudder to think what could have happened."

"I know," he soothed. "I feel the same. And I hesitate to say it, because I don't want to upset you any further, but a couple of things about this incident give rise to some suspicion."

I looked at him quickly. "What things?"

"Well, first of all," the words came slowly, "the driver of that runaway was highly skilled with the reins. He had to be to have made it down this street—at breakneck speed and in heavy traffic—without causing some damage. And an expert like that doesn't generally lose control of his animals. Then there's this business of the driver's hat being pulled down and obscuring his face."

My eyes narrowed as I considered what Jason had said. "Well, I can see where you might be suspicious. Still, runaways are fairly common; and as far as the driver's hat goes, it could have been pulled low simply to shield his eyes from the sun."

"True."

"And maybe, Jason, added to his driving expertise was a large degree of luck."

"Possibly. But for how long do you suppose his luck would hold out? For several blocks?"

"I wouldn't think so."

"Are you pressed for time?"

"No, not really."

"Well, then, if you don't mind I'd like to check out the street he turned onto and, just for the sake of curiosity, see if he made it through without mishap."

"Please do. I'm curious about that myself."

"It's the next street coming up," he informed me; then after a fractional pause he continued, "I also wonder, Abby, about that unmarked wagon. It was a lumber wagon, like this one, except that ours, of course, has the company name emblazoned on both sides."

"A lumber wagon?" I swallowed, and was certain, from the cautious note that had come into his voice, that he was thinking of Nicholas. That put me on the defensive. Nevertheless, I was determined to avoid another discussion on Nicholas and the accidents at the mill. "The streets are full of marked and unmarked wagons," I pointed out in the calmest voice I could muster.

"Yes, but that, combined with the driving expertise and the hidden face, in view of all that's happened to us, prompts me to be a little suspicious."

We turned onto the street Jason indicated and looked down its length. Traffic was lighter here and moving smoothly. "Nothing unusual," I remarked unnecessarily.

"I didn't expect there would be."

"The driver might have gotten the animals under control shortly after rounding this corner."

"If they were ever out of control." Jason's voice grew thoughtful. "It would have been very simple for someone watching for us to leave the restaurant to signal the driver up the street. He then put the team into action and deliberately tried to frighten our horses into bolting."

"Or the runaway could have been genuine."

"Oh, Abby, I'd like to believe that." He regarded me steadily. "Just as I'd like to believe the same about what occurred in the boiler room and the pot shot that narrowly missed me a few weeks ago."

Those grim reminders sent chills racing over my flesh.

Apparently Jason sensed my sudden apprehension, for once again he placed a comforting hand over mine. "Forgive me if I've upset you. I don't like thinking in suspicious terms any more than you do, but under the circumstances I don't think it would be wise to regard this latest incident lightly. Not that I mind rescuing you, you understand."

I heard the grin come into his voice and I knew he was trying to put me at ease. Grateful, I met his eyes and the gentleness I saw there was like a soothing salve. "I guess I'll always worry about you," he breathed, "and feel the need to protect you. Please, Abby, for your own safety, be doubly cautious, will you?"

I was overwhelmed by his concern and despite the unnerving occurrences that had come into our lives, happier than I'd ever been before. "I will be," I promised, and it wasn't until later in the afternoon, when I reflected on his protectiveness, that I remembered both he and Nicholas had stressed, in the exact same words: "For your own safety." Good heavens, in the twenty years of my life, no one had ever before said that to me and now, in less than a week, I'd heard it twice, and from men who vehemently accused each other of wishing me ill. Why, even in this incident there could be accusations from both sides, and there I would be again, stuck in the middle and on the defensive.

For those reasons I was immensely relieved when Jason didn't mention the runaway on our way home that evening. Maybe he also wished to avoid putting me on the defensive. In any case, we briefly discussed the mill, then the subject shifted to my work at Dr. Sims's office and Jason asked, "When do you plan to start training Dorothea there?"

"On Monday."

"I'm sure she'll do well."

"Oh, I know she will."

He grinned at me. "I suspect your optimism could move mountains."

"I'll settle for just helping Dorothea upgrade her employment."

We laughed, then fell to reminiscing over our childhood days. I listened with keen interest when Jason spoke of his family and I particularly noted how he carefully avoided mentioning the accident that had claimed their lives, and how the loss had affected him.

I thought of my father and to a small degree I could understand the pain of Jason's loss and I did not intrude on that which he was not yet ready to share.

As we neared home our conversation became sporadic and I gave more and more of my attention to enjoying the scenery. The numerous looming stumps reminded me of my logging discussion with Nicholas and I couldn't resist asking Jason, "Did you ever try balancing on a springboard?"

"Once," he replied simply, "when I was a child."

"How did you do?"

"Not too well, I'm afraid."

"Oh?"

"I fell off and broke my arm." He laughed.

"Oh, dear." I couldn't help laughing too. "I wouldn't have tried again either."

Jason hugged me close and as I settled against him, he planted a kiss in my hair.

It wasn't until the evening of the following day that the happiness I had known with him for such a short time crumbled before my eyes.

As with the previous days, it, too, was productive. In the morning I donned old clothes, secured a pail of water and some chamois skins and washed the windows and mirrors.

After a brief visit with Grandfather in the

afternoon, I turned my attention to addressing the party invitations. Occasionally a name, written in bold black ink across a white envelope, held my eyes and I tried to visualize how that person might look. It would be interesting, I decided, to see if my mental pictures coincided with actuality.

It was just before dinner when the sun appeared between patches of white clouds and cast its golden glow about. Unable to venture out at that time I waited until Grandfather retired for the night, then left the house for the gazebo.

I wandered along the path which zigzagged between the trees, enjoying the chirp of robins overhead. At that moment everything was perfect.

When I reached the edge of the clearing and was about to step into it, voices brought me to a stop. I pushed aside an evergreen bough and let my gaze sweep along the clearing to the gazebo. My mouth fell open and my feet felt as if they were frozen to the ground. Jason and Leah were in the latticework structure and he was kissing her.

CHAPTER SIXTEEN

I jerked my hand from the bough. And as it snapped upward, flicking droplets of moisture on me, I gathered up my skirts and ran blindly for the house.

In the solitude of my room I threw myself down on the bed and wept without restraint. Within seconds the crocheted spread beneath my face was drenched.

Desperately I fought to shut out the scene I had just witnessed, but the vision of Jason and Leah locked in an ardent embrace haunted me like a nightmare. Where was the worry, concern, and protectiveness for me then? It was all lies. What a fool I was. The warning signs were there right from the moment I entered this house, and I knew I would not have shunned them if Jason's emotions had been as obvious as Leah's. How cleverly he had masked them! All the old suspicions surfaced, rendering me weak and helpless.

In retrospect I could see that his aloofness toward me had changed suddenly, and I wondered what hidden motive had influenced the rapid change. Was his new show of emotion a cover-up, a means to distract attention from himself should anything happen to me? And how convenient for Jason that the sabotage began prior to my arrival in Seattle. Now, if he wanted me out of the way, he could use the mechanical breakdowns to his advantage. Certainly no one would suspect him of foul play if he and I had become good friends or, better yet, lovers. And that, along with the two rescues he could very well have masterminded, would, without a doubt, place him well above suspicion. Oh, yes, with me out of the way, everything would then be his, including Leah.

I paced the floor wishing for someone to confide in, but no one would understand. Jason had been an integral part of this household for eighteen years and no one would consider him capable of wrongdoing.

Even Nicholas I could not turn to. What could I say to him—that I had fallen in love with Jason and that he did not return those feelings? I'd sound like a whining child. And when it came right down to it, Jason had never said he loved me. I had simply deluded myself.

I pulled a chair to the window and sat down to stare into the darkness, remembering that evening when Nicholas had kissed me. Never would I have allowed that kiss to happen if I had known then that I was in love with Jason. Unless men viewed love differently, I had no alternative but to believe he did not love me.

Maybe Jason didn't love Leah, either. It was possible that we were both merely flirtations. Nevertheless, that thought did not soften the hurt.

As the days progressed I moved through them with a sense of detachment. My interest in the party dimmed and I had to force myself to take an active part in the preparations. How could I give the impression of a happy hostess, I wondered, when a cool liquid flowed through my veins?

Was it just my imagination or did Leah, too, seem different? Happier, almost friendly toward me. Her radiant smile served to sharpen my bitterness.

The days that followed appeared outwardly calm and peaceful, and I found that with Grandfather and the Brannons I was able to maintain a degree of lightheartedness. If they suspected my unhappiness they made no remarks, nor did it reflect in their faces.

Jason, however, was a different matter and avoiding him proved to be a trying experience—one I was not sure I could endure much longer.

To my dismay, for the first three days following my discovery, he came home from the mill earlier than usual. Each time he invited me to join him for either a walk or a canoe ride on the lake. He had regarded me with a boyish enthusiasm, which brought a fresh flood of tears to the back of my eyes. But the picture of him and Leah together always influenced me to fabricate excuses. Jason shrugged them aside with feeble smiles and then closeted himself in the study. If Leah joined him there, I purposely did not notice.

During the remainder of that week I carefully

avoided even a moment alone with him. Dinner was a strain and I dreaded it. There was no way I could avoid him then and for Grandfather's benefit I had to assume gaiety. Several times I caught Jason staring at me warily and there was no doubt in my mind that if we were alone he would shake the reason for my coolness from me. At times I wished he would, for then I would undoubtedly discover how he felt about Leah. I could not bring myself to boldly inquire, and actually it was none of my affair. Since the mill concerned us both I was free to query him there, but his private life was his own.

Bless Dorothea and her newly found outgoing manner, for during those dismal days she managed to rally my spirits. We spent hours together in the library, giggling like schoolgirls, while we worked on Dr. Sims's billing. Dorothea grasped bookkeeping rapidly and could have finished the billing alone, but I needed to be with her. At least within the confines of the library I found a measure of peace and there I did not have to face Leah.

On Monday Dorothea and I went to Dr. Sims's office and her first day of training progressed even better than I had anticipated. Dorothea was observant, listened carefully to my instructions, and carried them out with unerring proficiency.

At the end of the day Dr. Sims patted her affectionately on the shoulder. "You've done an excellent job, Dorothea. Keep this up and somehow we'll figure out a way to make this a permanent arrangement."

"Oh, thank you, sir." She beamed. "I'd like that more than anything."

I smiled at her happiness and let myself become engulfed in it.

By the next morning, however, the only emotion I

felt was dread, for today I could not avoid being alone with Jason. After breakfast I would board the carriage with him and head for a day of work at the mill. Perhaps I could pretend illness, I thought, and pulled the bedcovers to my chin. But that was ridiculous. I couldn't avoid being alone with him forever. Besides, as far as Jason Landry was concerned, my heart had become stone and nothing he might say or do could hurt me anymore.

Lips compressed, I left the bed and glanced out the window. It was overcast and drizzly, so I dressed in a winter skirt and a French lawn shirtwaist. Then I arranged my hair with tortoise-shell side combs and went down to the dining room. As I entered Leah was coming from the kitchen carrying a tray laden with a sprigged tea service and matching cup and saucer.

"Good morning," I greeted her simply.

"Good morning, miss." The reply was automatic, and without warmth.

"Is that for my grandfather?" I gestured to the tray.

She nodded. "He had a restless night and I thought maybe some hot tea might perk him up."

As she glided past me I could see she looked tired and I instinctively offered, "Would you like me to take that to him, Leah?"

She stopped and regarded me with a hint of appreciation. "That would be nice, miss, if you have the time. I could use a spot of tea myself."

"As soon as I saw my grandfather, I decided to spend the day with him. He looked peaked, and his joints were swollen.

When Grandfather was finished with the tea I told him of my decision. "No, Abby," he insisted again, "that's not necessary. Your place today is with Jason at the mill."

"You are my first concern," I told him truthfully,

and was certain in my own mind that I wasn't using Martin Justin's aliments as an excuse to avoid Jason. "And I want to do whatever I can to make you as comfortable as possible. Besides, there's still so much to do in preparation for the party, and I'm sure Mrs. Brannon would appreciate my being around to lend a helping hand."

Grandfather considered for a long moment, then finally relented. "Oh, very well, Abby. But you must promise not to neglect the mill for too long."

I promised, and when I left his room a short time later with the tea service in hand, I encountered Jason coming from the dining room. He looked me over with a cool sweep of his eyes and my heart thudded, informing me that it had not, after all, turned to stone where he was concerned. "I've been looking for you," he said, and I couldn't help noticing how ruggedly handsome he was in his maroon sweater and the gray trousers that molded themselves to his slim hips and long legs. "The carriage is ready anytime you are."

I swallowed hard, and when I spoke I was grateful that my voice sounded even. "I'm sorry, Jason, but Grandfather, as you know, isn't well, and I've decided to stay home with him."

What appeared to be an expression of disappointment briefly crossed his face, though his cool response indicated otherwise. "As you wish." He paused, regarding me intently; then his expression softened. "Abby," he continued, "I—"

The sound of approaching footsteps intruded on his words and we both glanced up as Leah came to a stop before us. She devoured Jason with her blue eyes, and quite clearly at the moment she did not look the least bit tired. With what appeared a great effort, Leah tore her gaze from Jason and addressed me. "Your breakfast is ready, miss."

I thanked her, though I doubted she even heard me, for her entire attention immediately returned to Jason. Seeing them so close together was a cruel reminder of the ardent kiss I'd inadvertently witnessed, and I knew that now more than ever, and in spite of everything, I still loved him. I still wanted him. But, dear heaven, that could never be and I couldn't bear to be near them.

As the sting of scalding tears came to the backs of my eyes, I excused myself and hurried off to the rear of the house. In the dining room, I set down the tray and wiped away the tears. I couldn't let the Brannons see me crying, and I couldn't help wishing that Jason would follow after me and somehow make everything right between us. But he did not come my way and worst of all several long and agonizing seconds passed before I heard him leave the house and then heard Leah open and close Grandfather's door. What had transpired between the quiet pair in those seconds? Not a kiss, I was certain. Not in the open where they might be observed. But whispered endearments?

I shook my head, dispelling those thoughts and determined not to dwell on them again. And I didn't—at least not until late that afternoon, when Nicholas came to call.

I hadn't seen him arrive and wasn't even aware he was in the house until I came down the stairs and saw him standing near Grandfather's closed door, talking with Leah. As always, her shoulders were drawn back, accentuating the heavy breasts that threatened to send bodice buttons flying and her eyes were fixed on the handsome masculine face. Briefly, I envisioned her with Jason; then I threw off the dismal picture and forced a faint smile. "Why, Nicholas," I said from the stairway, "how nice to see you."

He turned, and the smile that warmed his face did wonders for my flagging spirits. "Abby, I was hoping to see you. You've been so busy lately that I hesitated to disturb you."

"Oh, don't ever feel that way," I insisted, and the other woman shot me a frown. "I'm always home to you."

"Well, that's good to hear." He excused himself from Leah and as he came toward me, she turned on her heel and went into Grandfather's room.

"Is there a special reason for this visit?" I asked, noting the fine fit of his dark, vested suit and the gleam of his leather boots.

He came to stand before me. "Well, I heard from Zach Taylor this morning that Martin wasn't feeling well, so I rode out to see him."

"That was very thoughtful of you."

"I think a great deal of your grandfather, Abby."

"He feels the same about you, Nicholas."

"Thank God he doesn't listen to Jason's opinion of me."

"Or *your* opinion of Jason."

"Touché." He grinned down on me, then asked, "Have you a few minutes to spare?"

"For you, yes, of course. Shall we go into the parlor?"

He nodded, and let me lead the way.

As we seated ourselves on the sofa, I gestured to the wine decanters on the table before us. "Would you care for anything?"

"Thank you, a little port would be nice. Anything for you, Abby?"

"Nothing, thank you."

Nicholas sipped his wine, then inquired, "So, how have you been?"

"Oh, just fine."

"You seem a bit subdued."

"I guess I'm just tired," I lied, "from all there's been to do lately."

"No more trouble at the mill, I hope."

I thought of the runaway team and wondered if Nicholas might have heard of it. I hoped he hadn't, for I was in no mood for more questions and speculation and, undoubtedly, accusations. "No trouble that I'm aware of," I responded.

"Well, that's good to hear. Say, listen, Abby—" He glanced at the doorway, apparently reassuring himself we were alone, then resumed in a low, conspiratorial voice, "Have you perhaps uncovered anything of what might be behind the accidents there?"

I heaved a small inner sigh, certain that if Nicholas had learned of the runaway, he would have mentioned it by now. "No," I answered quietly, then informed him of Jason's superior managerial ability. "As for the mechanical breakdowns," I added, "I haven't had the chance yet to even casually question any of the employees. And unless something further were to happen, I'm not even sure if I should. After all, if Jason is innocent, I wouldn't want to do anything that might make him or the company look bad."

"I see." He was thoughtful. "Then you're going to adopt a wait-and-see attitude?"

"I think that's all I can do."

His brows knit in consideration. "Well, perhaps you're right. Let's just hope, though, that in the end no one winds up getting seriously hurt."

I nodded. "That is a major worry."

Nicholas consulted the grandfather's clock near the door, then set aside the wineglass. "I'm afraid I must go, Abby." He rose slowly and held out a hand to me. "I have a dinner meeting in town."

With my hand in his, he helped me to my feet, then

gently drew me close. "Will you have dinner with me some evening?" he breathed. "And maybe take in the theater?"

That pleasant prospect brought a smile to my lips. Nevertheless, I hesitated, uncertain at first if accepting while I was still in love with Jason would be fair to Nicholas. But then I firmly reminded myself that nothing would ever come of that love and I must not dwell on it. So I accepted the invitation, and I did not resist when Nicholas tenderly put his mouth on mine. It was a light kiss and yet at the same time his lips conveyed fire and his encircling arms were like a cradle of comfort and warmth. Yes, I felt safe and secure in his embrace. But I knew I must not linger in it. I must not earnestly encourage him or any other man until I had rid myself of this lovesickness for Jason.

After Nicholas released me, I walked with him to the front door. There, he asked when he might take me to dinner.

"After the party would be better for me, if you don't mind."

"Sooner would be nicer," he confessed softly. "But I understand. After the party it will be." We said our good-bys and he stepped out on the porch. I was just about to close the door, when Nicholas turned abruptly and addressed me again. "Oh, one more thing, Abby."

"Yes."

"Zach wanted to know if it would be all right for him to come out for a visit with Martin tomorrow afternoon."

"I'm sure that would be fine. Grandfather loves to have the company."

"I'll pass that along, then." He flashed a smile and as he turned back to the steps, the sound of a horse on the drive captured my attention. I glanced up and saw Jason coming home from the mill. Thankfully he was too far away for me to discern his expression upon sighting Nicholas. But then I knew what to expect and I pictured the dark scowl in my mind. I also knew from past experience, that Jason would presume the other man had come primarily to see me. And I couldn't help wondering, just a little, if Jason might be fuming over the fact that I'd managed to find time for this visit when I hadn't the time to spend with him. Well, let him presume whatever he wished, I decided, and with my lips set in a straight, unyielding line, I stepped back and firmly closed the door.

From that afternoon forward Jason took to avoiding me.

CHAPTER SEVENTEEN

It was about a week later when Grandfather summoned me to the library and confronted me with suspicion. "There is something wrong in this house," he insisted, with vigor in his voice, "and whatever it is, young lady, it seems to revolve around you. I want you to tell me what it is."

"I'm afraid I don't understand," I answered evasively.

"Quit hedging, Abby. What's come over you lately? Why, not too long ago you walked around here for days with your head in the clouds, then suddenly—" He slammed his fist down on the table beside him. "It has to do with Jason, doesn't it?" he persisted.

"Yes, sir."

"I knew it. I knew it. What in heaven's name is the matter with you two? You're behaving like ten-year-olds. It was obvious even to me that you didn't like each other at first. But then I could see all that change and I even came to believe—" His voice faded.

Now I was curious. "What did you come to believe, Grandfather?"

He sighed and I gained the impression he was formulating his thoughts. "I consider myself a perceptive person, Abby," he said at last, "but even if I weren't, it would still be apparent to me that you and Jason are in love. No, don't try to deny it because I won't believe you. And for the life of me I can't understand why either one of you would want to deny it. Why, it's all so perfect."

My head came up with a start. "What do you mean, all so perfect?"

He cleared his throat. "Well, you know how much I love you both."

"Yes, I know."

He hesitated, and I shivered slightly, even though the room was warm. "Who knows how much time I have left—perhaps days, hopefully years? But I don't want to dwell on that point. However, the fact that I may not be around much longer does exert pressure on me. My affairs must be settled without delay."

"You mean the mill?"

"Yes, but also you and Jason." His eyes became dreamy with remembrance. "What would I have done without him? He's been like a son—a loyal son, I might add. I want him to have the mill. I want you *both* to have it." He took my hand in his. "I've come to love you very much, Abby dear, and I cannot leave this world until I'm sure you'll be well cared for."

"You needn't worry about me, Grandfather. You've admitted yourself that I'm independent and we both know I'm capable of handling my own affairs. I love you and your concern touches me deeply, but as for the mill I have no right to it. It belongs to Jason."

The aged man smiled. "I knew I was right."

"About what?"

"You *are* in love with him."

I made my tone firm. "I'm not acting out of love, but simply from what I believe to be fair."

He shrugged that off. "Nonetheless, I want the mill to remain in the family, and I want you and Jason to share in it equally. Above all, I want to be assured you'll be well cared for. I can be guaranteed on all three points if you and Jason marry."

My head flew up, and I felt the color drain from my face. "Is this what you talked to him about? I mean, he mentioned that you had some plan in mind. Did you insist he marry me? Or in any way indicate that this would be the only means by which he could retain control of the company?"

"Yes, we talked about marriage between the two of you. But I don't think I gave the impression that his control was dependent upon it."

"Oh, Grandfather," I cried, "how could you have even suggested that he and I marry? I'll never be able to face him again." Now I knew why Jason had scoffed at this absurd idea. He didn't want me—the mill perhaps, but not me. Was Nicholas right about Jason not being able to simply walk away from something he'd given half of his life to? Oh, Lord, I thought, and held my breath. If I were out of the way the mill would be his. He would not be bound to a wife he did not love.

"Calm down, Abby, you look as if you're going to explode. Surely if you love each other, then what difference can my suggestion make?" He leaned closer, and I braced myself for his next words. "It would make me happy and also put my mind at ease if you and Jason would announce your engagement at the party next week."

It took all my self-control to keep from shouting at him. "Aren't you being presumptuous? He hasn't asked me to marry him, or are you proposing on his behalf?"

"Don't be sarcastic, Abby. Mark my words, Jason will soon propose to you, and when he does I want you to give my suggestion careful consideration. I realize you haven't known each other long, but at my age important matters have to be rushed along."

"Did Jason ever tell you he loved me and wanted to marry me?"

Martin Justin lifted his chin. "No, but then we haven't discussed the matter since your arrival." He grinned. "I knew the moment I saw you he would change his mind. He'd be a fool if he didn't."

"Well, he has not changed his mind." I hesitated, wondering if he might have. Could this explain his sudden change toward me? Did it after all seem easier to marry me, *then* contrive a way to get rid of me? "We are not in love," I insisted. "There will be no engagement! I will not marry for the sake of convenience. If you must settle your affairs immediately, then leave the mill to Jason. Even if I wanted it, which I don't, managing it is out of my realm."

"Jason's a fool," Martin Justin muttered, and pounded his fist on the arm of his chair. "A damned fool for letting you slip through his fingers. And you, young lady, are not at all perceptive. I've known Jason Landry from the day he was born and I know him as well as I know myself. He loves you, and I'd be willing to bet you're in love with him. But I'm not going to argue the point. Obviously something happened between you two, something you don't want to talk about. A lover's quarrel perhaps?" A spark of hope tinged his voice.

I was angered by his persistence. "There can be no lovers' quarrel where no love exists."

He waved an impatient hand. "All right, Abby, have it your way. If you will not marry Jason, then you will share in the mill equally, under a joint-partnership agreement. Surely you can't object to that?"

I knew a partnership would never work—not under the present circumstances—but I said nothing. To reject Grandfather's offer would sound unreasonable and to pursue the matter would unlock doors to questions I did not want to answer—at least not now.

The man at my side took my silence as a sign of acceptance. "Jason's birthday is coming up in two months. I'll present him with the partnership papers then. As of July 25th, the date of his birth, the sign over the mill will read: Justin and Landry Mill Company."

"When are you going to inform him of the partnership?" I wanted to know.

"I don't intend to verbally inform him. He'll find out for himself when he goes to the mill on the 25th and sees the sign."

"Wouldn't it be better to tell him right away? Perhaps even announce it at the party?"

He pondered for a moment. "No, I like my idea better."

"But just think, Grandfather,"—I tried to sound excited—"if you'd announce the partnership at the party, then his friends could share in his excitement and good fortune." It was not for Jason't sake that I pressed the issue, but my own. Logic told me that if he was up to something underhanded, perhaps knowledge of the partnership would terminate any wrongdoing and I would be able to breathe easier.

However, Martin Justin did not relent; there would be no announcement at the party.

For several days after our talk, nothing really changed. Grandfather did not mention the engagement again. But he looked at me as though he were confident that eventually he would have his way.

His manner annoyed me, but for the most part I ignored it. When he discussed the matter with Jason, as I knew he would, there would be no doubt left in Martin Justin's mind that marriage between Jason and me was a dead issue.

It was on the evening prior to the party that I saw Jason angrier than I had ever seen him before. I was on my way from the parlor to the stairs when the study door burst open and he stormed out. Grandfather shouted after him, "Jason, come back here."

Jason's face was white with fury. He pulled up short when he saw me at the base of the stairs and threw me a hateful look. "You'd better go to him," he ordered, then crossed to the front door and jerked it open. For what seemed like a long time I stared at the dark panel, wondering when and where this was all going to end and what more would occur before it did.

Grandfather sat near the partially opened French doors in the study. His face was white and drawn, but he appeared calm. "Where did Jason go?"

"Out the front door." I kept my voice even. "You talked to him about your plan, didn't you, Grandfather?"

"Don't put it that way, Abby; you make me sound like a meddler. I only want what's best for you both."

"I know you do, but you can't plan the lives of others."

"I wasn't really trying to plan your lives, just guide them along."

"Oh Grandfather, there's not much difference between the two."

"I suppose you're right. But you know, Abby, he didn't even get angry until I told him you didn't want to marry him."

You had no right to tell him that. No wonder he was furious. You humiliated him. You ground his self-respect into the dust." My voice broke.

"I'm sorry; I didn't mean to hurt either one of you. I just wanted to impress upon Jason that he'd have to be very persuasive in order to win you back. I'll apologize to him in the morning, and I promise not to mention the subject again." He looked at me with pleading eyes. "Can you forgive a foolish old man?"

I knelt at his side and put a hand over his. "You're not a foolish old man. You meant well, and I love you all the more for caring so profoundly."

On the night of the party Dorothea came up the stairs to assist me with my hair. She had arranged it in a becoming style, piled high on my head with cascading curls down the back. Our gazes met briefly in the mirror, and I smiled my approval. "You're a talented young lady, Dorothea Brannon."

She smiled, pleased, then flipped a dark strand of my hair around her forefinger. "There, you're all ready." She laid the brush on the dressing table; then stepped aside. "Walk around the room and let me see how you look."

I rose to my feet in a silken rustle and whirled about.

"Oh, you're beautiful," she breathed. "You won't have one free moment this evening. Every man will want to dance with you."

"In that case,"—I grinned—"I hope they're all handsome."

A knock sounded on the door, and Dorothea responded to it. Jason stood in the hallway dressed immaculately in faultless evening clothes. The lapels of his jacket were satin and his shirt front was stiff with pearl buttons studding it. His face was masklike. "Our guests will be arriving soon. If you're ready I'll escort you down the stairs."

"I'd better get down to the kitchen," Dorothea piped up, her eyes admiring Jason. "I hope you both have a wonderful time."

I put an affectionate hand on the sleeve of her black sateen uniform. "Thank you, Dorothea, for arranging my hair."

She nodded with a smile and then left the room, brushing past Jason in the doorway. He was still watching me with cool brooding eyes. This was the moment I had dreaded all day. Did he know I was aware of his humiliation? Dare I make any attempt to gloss over Grandfather's words? More to the point, did Jason despise me for flatly refusing to even consider a marriage proposal? Did he feel I had deliberately usurped him?

I didn't want to believe that any more than I wanted to believe he was responsible for my encounter with the feather duster and the faulty equipment at the mill and maybe even the runaway. Despite everything, I still loved him and I didn't want him to be unhappy.

"Well, are you going to stand there all night?"

His sharp tone shot a bolt of annoyance through me. He was impossible and didn't deserve one iota of sympathy. At that moment I resolved to expel the wretched misery that had tormented me for the last several days. Too much effort had gone into this party and I would not allow it to go to waste. Tonight's ball would be a success—of that I was determined.

I forced a bright smile and allowed Jason to escort me from the room. At the second-floor landing I noticed my grandfather waiting for us below. Leah, who was dressed identically to Dorothea, stood at his side. She flicked me a casual glance, then turned her attention to Jason. All the way down the stairs I wondered if she possessed what I wanted and would never have—Jason.

CHAPTER EIGHTEEN

A warm gentle breeze drifted through the hallway from the open French doors in the dining room, bringing with it the fragrances of dahlias, roses, daffodils, and tulips, which filled the crystal vases on the mahogany tables scattered along the walls.

Grandfather, attired in a dark suit and stiff white shirt, stirred in his chair. "I have something for you, Abby." From his inside coat pocket he withdrew a heart-shaped pendant, outlined in fiery diamonds. Suspended in the heart's open center was a single ruby. "I gave this to your grandmother on our wedding day and now I want you to have it."

Tears clouded my vision as he gently laid the delicate pendant across the palm of my hand. As I held it lovingly and tenderly, sunbeams which spilled through the window near the front door played on the precious stones.

I closed my fingers lightly over the most cherished gift I had ever received and threw my arms about his neck. "I shall treasure this necklace forever." I told him in a voice that fluctuated from feeling as my eyes filled with tears of joy.

He held me in his embrace for a long moment, then put me apart from him. "Let me see how it looks on you."

As I came erect he lifted his eyes to Jason. "Well, don't just stand there, young man," he reproved. "Help Abby fasten the clasp. Oh, and Leah, you can go now. My granddaughter will see to me."

She swung around, her nose in the air as if offended by the dismissal, and hurried to the rear of the house.

There was a strange expression in Jason's eyes as he took the necklace from the palm of my hand—a look that gave me the impression he had come to a decision, one he had pondered for some time. His hands warm on the back of my neck seared my skin like a branding iron. I moved away from him the moment the pendant was secured.

Martin Justin smiled at me through filmed eyes. "You're beautiful, Abby, simply beautiful. Isn't she, Jason?"

"Yes, sir," he agreed in a scarcely audible voice.

Beyond the door we could hear the rattle of carriage wheels and the exchange of merry voices as the guests began to arrive. Stephen, the butler hired for the weekend, took up his position at the front door.

For what seemed like hours I stood between Grandfather and Jason while we welcomed our guests. The only faces that were familiar to me were those of Dr. and Mrs. Sims, Mr. Taylor from the mill, and Nicholas. After a while all the other faces became a blur.

At last the greetings were over and we joined our guests in the ballroom. It was alive with the sound of happy voices. Overhead chandeliers glittered under the glow of white tapered candles and gilt chairs were arranged along the walls of the high-ceilinged room.

Near the entrance were long tables loaded with canapés, crystal glasses, liquor decanters, and four immense punch bowls filled to their brims with champagne, rum, and Madeira punches.

Warm night air flowed through the open French doors on the south and east walls. Through the openings I glimpsed the lighted Japanese lanterns strung along the porch.

So that he would have a clear view of the dancers, we positioned Grandfather's chair along the wall near the center of the room. He signaled to the orchestra and they began to play a Chopin waltz. The voices grew quiet and it seemed as though everyone stared at us. "It's up to you two to start the dancing," Grandfather told Jason and me.

Without a word he took me into his arms. We circled the room once and then the other couples moved out onto the floor to join us. For a man who did not enjoy parties, I was surprised to discover that Jason was an excellent dancer.

When the waltz was nearly over he broke the uncomfortable silence between us. "You had the most curious smile on your face while we were greeting our guests. What were you thinking?"

I felt like a young girl who had been caught drawing her finger through the icing on a layer cake. "It was just a silly game I made up." I smiled faintly.

"Oh?" His brow shot up. "May I ask the nature of the game?"

I hesitated. "I'll tell you if you promise not to laugh."

Amusement flickered in his dark eyes. "I promise."

"Well, when I was addressing the invitations I conjured up pictures of people to match some of the names on the list. For instance, I envisioned Mr. Pendergast as a small, heavyset man with twinkling eyes."

Jason laughed, despite his promise. "I'm sorry. I couldn't help myself. You hit that one right on the nose. Did you guess as well on the others?"

A tender smile spread across his lips and I yearned for him, unable to maintain an air of indifference. "No." I shook my head, matching his expression.

The light moment between us was broken when Nicholas approached for the next dance. I moved into his arms with a bit of reluctance. Over his shoulder I watched Jason make his way to the bar.

"You're exceptionally beautiful this evening," Nicholas complimented. "I must say I envy Martin and Jason having you around all the time."

"It seems to me," I teased, "that I've already observed you flirting with several attractive young ladies."

He smiled into my eyes. "Do I detect a note of jealousy, I hope?"

I grinned. "Perhaps."

It seemed as though I danced with every man in the room. They were all friendly and complimentary, and as much as I tried to give them my undivided attention I found myself darting glances at Jason. He appeared to be spending most of his time at the bar. He wasn't a heavy drinker. At least, until now I had never seen him take more than one glass of wine before dinner.

Jason did not ask me to dance again. However, when the orchestra took a brief intermission, he saw to it that I became acquainted with most of the young ladies in the room. After all, I recalled as I chatted with them, it was for this reason he had suggested the party. I did enjoy their company, and when I found myself inviting several of the ladies to tea the following week I noticed the look of triumph in his eyes.

Later in the evening, while I danced to the strains

of the "Emperor Waltz" with Mr. Taylor, Jason cut in on us. His face was flushed and his eyes were bright. "Zach, do you mind? I'd like to speak with Abby for a minute."

I was annoyed by his rude intrusion. "Can't it wait, Jason?"

"No! there's something we should settle right away."

Mr. Taylor released me. "It's all right, Miss Justin. Be sure to save me a dance later, though."

With a smile of embarrassment, I acknowledged his request and watched him for a moment as he departed.

Jason seized my arm in a rough grip and steered me through the open French doors, across the lantern-lighted porch and down the steps onto the lawn. Halfway between the house and the lake he came to a halt. In the moonlight I could see his face clearly. There was thunder in his look.

I jerked my arm from his touch and hugged myself. "It's cold out here," I protested.

"What I have to say won't take long."

The cold look in his eyes influenced my backward steps. His hand flashed out and clamped over my wrist. Jason pulled me to him. He reeked of whiskey. "You're beautiful, Abby," he murmured in a husky voice against my cheek. I struggled to free myself, but his embrace held me fast. His lips left my cheek and came down on my mouth. At first his kiss was gentle, and when I did not resist, his arms about me tightened and his kiss became fire that made my heart hammer. In one last desperate attempt I pushed at him. He freed me abruptly, knocking me off balance. Jason's strong hand reached out to steady me.

"What is the matter with you?" he exploded. "I can recall not too long ago you came into my arms eagerly. Now you're a block of ice. What is wrong?"

Hastily I looked around and was thankful to find that we were alone. I wanted to shout at him that I knew about Leah, but foolish pride imprisoned the words in my throat.

His grip tightened. "Answer me!"

I grimaced. "You're hurting me, Jason."

He thrust my arm from him as though he loathed me. "I should have known better than to fall in love with you. You played me for a fool."

I caught my breath and stared at him in disbelief. "What did you say?" I sputtered.

He regarded me with scorn. "Don't play innocent. You don't fool me anymore. And what about Wells? He's part of this game, isn't he? You used him to torment me."

"Please, Jason," I pleaded. "I wasn't trifling with your affection. I didn't know how you felt. You never gave me any indication."

His eyes flashed. "Oh, come on, Abby. Either you're awfully naïve, or you believe me a credulous fool. Didn't my kisses tell you anything?"

I spoke between stiff lips. "Yes, they told me you desired me, but that emotion doesn't necessarily indicate love. You should be well aware of that!"

"Well," he scoffed, "obviously you're not as naïve as I thought."

"I'm not stupid!"

He drew a long angry breath. "Oh, Abby, will we always be at loggerheads?"

"Probably. I've tried to understand you, Jason, but you're remote. You won't share yourself with me."

"What made you turn away from me?" he asked softly, and I felt an overwhelming desire to reach out to him. I shook it off. There were still too many unanswered questions between us.

"I'll tell you," I said, "but first would you answer one question for me?"

"If I can."

"When did you realize you loved me?"

He became thoughtful. "I guess I've loved you from the moment I saw you standing there in Charlie Olson's office. You were drenched, the feather in your hat drooped, and you were as angry as—" A grin interrupted his flow of words.

My body went slack. "If you love me, then why were you kissing Leah the other day?"

That erased the grin from his face. "Is that why you withdrew from me?"

"Yes, If you really loved me, Jason, you wouldn't want to be with another woman."

He put a hand at the back of his head and gazed at the stars, seemingly deep in thought. "Yes, I agree," he said at length; then paused as if groping for words. "Please don't ask me to explain now. A lot is involved and I—"

"No, Jason, don't put me off."

"I love you, Abby; trust in me."

"You're always asking me to do that."

"All right, forget it! No man wants a woman who won't trust in him. It's clear to me now that you and I will never get along. Obviously we can't live in the same house, either."

I glared at him. "Just what do you mean by that?"

"I'm leaving here. After tomorrow you won't have to see me anymore."

"But you can't leave. This is your home."

"It's your home now."

"But my grandfather will be heartsick. He thinks of you as a son. What will you tell him?"

He shrugged. "I don't know, but I'll think of something."

Regardless of how I felt about Jason, I did not want to turn him out of his home. "I'll leave," I told him.

"I'll go back to San Francisco."

"Don't be an idiot. You'll do nothing of the kind. I'm not blind, Abby. I've seen how much Martin loves you. Right now he needs you more than he does me. Besides, do you really believe you could leave him?"

"No," I whispered. "I guess not. But where will you go?"

He took me by the shoulders. "Why should you care?"

I moistened my dry lips. "I don't want to be the reason for your leaving, and I'm worried about my grandfather; he'll be upset."

His hands fell to his sides. "I see. Well, don't feel guilty, Miss Justin, and don't pace the floor nights worrying about me, either. I'll find a place to stay. I'll be out of here by the end of the week. If I could make it sooner, I would, but I'm leaving Monday for logging camps along the south bank of the lake. I probably won't return until Thursday. I'll pack then and be out of your way."

Tears ached in my throat, preventing speech. I didn't want Jason to leave, but I couldn't bring myself to verbally react to the urgings of my heart. I couldn't let my lovesick feeling for him make a fool of me.

My silence irritated him. "Come on, we'd better get back inside; they'll be bringing in the buffet supper soon."

The thought of food repulsed me. "I'm not hungry."

"It doesn't matter if you're hungry! You're the hostess; act like one."

My lower lip trembled. "You're cold, Jason Landry, as cold as stone."

He looked smug. "I can vividly recall a few occasions when you didn't think so."

Hot blood rushed to my face and I wanted to

double up my fists and pound on him, but I restrained the impulse. I would not give him the satisfaction of knowing how deeply he had hurt me. Without a word I gathered up my skirts and hurried back into the ballroom ahead of him. Not once during the remainder of the evening did I address him, or even allow my gaze to wander in his direction.

When I crawled into bed in the early-morning hours I was unable to sleep. I couldn't stop thinking about Jason and his declaration of love, and I remembered the happy time we'd had. Could he have so skillfully feigned light-heartedness if he had wanted me out of the way? Grandfather and the Brannons loved him and trusted him and his business associates held him in high esteem—except for Nicholas. And he didn't really know Jason all that well. Nicholas only presumed Jason desired to inherit the mill, just as Jason presumed Nicholas was involved in the sabotage. Was it unreasonable of me to have lashed out at Jason without giving him the opportunity to explain why he did not want to discuss Leah at this time? Had I allowed jealousy to influence my judgment? And why didn't Jason leap at my offer to return to San Francisco? If he wanted to be rid of me, he would have. He wouldn't have cared whether or not my departure made my grandfather unhappy.

The following day dragged by. The guests who had stayed the night moved about languidly and did not leave until mid-afternoon.

Grandfather was exhausted and irritable and retired early that night, too tired to even eat his dinner.

I saw little of Jason that day and it wasn't until I was alone in the parlor with my head bent over needlepoint that he approached me. "Abby," he said, from the doorway.

His unhappy voice slashed at my heart. "Yes." The word was a whisper.

"While I'm away I'd prefer you not to go to the mill."

"Why not?" I looked at him. "Has there been further trouble?"

"No, but the men are restless and I'd feel better if you didn't go alone."

Why should he care? He was going to be leaving and as far as he knew he would eventually have nothing. "Very well," I said quietly, "I'll spend the extra time with Dorothea at Dr. Sims's office."

He took a step into the room. "How is she doing there?"

"Extremely well. Dr. Sims is very pleased with her work."

"I'm glad to hear that. Dorothea is fortunate to have you for a friend."

My lips parted in astonishment. After last night how could he regard me with any kindness? "Jason," I ventured, "are you really going to move out?"

"Yes."

My heart overruled my brain. "I don't want you to leave."

His dark eyebrows rose in surprise. "It's best if I do. Maybe you and I will get along better if we don't see each other often, at least for a while." He paused, studying my face. "I'm sorry for the way I behaved last night, Abby. I guess I had too much to drink."

"I'm sorry, too, Jason." I put aside the needlework and clasped my hands tightly together to keep them from trembling. "I shouldn't have screamed at you."

He came closer. "I meant what I said about loving you." His voice was soft.

My mind went blank and I sat dumbly. Apparently Jason took my silence as a sign of rejection. "Well, I'll leave you to your needlework. Good night, Abby." He turned on his heel.

A sharp breath caught in my throat and my mouth went dry. For weeks I had thought him lost to me and now I was being given a second chance. If I let him go this time, would I lose him forever? I didn't want to take that risk. Regardless of what Nicholas said I would have to presume that my grandfather's love for Jason had not been abused. "Don't go," I choked, and he stopped dead. "I'll not question your judgment again. I promise."

Jason looked at me over his shoulder. "At this moment that is not what I want to hear."

"But you've been after me to make you that promise for weeks now."

He closed the door, then sat down beside me and took my hands in his. "How do you feel about me, Abby?"

I wanted to profess my love; yet I couldn't seem to find my voice.

"Are you still concerned about Leah? Because if you are, then don't be. She and I have been close, I won't deny that. After all, she is attractive and she did make herself available. I had no attachments at the time, so I saw no reason to turn my back on her. But I have no warm affection for her, Abby."

"Why didn't you tell me that last night?"

He grinned. "You didn't give me much of a chance to say anything. Besides, last night you probably wouldn't have been satisfied with a brief explanation. It wouldn't have answered your question about the kiss and I'd rather not go into that right now. A lot is involved and I don't want to say things about Leah that might not be true. I owe her that much."

I was perplexed. "What kind of things? Is she in love with you?"

"No." He shook his head. "I suspect her interest in me was generated by the wealth and power I have at my command."

"In other words, she's out to get a rich husband."

"That's the impression I've had."

"Well, no wonder she's been so jealous. She has a lot to lose." I told Jason about my suspicion of Leah spying on us in the woods. "And I can't prove it, but I'm sure she's the one who was banging around in the attic, harassing me. Undoubtedly she hoped I'd go all to pieces and make a fool of myself so that you'd be repulsed by me."

"It could have been her that I heard in the woods, which doesn't surprise me because she's been watching me like a Pinkerton detective. And I have to admit, Abby, that it was your accusation about Leah and the attic that started me to thinking." His voice faded.

"Thinking about what?"

He frowned at my persistence.

"Please," I beseeched. "I don't mean to pry. It's just that I'd like us to share and to be able to communicate freely."

"Is that why you like Wells so much, because he communicates freely?"

I nodded. "Yes."

He gave me a crooked smile. "Well, if you and I are going to communicate freely, then you'd better tell me how you feel about me and quit avoiding the subject."

"I wasn't avoiding it. I was sidetracked."

"Are you going to tell me?"

I lowered my gaze, suddenly shy. "I love you, Jason." The declaration came out a whisper.

"Don't mumble," he teased, and forced me to meet his eyes. His mouth was so near that I felt his breath on my face. "Now, what did you say?"

My respiration grew shallow and I wished he would stop wasting time and kiss me. "I said I love you."

"I love you, too," he breathed, and finally put his

mouth on mine. Jason kissed me with a tenderness that brought tears to my eyes.

When at last we separated I was nearly breathless and delirious with joy. For a long while I snuggled against him; then I raised my and asked, "How did my accusation about Leah and the attic start you to thinking?"

"Well,"—he sighed—"after you arrived Leah grew even more aggressive, which only served to hasten the waning of my interest in her. It seemed like every time I turned around she was there, intruding on my privacy. Other than being annoyed I didn't give much consideration to the change. I had too many other things on my mind. But then I began to think back, particularly to the day or two prior to your fall on the stairs. She fussed over me a lot then, trying to draw me from indifference and when I didn't respond she shouted at me that I'd used her, that I was no different than any of the others she had cared about. I had trampled on her, just as they had. When I reminded her that she had approached me first she stormed out of the study. Later, after she calmed down, she apologized to me, so I thought no more about it. I expected then, that our relationship would revert to employer—employee, but it didn't. She continued to fuss over me, but eventually for another reason, it appeared."

"Another reason?" I echoed.

"Yes, she seemed very interested in the company and what it was that kept me so occupied in the study. Naturally she didn't come right out and ask; she was very coy about it."

"I should think talk of the company would bore her."

"That's exactly what I thought. Why should the Kimberley bid concern Leah? Unless, of course, she considered selling my calculations to one of the other mills. No doubt she could receive quite a handsome sum, if it were to win the contract."

"But how could she be sure that your bid would be awarded the contract?"

"Well, as I told you a couple of months ago, the Justin Mill can afford to bid lower than the majority of others. And I guess I've been pretty lucky with my calculations because we've been awarded a vast number of contracts."

"Not luck, Jason," I corrected with a smile, "intelligence."

"If you insist." He laughed, then gave me a long kiss. "Anyway, I decided to set aside indifference just long enough to find out if she was up to something."

"I know Leah is quite intelligent, but is she clever enough to contrive a scheme like that?"

"I doubt it. I'm sure she's in on this with someone."

"Have you changed your mind about Nicholas, then? Do you suspect someone else now?"

"No."

"But, Jason, you—"

"I've seen Wells and Leah together a couple of times, Abby."

"Nicholas with Leah?"

"Yes; it was before she came to work here, and since she does have a reputation for being a flirt, their being together may have absolutely no bearing on the Kimberley bid."

"But you don't think so, do you?"

He shook his head, then gathered me to him. "You know, I really hate to go off and leave you here with her. That's one of the reasons why I planned to move out. I hoped if I left, she might also leave."

"Can't you just dismiss her?"

"No; I have no cause. She performs her duties well

and I can't let her go merely on a supposition. What if I'm wrong?"

"Yes, I see your point. Anyway, don't worry about me, Jason; I'll be all right. After all, it's been weeks since she last disturbed me." I looked at him. "What about the feather duster, do you still think it was a careless oversight by a servant?"

"Well, if it wasn't, then it was undoubtedly placed on the stairs for me to stumble over and not you. With me out of the way and Zach in charge, the business would most likely falter and the contracts would be a total loss—much to the advantage of our competitors." He held me at arm's length. "Take good care of yourself while I'm away, will you?"

The worried note in his voice tightened my nerves. "I will," I promised, and wondered if he suspected any one person of using the feather duster as a weapon. Before I was able to inquire, his lips were on mine again and the question vanished from my mind in the heat of passion.

Early the next morning Jason left on his business trip and the rest of us continued as usual. Having regained some of his strength, Grandfather was in a much better mood.

Twice during that week Dorothea and I worked in Dr. Sims's office, and it was there on Wednesday afternoon that we were startled out of our wits. The last patient had left and it was quiet. Without warning, the door burst open and a husky man with grizzled hair and beard stormed in. "Is the doctor in?"

Before I was able to respond, Dr. Sims stepped from the examining room. "What is it?" he asked, looking as though he were ready for the worst and prepared to grab his Gladstone bag and make a hasty departure.

The man crossed the room, leaving the door wide

open. Crisp air rustled the papers on the desk and scattered them to the floor. Dorothea hurried to close the door, while I gathered up the papers. "You've got to come right away, Doc." The man spoke between deep gulps of breath. "There's been an accident."

Dr. Sims took the man by the shoulders. "Calm yourself!" he insisted. And after the man took a few more deep breaths, the doctor resumed, "Now, tell me what happened and where?"

"Up at the Brandon logging camp. A man was hurt real bad." He wheeled. "Is one of you Miss Justin?"

I stepped forward. "Yes, sir, I am."

"You've got to come, too, miss. It was Mr. Landry that was hurt."

"What?" I choked.

"Mr. Landry was hurt and he's calling for you."

"But that can't be. You must be mistaken. Mr. Landry doesn't work there, so how could he have gotten injured."

Dorothea threw her arm about me. "Oh, miss, you look like you're going to faint. Please, sit down."

I pulled away from her. "No, I'm all right."

"Quit wastin' time," the man hollered. "He needs help right away."

Dr. Sims seemed suspicious. "Why did you travel all this way for a doctor? Surely there's one closer to the camp."

"Well, there is, but he's gone to Tacoma. Someone in his family took sick. My boss told me to go for Miss Justin and you."

"How did Mr. Landry get injured?"

"You're wastin' time with all this talk."

"I need to know, so I'll know which medical supplies to bring with me."

The grizzly-haired man ranged the room. "Mr. Landry was watchin' the logging operations. He was standin' in what should have been the safest spot, but a crazy thing happened. A fallin' tree hit another tree, fellin' it at an angle. The second tree broke off another right near where he was standin'. He ran, but he couldn't get far enough away before it hit ground, and he was struck down. Like I said, he's hurt real bad. The boss says it looks like Mr. Landry will die."

"Oh, God." I moaned, and buried my face in my hands. Dorothea hugged me to her and urged me to a chair. "Jason can't be hurt. He can't be dying."

The young girl held me to her breast. "Hush, Miss Abby," she soothed, and her own voice was choked with tears.

CHAPTER NINETEEN

After a brief bout with tears I put Dorothea from me and regarded Dr. Sims through moisture-filled eyes. "I'm going with you to the logging camp. I'm going to Jason."

"A logging camp is no place for a lady," he insisted. "Besides, it's a long and rough trip."

"I don't care! Jason needs me and if you won't take me, I'll find someone who will."

"You're that determined?"

I nodded.

"Oh, very well, then," he relented, with a note of reservation in his voice. "But can you ride, Abby? We can't take the buggy."

I dabbed at my eyes with a lace-trimmed handkerchief. "Yes, sir."

Footsteps clattered, bringing our heads up with a

jerk. The grizzly-haired man was at the door. "Aren't you going with us?" the doctor inquired.

"No, I have to get right back; we're short-handed. You won't have any trouble finding the camp; it's along the main road." With that he pulled open the door and was gone.

While the doctor checked his medical bag, reassuring himself it was well-supplied, Dorothea ran next door to inform his wife that we would be leaving, and I closed up the office.

Words rushed out as we made our plans. Since we would be traveling south, past Justin property, Dr. Sims suggested I make a hasty stop at the house, change into proper riding clothes, and inform my grandfather that I would be away from home, at least overnight.

"Don't tell anyone in the household about the accident," Dr. Sims cautioned. "If Martin should get wind of it I just might have to remain here and care for him."

I agreed, and it was decided that I would simply inform him that Mrs. Sims was bedded down with influenza and that I planned to care for her and the children.

Grandfather loved the Sims family and accepted my story of rendering assistance with pride. "Just take good care of yourself, Abby," he urged. "I wouldn't want you to get sick, too."

I told him good-by, then left his room for my own. In it, I changed into my one and only riding habit, threw a few overnight articles into a carpetbag, then hurried out to the stables. Dorothea waited inside its entrance, with a saddled chestnut mare. At the far end of the building a young boy was busy cleaning out one of the stalls. "I didn't say nothing to him, miss, or anyone else," Dorothea stated, her eyes misting.

I gave her a thin smile of appreciation and briefly touched her hand, comfortingly. Then I secured the carpetbag to the saddle and mounted.

Dorothea looked up at me. "He'll be all right, Miss Abby," she choked. "I just know he will be."

I nodded, repressing my tears. Then, lest I attract the attention of the household and arouse suspicion, I urged the horse slowly across the drive. It wasn't until we were well out of earshot of the house that I gave a snap to the reins and the horse broke into a gallop. Within seconds I joined Dr. Sims on the main road and we headed for the Brandon logging camp. For miles we rode side by side over the winding and rutted road. At first there were houses here and there, but they eventually gave way to a dense wall of firs and hemlocks that provided gloomy shade and made the air cooler.

It was after seven o'clock now and the roadway was devoid of other travelers. Numerous logging camps marked the landscape and the air came alive with the cries of "Timber," the swoosh of trees crashing to earth, and the grating sounds of cross-cut saws chewing through the butts of trees. Puffs of white smoke billowed from a donkey engine as its wheel turned to wind a taut line attached to a fallen tree. And there were loggers everywhere, most of them balanced on springboards as they worked.

Finally, after three hours in the saddle, we reined to a halt in front of a long, unpainted structure and alighted. "Wait here, Abby, while I go inside and see what I can find out."

I responded with a nod and watched him enter the building. My hand clutching the reins was slippery with perspiration and my stomach felt as though it were on fire. My gaze darted over the clusters of unpainted buildings in search of a sign indicating the infirmary, but there were no markings on any of the structures. Men in dark clothing and rumpled felt hats seemed to be everywhere and I felt a trifle self-conscious under their curious stares. Off to my right was a corral, enclosing a herd of oxen, and logs were stacked here and there.

The door behind me closed and I wheeled about.

Dr. Sims shrugged. "He isn't here."

"But that can't be." I felt tears run down my cheeks. "We're at the right camp."

"Don't cry! That won't help us locate Jason." He withdrew a handkerchief from his coat pocket and dried my tears. "Now, get up on your horse."

"But where are we going?"

"The man inside told me this is camp one. Jason could be up the road at camp two. There's something strange, though." He put a hand to his chin. "No one has heard of any accident."

"But then—"

"Please, Abby, let's not waste time on speculation; we'll find out soon enough what's going on."

At camp two we dismounted and once again I waited while my companion inquired at the office. My nerves were in tatters. I paced back and forth with my eyes fixed firmly on the ground. So intent were my thoughts that I was oblivious to all that went on around me.

Somewhere off in the distance I thought I heard a voice, but I paid it no heed and I did not hear the footfalls behind me. Without warning strong hands came down on my shoulders. I jumped with fright and in one quick motion twisted myself free and whirled about. The ground and trees wavered. In that instant, before darkness closed over me, I saw Jason.

When I regained consciousness and my eyelids fluttered open, I found I was lying on a bunk in a dimly lit room. The air was sharp with the heavy odor of kerosene. Jason sat beside me, his expression grave. "You are the most aggravating female,"—he scowled—"always passing out on me."

"Oh, Jason." I sat up and threw my arms about his neck.

"Say, I didn't know you were so strong," he teased, his mouth in my hair.

I pulled away from him slightly so that I could look into his eyes. "We were told you were hurt, maybe even dying." My voice broke.

He ran a gentle finger over my wet cheek. "Yes, I know. Doc told me the whole story."

"But I don't understand it, unless they had you confused with someone else. But then that doesn't make sense either."

"It surely doesn't, because there was no accident of any kind."

"Well, now I really am bewildered."

"I think I know what's going on, but we'll talk about that later. Right now I want you to tell me why you came here with Doc Sims. Obviously you didn't inform him that you're not skilled rider."

"He's aware of that now." I grinned.

Jason frowned. "Don't you know this is no place for a lady?"

I turned from his reproving eyes and let my gaze wander over the dingy wet socks and long underwear that hung on lines strung around the bunkhouse. "The doctor warned me, but as I told you, Jason,"—I looked at him—"a man said you were dying. I had to come. I had to be with you. Are you furious with me?"

"Oh, Abby." He sighed, and hauled me to him. "How can I be angry with you for loving me.

Besides,"—laughter came into his voice—"I'm getting used to your self-determined ways. Somehow I don't think life will ever again be dull." He gave me a long and breath-taking kiss, then released me and darted a look around. "Come on." He rose, and pulled me to my feet. "We'd better get out of here; we're keeping a lot of men from sleep."

He led me between lines of damp laundry and out the bunkhouse door. A group of men stood in the shadows nearby, and I offered them an apology for having disturbed their rest. I heard some murmured responses, but the voices were weary and the words unintelligible.

When Jason and I entered the cookhouse we saw Dr. Sims seated alone at the far end of the room. He motioned us to his side and then leaned back and peered through the open doorway beyond. "She's here now," he called. "You can bring in her dinner."

Within seconds a plate of ham and eggs, accompanied by a thick slice of buttered bread and a glass of warm milk, were on the table before me.

Dr. Sims stood up. "Well, I'm anxious to hear what this wild-goose chase was all about, but at this moment I'm too tired to get into it. I'm going to scout up an empty bunk. I'll see you both in the morning." We watched him saunter from the room.

It was eerie with just the two of us sitting in this huge, faintly illuminated room. The walls were laced with the strange patterns cast by the flickering kerosene lamps. Jason moved at my side. "Well, now I'm certain that Leah is involved in the scheme to acquire the Kimberley bid. What occurred today confirms my suspicion."

"I don't see the connection."

"Doc Sims told me nobody at the house was informed of my supposed accident. If that's the case, then how do you explain that man knowing exactly where to locate you?"

"Why, I never thought of that, but you're right. The Brannons would never inform a stranger of my whereabouts. Inquiries of that nature would be referred to my grandfather, and he said nothing to me about a strange man seeking me out. I wonder who he was. He was so coarse and dirty; I can't picture Leah becoming acquainted with somebody like that."

"I expect her partner probably hired him and undoubtedly a couple of others to carry off the machinery breakdowns."

"Not Nicholas," I reiterated slowly, "he can't be her partner."

"It has to be him, Abby. He's the only logical suspect. He and Leah have been together, and he's been struggling for over two years now to secure larger contracts. On top of that, he's gone out of his way to strike up a friendship with Taylor."

"Nicholas doesn't have to go out of his way to strike up a friendship with anybody. He's so amiable that people are naturally drawn to him."

"Perhaps. Nonetheless, that's a very convenient friendship for Wells. If anything were to happen to me it wouldn't surprise me at all if Zach approached Wells for business advice. And since you and Wells are also friends you'd probably seek him out, too."

"Yes, I suppose I would. But why this tale of your being injured?"

"I imagine it ties in somehow with the incident two weeks ago, when someone snooped around the study. Whoever the culprit was, he didn't get what he came for: the Kimberley estimate. I suspect he believes it's still locked in the study safe, and he probably intends to break into it this evening."

"Are you saying you believe someone might be

prowling around the house tonight?"

"I'm afraid so. Why else this ruse to get you away from there? With you gone there's no one to hamper his search. He won't have to rush trying to get the safe open—not that he'll find anything when he does. I transferred the papers back to the office safe."

"But what about my grandfather?" I came to my feet. "We have to get back to the house; they might hurt him."

Jason's hands flew to my waist and he returned me to the bench. "Calm down, Abby. Don't you suppose Martin was my first consideration? It would be foolhardy to attempt traversing that treacherous roadway in the dark. Even with lanterns it would be an impossible journey."

Reluctantly, I had to admit he was right. There was nothing we could do until morning. "Do you think they'd hurt my grandfather?" My voice broke.

There was a soft reassuring expression in his eyes. "I can think of no reason that would compel anyone to hurt him. Martin is defenseless. He can't get in anyone's way and unless the intruder goes into his room, which isn't likely, Martin wouldn't be able to identify him. Now, come on, let's get you to bed; you look exhausted. I was using that room over there, next to the kitchen. You take it for the night and I'll put up a cot near the door."

"Very well," I agreed, feeling utterly helpless. "I had a carpetbag."

"Go on to the room. I'll look for it."

I nodded, and as I obeyed the instructions, Jason caught up the dirty dishes and returned them to the kitchen.

I slept fitfully that night and had just dozed off for the dozenth time when the deep throaty growl of a man shouting, "Daylight in the swamp," brought me bolt upright in the lumpy bed.

"What on earth?" I gasped, and stared wide-eyed into the dusky room. The call came again, and when it faded, I became acutely aware of muffled voices, from beyond my door, and the clatter of pots and pans. Was it time to get up?

Groggily, and with cold air stinging my face, I lighted the kerosene lamp on the bedside table. As I consulted my pendant watch, noting it was only 4:15, the building began to vibrate and there was a rumbling sound, like that made by a herd of stampeding cattle. Within seconds the clamor gave way to the clinking of utensils and the curses of men, apparently fighting for places in the food line.

Well, obviously it was time to be up—and more importantly, time to be on the way home to Grandfather.

Motivated by the cold air and the aroma of piping hot coffee, I dressed as quickly as my sore muscles would allow, then stepped to the door. There was incredible quiet beyond it now. Curious, I eased open the rough panel and peered out. The dining room was filled to capacity with scraggly-looking men, and my eyes grew round at the mountains of food heaped on their plates.

My gaze dropped to the cot where Jason had spent the night. It was empty, and I was about to scan the dining room in search of him, when he approached from the kitchen area. He gave me a faint smile, then said "We'll wait, Abby, until the men are finished, then—"

My spine stiffened. "Wait? But why."

"Because I said so, that's why?"

My lips parted to utter another protest, but he put a silencing finger over my mouth. "It's not light enough yet to travel safely," he explained in a firm voice. "And we are not traveling without some nourishing food to give us strength. Now,"—he frowned down on me—"are you going to argue? Or are you going to trust in my judgment?"

I didn't have to consider the matter to know that Jason was right about both the travel and food, and I told him so. "I guess worry for Grandfather has dimmed my own judgment," I admitted quietly.

"Oh, Abby," he soothed, "don't worry."

"I'm sorry, Jason, but I can't help it."

He drew me close and gave me a long and comforting kiss, then held me near until we heard the loggers noisily filing from the dining room.

Shortly after we entered it, Dr. Sims came in and joined us for breakfast. Over the hearty meal, which I forced myself to consume, Jason explained to the other man his suspicion of Nicholas and Leah.

"Hm," the doctor rasped, "that's hard to believe. Why, Leah always seemed so conscientious and caring. As for Nicholas Wells, I hardly know him. But he seemed nice enough—honest-looking anyway."

"I still can't believe it about Nicholas," I murmured.

Dr. Sims frowned. "Frankly, I'd like to get my hands on the necks of those responsible for this wild-goose chase."

"Amen," Jason muttered.

We finished the meal and at long last commenced our journey home.

When we reached the base of the drive leading to the Justin home, Jason and I apologized again to Dr. Sims for the inconvenience caused, then bade him farewell.

We entered the stable and dismounted. Where was Mr. Brannon, or at least one of the stable boys? I wondered, and began to feel rising panic. Without taking the time to unsaddle our horses we turned them into the stalls, checked their food and water supply, then made our way to the house.

Inside the entrance Jason grasped me by the arm. "We'll go in to see Martin together. I'll do the explaining."

While he closed the front door I looked around the hallway. I suppose I had expected everything to be turned upside down, but all was as it should be, except for the utter dead silence.

Hand in hand we hurried toward the rear of the house, our footsteps like thunder in our ears. At the study Jason stopped short. "Let's see if I was right." He threw open the door and stiffened perceptibly.

I leaned forward and stared past him. "Oh," I wailed, "the room's a mess." Papers were scattered around on the maroon rug, books were pulled from shelves and piled helter-skelter on the leather chair, and empty desk drawers were stacked on top of the desk.

Jason crossed the small room, dragging me along behind him. Paper crackled beneath our feet. "I have to find my grandfather," I insisted, and tried to twist my hand free. He tightened his grip and swung me around before the open closet.

Centered in its interior loomed the monstrous black safe, its opened door disclosing emptiness. Jason scoffed. "Wells must have hired someone to open it."

"Let go of me, Jason!"

He turned on his heel. "No, Abby, we'll locate Martin together." He led me from the room and down the hall to Grandfather's door. Jason knocked sharply. After a brief interval of silence he opened the panel just wide enough for him to peer in. Hysteria burned in my throat. Jason, too, was frightened for the older man. I raised up on my toes, but I was unable to see over his shoulder. "Well, he's not in there." He pushed open the door. "Come on, we'll check the other rooms."

On our way past the entrance I looked in. The draperies were open and the bed made up. The corners of my mouth trembled. Had Grandfather slept there at all last night?

We investigated every room on the first floor with the exception of the kitchen and Jason was now leading me through its entrance. In the middle of the room we came to a sudden halt, for through the screen door we saw Grandfather on the porch gazing across the lawn.

Jason released my hand and I ran across the linoleum and out the door.

Startled by my commotion the man in the wheelchair jerked his head around and observed me over his shoulder. "What are you doing home so soon?" His eyes widened in alarm. "You're trembling, Abby."

Jason came out on the porch and Grandfather surveyed us both. "What's going on here? Something is wrong; you're both chalk-white."

The other man sighed deeply. "Martin, before I begin, tell me, where is everyone? The place seems deserted."

Grandfather waved a hand toward the lawn. "The Brannons are out there, picking peas in the garden. Dorothea is somewhere along the road picking red raspberries. Didn't you see her when you rode in?"

I shook my head. "No, we didn't."

He put a hand to his chin. "That's odd, she was there awhile ago. Nicholas saw her, even spoke with her."

Jason's head came up. "Wells was here?"

"Why, yes, he came to see Leah."

"Leah?" I echoed, and my heart thumped.

Martin Justin shook his head in bewilderment. "Yes, he came to see Leah, and frankly I'll never understand you young people. I thought Nicholas was sweet on you, Abby, but now he's gone off with her."

Jason jumped to his feet. "What do you mean, gone off with her? Did they say where they were going?"

"No. Leah came to me a short time ago and asked if she could have the remainder of the day off; said she had urgent business in town. She seemed upset. Come to think of it, when Nicholas came into my room a few minutes later to pay his respects he seemed preoccupied and restless." A frown creased his forehead. "Why all the questions?"

Jason spoke in a rush of words. "I can't discuss it now, Martin. You'll have to excuse me; I have to go into town." He turned his eyes to me. "Don't say anything until I return."

The fury in his eyes told me he was going to seek out Leah and Nicholas. Jason was going to confront them with his suspicion. How would they react? Would they panic? And if they did, what then?

Before I could make an attempt to dissuade this man I loved, he wheeled and went down the steps two at a time.

"Jason," I cried, and ran past my grandfather. "Wait!" My plea didn't even slow his step, nor did he even cast me a look over his shoulder. I was terrified for him. I had to stop him, but how? There wasn't time to really think so I grasped the first thought that leaped to mind. I came to an abrupt halt and stood stock-still, my fists clenched at my sides. "Jason, if you go after them, I'll hate you forever!"

He pulled up short and swung around to give me a slow searching look. Salty tears streamed down my face and I flicked them away with the back of my hand. Out of the corner of my eye I noticed the

Brannons step to the edge of the garden. I felt sick inside. I had screamed like a fishwife and undoubtedly they thought me a shrew. But that didn't matter, as long as I had arrested Jason.

"Jason! Abby!" Grandfather shouted. I looked from one man to the other. Martin Justin's face was white with anger, while Jason stood rigid, his feet planted firmly in the grass. There was frustration in his intense eyes.

I didn't know which way to turn. I could not allow my grandfather to become upset. On the other hand I couldn't let Jason confront Nicholas and Leah. "Quit dillydallying!" Grandfather ordered. "Come back here! Both of you."

Jason went to the porch and regarded the older man. I sighed with relief, confident that he would not leave Grandfather in his present agitated condition.

After several seconds Jason came toward me, defeat pulling down the corners of his mouth. I was elated that I had deterred him and yet at the same time I felt miserable. "I'm sorry," I apologized when he came to a stop in front of me. "That was a dumb thing for me to say."

To my amazement he slipped an arm about my shoulders and hugged me to him. "You don't have to apologize, Abby. I know why you did it."

On our way back to the porch I saw the Brannons resume their work in the garden.

Martin Justin eyed us in bewilderment. "What is going on here?" he demanded

Jason went to the wheelchair. "Let's go inside where we can talk undisturbed."

I reached for the knob on the screen door, but the sound of someone running along the porch halted my hand in midair. Dorothea bounded around the front corner of the house, her dark-brown plaits flying and her cheeks bright with color.

She stopped momentarily to let her gaze go over Jason, apparently reassuring herself that he was unharmed, then continued forward at a brisk pace. "Dr. Sims passed me on the road." She was breathless, as if she had run the entire mile up the drive. "He told me what happened." Dorothea's broadcloth dress was smudged with dirt and there was jagged rent near the hemline.

In an effort to relieve the tension that had sobered our expressions, I feigned a frown and teased her. "I'd say from the appearance of your dress, Dorothea, that berry-picking is a hazardous task."

She bent and attempted to brush off the dirt. "Oh, those horrid, thorny vines," she grumbled, noting the gaping tear.

Jason cleared his throat. "Dorothea, what did Mr. Wells say to you?"

She straightened and looked at each of us before responding to Jason. "He told me that he was on his way past Dr. Sims's office and decided to stop in for a visit. That's when Mrs. Sims informed him of your accident."

"What accident?" Martin Justin blustered.

I placed a reassuring hand on his. "It was a mistake, Grandfather, there was no accident."

"Go on, Dorothea," Jason persisted.

"Well, Mr. Wells asked if I'd heard how you were." Her lower lip trembled. "He knew the whole story so I couldn't pretend it wasn't true."

Jason went to her side and slipped a comforting arm about her shoulders. "It's all right, Dorothea. I'm sorry you were dragged into this."

Dorothea continued on her way, a north wind whipping at her skirts.

In the library, a few minutes later, we explained

the entire situation to my grandfather. He was outraged. "You faced possible danger, and you told me nothing?"

Finally, after two hours, we were able to calm him, but he still refused to believe Nicholas was involved. "That's just not possible," he insisted.

"I know, Grandfather; believe me, I feel the same."

When Jason told the older man about the study being ransacked, his shaggy white brows drew together in a straight line. "I knew it! I was sure I heard noises last night. Darn that Leah! I called her into my room and questioned her about it, but she shrugged it off. She said I must have been dreaming. If only the Brannons had been around," he mused, "but, of course, by then they had retired to their cottage for the night. Just wait until that young lady gets home!"

After lunch we sat at Grandfather's bedside until he fell into a deep sleep and then Jason and I went to the study. It was still a shambles. Dorothea had offered to restore it to order, but I raised a protesting hand, citing the half-full bushelbasket of peas in the kitchen—her task for the afternoon.

The empty safe seemed to renew Jason's determination to confront our housekeeper. After several minutes of pacing the floor he strode to the door and yanked it open. "I'm not standing around here waiting for Leah to return. I'm going out to find her and Wells."

I rushed around the desk and clutched his arm. "Even if you locate them, what could you do? You have no positive proof."

The muscles in his face hardened. "If I have to, I'll beat the truth from Wells."

"But, Jason—" The sound of hurrying feet interrupted my plea. Dorothea pulled to a stop before us.

"Seattle is on fire," she cried between gasps of breath.

Jason took her by the shoulders. "Who told you that?"

"A man from the mill." Her voice was shrill. "He was at the kitchen door a minute ago. He said to tell you to get to the mill right away. You can see the smoke from the porch."

Jason put her aside and bounded for the front door, his footfalls hammering in our ears. I started after him, but Dorothea put a detaining hand on my arm. "Mama and Papa are on their way to town. My sister—" Her voice broke and sobs shook her shoulders.

I hugged her to me. "They'll be all right," I said comfortingly. "Please don't allow yourself to believe otherwise."

Several seconds elapsed before she was able to bring her tears under control; then we followed after Jason. By the time we reached the porch he was running across the lawn toward us. A bluish haze filtered through the trees and columns of purple smoke hovered directly over Seattle.

Jason came to a stop in front of me. "I'm going to town. Take care of everything here."

"I'm going with you. Dorothea can look after my grandfather."

He gripped my arms, his fingers biting into my flesh. "You'll do nothing of the kind!"

"People may be hurt and in need of help. I've had plenty of experience. Please, Jason, let me go."

"All right, Abby, all right." He dropped his hands to his sides. "But we'll have to take horses. Will you be able to ride hard and fast?"

I ignored my aching muscles. "Yes."

In rapid strides we went to the stables. Fortunately

I was still attired in my riding habit, for I knew Jason would not have waited for me to change.

He saddled up two horses, and after mounting, we left the structure in haste. Grayish-white ashes now floated down from the smoke-infested sky and settled over everything.

CHAPTER TWENTY

Even before we left the drive for the main road we could hear the roar of the flames and the steady shriek of steam whistles from the mills and the ships anchored along the waterfront.

Just as we reached the summit of Yesler Avenue a thunderous explosion ripped through the air and flames shot upward, smearing the sky amber. We reined in and stared aghast at Seattle. A brand of flames spread through the heart of town. "Oh, my God," Jason rasped, his face pallid.

We urged our horses on, moving into the billows of black smoke. Wagons loaded with goods rumbled past us; people carrying what they could on their backs struggled up the hill into the outlying residential district. The shriek of steam whistles now mingled with the toll of church bells and the clang of fire-station bells. Businessmen and homeowners ran in and out of buildings stacking goods on street corners. Planks from the streets were being removed and hauled off. Everywhere there were bucket brigades, hosecarts, and fire engines.

On Coleman block, a group of men flagged us down. "Better get out of here," bellowed a tall, lean man covered with soot. "We're putting a charge of dynamite under the Nugget." He flicked a hand toward the restaurant on our left. "The mayor ordered us to blow up this block. He seems to think that'll stop the fire. God, I hope he's right."

In compliance, we turned our horses toward Puget Sound and Justin Mill. So far, to my relief, I saw no casualties; and even though people ran in all directions, those fighting the fire appeared in control.

Another explosion rocked the ground and I gasped and stiffened in the saddle. Jason looked past me, raising a hand to shield his eyes from the intense heat. "That must have been one of the saloons on Madison," he said grimly. "Alcohol will keep this fire burning for hours."

Along the sound, ships were being hastily loaded and many of them were already making their way into deep water. One of the mills was on fire and a fire company worked frantically pumping water from the bay, while mill workers slapped wet burlap bags on the cedar-shingled roof.

Jason looked at me, a hopeless expression in his eyes. "The wind is rising. There'll be nothing left of Seattle but charred rubble. We'd better save what we can from the mill and then, if you want, you can see if help is needed with the injured and I'll go to work on the fire lines."

I acknowledged his statement with a nod and we urged our horses forward. A few minutes later, when we passed the Wells Mill Company, my heart twisted with pain. With tongues of flames hissing just a quarter of a mile behind us, Nicholas' business would soon be a powdery heap of ashes: the grim reaper, fire, destroying four years of arduous work.

At Justin Mill we reined to an abrupt halt in front of the office, dismounted, and let our eyes scan the area. The place looked deserted. It was eerie standing within the circle of buildings, the ground white with ashes and the sky shrouded with thick clouds of inky smoke. Over the cedar-shake roof of the sawmill I could barely make out the masts of ships in the harbor.

"Abby, here's the combination to my office safe." Jason was scribbling numbers on a slip of paper. "Go in and empty it out. I'll join you as soon as I'm certain everyone is out of here."

I accepted the paper and darted for the building. Inside, I hurried noisily across the wooden floor and flung open Jason's office door. Involuntarily a hand went to my mouth and I froze in horror as if every nerve in my body had turned to ice.

Without looking for Leah I had found her. She stood beside Jason's desk, her brow arched in defiance. "Come in, Miss Justin," she ordered. "How was your trip to the logging camp last night?"

"Shut up, Leah." Startled, I jerked my head around see a tall and husky blond-haired man standing in the corner, one hand resting on the safe and the other brandishing a snub-nosed revolver. "Come in, Miss Justin." He motioned with the weapon. "And close the door behind you."

Without taking my eyes from his tanned face I shut the door and leaned against it for support.

There was a brief silence while he looked me up and down with a quick sweep of his deep-blue eyes. "Allow me to introduce you to my brother, Carl," Leah said with a hint of malice. I could see she was enjoying my misery.

"What are you doing here?" I could hardly speak due to the hammering pulse in the hollow of my throat.

Carl stepped forward. "Shut up." His eyes lowered

to my hand that lay on the front of my riding habit. In my fright I had forgotten about the slip of paper Jason had given me. Before I could clamp my perspiring fingers over it, Carl's free hand shot out and snatched it away from me.

He moved back a step, cold-steel revolver pointed at my stomach, and glanced at the numbers. "Well, Leah, we must thank Miss Justin. She was kind enough to provide us with the combination to the safe."

"How accommodating." She smirked, then suddenly sobered. "Where is Jason?"

My heart leaped to my throat and my legs felt as though they would no longer support the weight of my body. "I don't know . . . exactly. He's out there somewhere fighting the fire."

"Don't give me that! He'd never permit you to come here alone."

Carl shoved the gun at Leah. "Never mind! Keep an eye on her while I open the safe."

With the revolver leveled at me she perched herself on the corner of the desk, a triumphant look in her eyes. "I must say, I'm a pretty good actress. You really thought Jason was in love with me, didn't you?"

I gave her a slow nod, then turned my attention to Carl, who knelt before the safe. "What good will those papers do you? By now Wells Mill Company is probably on fire. It'll be months before it's rebuilt, if Nicholas can afford to rebuild at all."

Leah cocked her head to one side, her blond brows knit together. "Nicholas? What has he got to do with—" Her voice dwindled and her mouth gaped in wonder. "Why you think he's in on this, don't you?"

"It looks that way." I gulped.

"And here I thought you were so smart," she ridiculed with delight. "You, Miss Justin, are a miserable judge of character. How could you honestly believe that that spineless man could devise and carry out such a clever scheme? Nicholas Wells"—she spat out the name contemptuously—"hasn't one ounce of courage in his whole body."

"Shut up, Leah," Carl shouted over his shoulder as he pulled papers from the safe and stacked them on the floor.

"What difference does it make?" she countered. "We can't allow her or, for that matter, Jason to live." Carl was too engrossed in the papers to utter a remark.

Oh, God, I inwardly cried, and ran my tongue around the inside of my dry mouth. This couldn't be happening. It was all so unreal. And what of Nicholas? I still wanted to believe him innocent, but at this point I wasn't sure of anything anymore. And the fact remained that neither Leah nor her brother impressed me as individuals who possessed the sharp, keen mind required to mastermind industrial espionage.

"I don't believe you about Nicholas." I prodded her in an effort to determine if she was simply trying to protect him. "I happen to know that he's a shrewd and aggressive businessman."

She lifted her shoulders in indifference. "I suppose he is, but he's disgustingly honest. Someday he'll probably be financially well off, but I'm not sitting around biding my time while he struggles toward that end."

"Then you *were* seeing him. Socially, I mean?"

Leah came to her feet, the revolver still leveled at my stomach. "Sure, I encouraged him. Why not? His mediocre success would have been better than nothing. But then this plan came along and if it worked out, I wouldn't need him or any other man I didn't particularly want. As for Jason, I never cared about him. Frankly, we needed him out of the way. You even ruined that! He was supposed to trip on the feather duster and break his neck tumbling down the stairs."

"But why?" I inched my hand over the smooth doorknob.

"Because he was getting suspicious." She arched an eyebrow at me. "Did I frighten you with my antics in the attic?"

I tightened my hand on the knob, wondering if I dared pull open the door and make a run for it. From the corner of my eye I saw Carl stand up. I held firm. "What did you hope to accomplish by thumping around in the attic?"

She sat back down on the desk. "I was just amusing myself. I saw the way Jason looked at you that first day, and I decided it would be fun to make you look like a hysterical schoolgirl. I knew that would turn him against you. Besides, we didn't need you snooping around. But we couldn't scare you back to San Francisco, could we? I'll bet you're sorry now that you didn't make a hasty retreat."

Carl moved to Leah's side and placed the papers from the safe on top of the desk. He took the gun from her hand. "All right, miss—" His words were cut off by the clatter of footsteps in the outer office.

I sucked in my breath and flattened myself against the door, the knob hard against my back jabbing my sore muscles.

Carl gestured with the weapon. "Get over here, and if you scream I'll shoot right through the door."

Shakily I obeyed his order. Eyes wide with fear I watched the silver knob turn and then Jason swung open the door.

At first he saw no one but me, standing wan and

statuelike, but then in one rapid motion as if he'd heard a noise, he flipped his head sideways. His eyes blazed with anger. "You don't give up do you?"

Again Carl waved the gun. "Get over by Miss Justin!" Jason stood his ground. "Move! Or I'll kill her!" Jason looked at me quickly, then stepped to my side and slipped a protective arm around my shoulders.

"How touching," Leah jeered.

"Stop your chatter," Carl grumbled. "There's some rope out by the blacksmith shop, go get it."

She looked at him in bewilderment. "Why rope?"

"We'll tie them up in here and let the fire take care of them."

"You won't get away with it," I cried.

Jason started toward Carl.

He jerked his hand. "Get back!" He threatened with the gun. "Get—" The shattering of glass cut him off. I spun around to the window just as a shot rang out, and I heard Carl's body slam against the wall as if hurled with tremendous force, then drop to the floor. In that one fraction of a minute, before strong fingers pushed me to the narrow boards, I glimpsed a strand of silver blended with a sprinkling of gray hair. It was Mr. Taylor at the window with his head hard against the butt of a rifle.

Another shot cracked, vibrating in my ears. Before my hands went up to cover them, I heard an agonizing moan and then someone behind me thumped to the floor. Jason! His name streaked across my mind and for one horror-filled moment I lay frozen, eyes squeezed shut and hands pressed over my ears, too terrified to raise my head to the unmoving figure nearby.

Arms went around me and pulled me close. "Abby," Jason rasped, and held me so tightly that I could scarcely breathe, "are you all right?"

"Oh, Jason," I choked, "I thought maybe you—"

"I know. I know, darling. I'm fine. Are you all right?"

I nodded, then hesitantly lifted my head to the two blood-spattered bodies sprawled side by side on the floor. The snub-nosed revolver lay at Carl's feet. My gaze moved to Leah and lingered on her colorless face, the crimson splotch on the bodice of her dress heightened her ashen complexion. Leah's eyelids fluttered. "Jason," I gulped, "she's alive. Oh, help her. Please help her."

He released me, darted a look to the window, then hurriedly crawled to her side. Jason leaned over Leah and gently lifted her head. For a long moment the only sounds that pervaded the room were those of scuffling from beyond the window; then Leah drew a breath, as if fighting for survival. "Tell my mother—" She coughed twice; then Leah was still.

Heavy footfalls came to me from the outer office and Mr. Taylor demanded, "Take your hands off me! I saved their lives. Don't you understand! I saved their lives."

"Here's the man behind your sabotage," Nicholas insisted, and shoved the outraged bookkeeper into the office.

I shouted at him. "You killed her! You killed an unarmed woman." Sobs shook my shoulders, and I was only dimly aware of Jason helping me to my feet. Murmuring words of comfort, he led me from the room.

For what seemed like a long time after that I waited alone on the office porch while Jason conferred with the two men inside. How gruesome it had been sitting there with my back to Leah and Carl's lifeless bodies, while before me the city of Seattle was being devoured by great tongues of flame.

When Jason reappeared he made no attempt to explain Mr. Taylor's involvement and I had been too dazed to inquire. Jason brought me home immediately, placed me in Dorothea's care, then returned to town.

The grim news reached us early the next morning. The fire, caused by a pot of glue that had boiled over onto a gas stove, was extinguished; but not before it had burned through one hundred and twenty-six acres. Twenty-five city blocks were now charred rubble. Justin Mill Company, Wells Mill Company, and Jason's house were leveled to glowing embers.

The sawmills had been reduced to a handful of ashes—so had the prospect of wealth that had spurred Leah and Carl to the verge of murder.

It was sunup, Mrs. Brannon told me over breakfast, before Jason came home and went directly to bed.

It was late afternoon now and from my seat on the lawn swing I stared over the lake, wondering how he could still be asleep. The house was alive with the sounds of guest rooms being readied, and the footfalls of homeless friends trudging up and down the stairs, lugging suitcases and cherished household items.

A door behind me banged shut and I turned to see Jason crossing the lawn toward me. On the porch behind him Dorothea was playing with her niece. I jumped up and ran into his arms. He kissed me and then with his arm about my waist we strolled along the rim of the lake, while he related the events of the night.

At the same time that Jason and I were on our way home late yesterday afternoon, Nicholas, I was told, was in the process of removing the bespectacled accountant to the courthouse, where he adamantly denied any wrongdoing. Repeatedly he went over his story that it was the sight of two horses tethered at the rear of the mill which prompted him to investigate the premises, fearful of looters. And, he told the authorities that he had fired upon the intruders because it was the only way in which he knew to save the lives of his employers.

However, after many hours of interrogation during which he could not justifiably explain why he had shot an unarmed woman, Zachary Taylor confessed.

It was not the promise of wealth that had motivated the soft-spoken man, but rather hatred. A hatred for Martin Justin and Jason Landry, the young man whom he had been forced to train in the operations of the company and who in the end had gained its sole command.

For all these twenty-seven years Zachary Taylor had worked and struggled alongside his employer with the one predominate hope that in time he would be offered at least a junior partnership in the sawmill. But instead, in the bookkeeper's estimation, his loyalty and dedication had gone unnoticed. Jason, who, by comparison, possessed far less business experience, had been favored with the choice position in the company.

It was Zachary Taylor who had formulated the plan to discredit Jason Landry, and to accomplish this end he had enlisted the aid of Leah's brother, Carl, a man whom Zach Taylor knew held no scruples regarding the manner in which he earned additional money.

It was Carl in fact who had brought the meek-appearing man into contact with the owner of a small mill. And in exchange for Jason's Kimberley estimate, which that mill owner felt certain would be awarded the contract, Zachary Taylor would have received a partnership in that small company. Since owning a portion of a business was all he had desired, he willingly agreed to relinquish his share of any monies derived from the contract to Carl.

The equipment breakdowns at Justin Mill continued, of course, in an attempt to diminish the reliability of the company. Since Zachary Taylor did not have access to the safe in Jason's private office it was arranged that Carl would break into it. But the estimate always eluded them and Mr. Taylor grew anxious and apprehensive, fearful that his last opportunity for success would again be snatched away.

There was only one other place he knew where those calculations could be — in the Justin home. So Carl urged his sister to employ her feminine wiles on Jason, hoping that she perhaps could ferret out the elusive figures. Half-heartedly she agreed, though in the back of her mind she dreamed of marrying Jason and having it all to herself.

In the end, when Mr. Taylor saw the raging inferno ignite the company which was to have been partially his, and all appeared lost, he sought in desperation to save his job at the Justin Mill.

It had indeed been the fear of looters which had brought him to the office window, but when he saw that his partners had given themselves away he panicked, and shot and killed the only people apt to reveal his involvement.

We stopped at the edge of the lake near the Brannons' cottage. "Why did Nicholas take Leah to town with him yesterday morning?" I wanted to know. "Was he suspicious?"

"Yes, though he didn't have much to go on. You see, Wells told me that he saw Carl and Zach together in a tavern a few nights ago. He said they seemed very friendly and totally engrossed in conversation, prompting him to wonder what two men who were such complete opposites could have in common. Wells said he knew that Zach was jealous of me and my command and it was then that he began to suspect that our company problems were caused by internal forces. When Mrs. Sims told Wells of my accident in the woods he said he had felt disgusted with himself for not consulting with me immediately, even though he wasn't sure my supposed accident related to those at the mill. That's when he came by here for Leah. From past experience with her, Wells also came to the conclusion that she was out to snare a husband of means. He shunned her for that reason and figured that I might have shunned her too. So he wondered if she desired money desperately enough to do almost anything for it. And he hauled her off to town to question her. She flatly denied his accusations and then the outbreak of the fire disrupted his questioning. He never saw Leah again . . . alive."

"But what brought Nicholas to the window of your office?"

Jason ran a hand over his face. "Well, he told me that when his mill caught fire and there was absolutely nothing he could do to save it, he decided to ride over and see if he could be of any help. That's when he spotted Zach skulking around the office building, armed. Wells followed after him, but the two shots were fired before he had gotten close enough to jump Zach." He paused and grinned at me sheepishly. "I was certainly wrong about Wells, wasn't I?"

"Yes, but he was just as wrong about you," I pointed out. "In any case, you were right about everything else. And I can understand why you didn't suspect kindly appearing Mr. Taylor, but what about Carl?"

"I never linked him to the breakdowns because he

didn't possess much knowledge of the machinery. It's amazing he didn't kill himself rigging the equipment to malfunction."

I drew a short breath. "What about the runaway, Jason? Did you find out if that was a deliberate attempt on us?"

"That question was put to Zach and he didn't know anything about it, so apparently it was genuine."

"I see," I murmured, "and what about Nicholas? Can he afford to rebuild?"

"I'm afraid not. Oh, he's by no means penniless. He told me he has some insurance, but it's not enough to rebuild. Anyway, he's decided to try his luck in Portland. I guess he has a business connection there. But let's not talk about him anymore. He'll be out for a visit with you and Martin before he leaves and he can tell you his plans then."

"I have so much to say to him, Jason. He's been so kind to me."

"He guessed about our feelings for each other."

"I think he suspected all along that I was in love with you."

Jason gave me a long kiss, then smiled down into my face. "Did you grandfather mention our plans to rebuild the Justin and Landry Mill Company?"

I also smiled. "When did he tell you about the partnership?"

"Just before I came out to join you. We're going to start construction immediately. Why, before you know it we'll be back in business. Now, tell me, what have you been doing all day?"

The corners of my mouth drooped. "Making up beds in my room. The guest rooms are full and there are at least a half-dozen beds in mine. It looks like a dormitory. I can hardly move around. Oh, well, I suppose I can put up with it, at least for a little while."

"And to think I have an entire room to myself."

"You mean you don't have to share it with anyone?"

He shrugged. "I guess not. From what I heard last night most of the men are going to put up tents and live in town. They'll be working long hours rebuilding and apparently they're not interested in traveling back and forth." A devilish gleam came into his eyes. "You could move in with me."

I felt a flush pink my cheeks. "Why, Jason Landry! Grandfather would have us both thrown out of the house."

He tilted his head back and laughed, then caught me in the circle of his arms. "I'm asking you to marry me, you sweet idiot. You know, if I leave now I could be back with the minister within the hour."

"But we can't get married in an hour."

He raised a hand. "I know, don't tell me. You want an elaborate church wedding and you want your family here from San Francisco. That will take weeks or maybe even months to arrange. As I see it, Abby, you have one of two choices. You can spend tonight and every night with me in our room. Or you can have a big church wedding months from now, sharing, for who knows how long, your room with a bunch of chattering ladies." He gave me another kiss, one that set me atremble.

"That's not fair," I protested with a feigned frown.

He grinned. "Well, I was only trying to point out it will be impossible for us to keep our emotions in check for even a few more days, let alone several months."

Suppressing a smile, I turned away and started for the house. Jason fell into step beside me. "Where are you going?" He sounded worried.

"To move my things into your room, of course."

He caught me by the arm and swung me into his embrace.

I nestled my head against his chest. "I'll wager not

many newlyweds spend their wedding night in a house full of noisy ladies."

Jason lifted my chin and put his mouth near mine. "Really, Abby, do you think we'll hear them?"

In case you're wondering, we didn't.